THE SKEPTICAL MAN

A Q.C. DAVIS MYSTERY

LISA M. LILLY

SPINY WOMAN PRESS

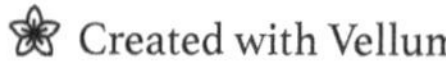 Created with Vellum

CHAPTER 1
THE MURDER WISH

I NEEDED A MURDER. The thought darted through my mind before I could stop it. But I was appalled. It was a terrible thing to wish. Plus my last investigation was why I was in my law office late tonight. I devoted months to looking into the long ago murder of my sister, the original Quille C. Davis, during spring. It was worth the time, no question. But it led to my working long hours all summer.

And summer is my favorite season in Chicago. Neighborhood festivals and parades take place every weekend. There's blues music, jazz, beer drinking and loud bands (I skip both of those), art and antique fairs. No matter what you love, it's out there. Cheese and caramel popcorn, Vienna beef hot dogs, and every other type of food you could want. The weather is warm and sunny, but the wind off Lake Michigan keeps downtown from turning into an oven.

But I was inside. I needed to meet the deadlines on my cases. And I needed the money from those cases.

My love life, or lack of it, stood in the way of a great summer, too. My boyfriend, Ty, was in Dubai for a two-year work project. His company promised he could visit every few months or I could fly there. So far, we'd seen each other once.

At the thought of Ty, I stopped typing mid-sentence. It was barely six, too early to call it a day. But I wasn't missing yet another outdoor concert with my friends. If I did, I'd feel too much like that person who can't have fun because she's not part of a couple, which I never wanted to be.

The humidity made leaving the building feel like stepping into a sheet of warm rain. I took off my blazer and wound my long, wavy hair into a clip at the back of my head.

My phone rang as I crossed Michigan Avenue and strode past the giant stone lions that guard the Art Institute. I was tempted to ignore it. I could already hear the orchestra warming up. But I was waiting to hear from a lawyer about a case I hoped to settle. I veered into the art museum's garden and answered.

It wasn't the lawyer, but it was a judge.

"Quille, so glad you picked up," Judge Julia Lopez said. "I need your help."

"Anything."

I met Julia over a decade ago when I started thinking about law school. She's the main person who encouraged me to go. I still turn to her for career advice from time to time.

Her husband had died this summer. I sent a sympathy card— paper, not digital, as my Gram taught me to do—and left her a voicemail. But this was the first time I'd heard back.

"I need you to investigate Randall's murder," she said now.

"You—Randall was murdered?" I sank onto a concrete bench, knees shaky as I thought of my wish for a crime to look into. But Julia's husband was already gone when I thought that. Not that I believed my thinking could make something happen. "What about the police?"

"It's— I—I'd rather talk in person. Can you come to my chambers? Now?"

I rubbed the back of my neck, which felt tight and sore, often the sign of a migraine to come. I longed to meet my friends, who were waiting on blankets spread out before the Millenium Park bandshell. No doubt with a bucket of fried chicken and biscuits and home baked brownies. But Julia needed to talk now. Not tomorrow morning or later in the week.

"Will the guards let me in?" I said.

The Daley Center, which houses state courtrooms downtown, closes at six.

"Oh, I—sorry," Julia said. "I've lost all sense of time lately. I'll make sure they do."

"Can I bring you anything? Coffee? Dinner?"

They must have coffee in the judge's chambers, but maybe not after hours. And I knew firsthand that people don't always take care of themselves after someone they love dies.

"Oh, no—well—you're a tea person, aren't you?" Julia said. "Is there some sort of calming tea?"

It was so like Julia to remember despite her grief that I drink tea, not coffee. I told her I'd be there in twenty minutes.

The tea was literally called Calm. The last tea shop in downtown Chicago closed a few years back, but many coffee places remain. The third one I tried had herbal tea. While I waited in line I reread the news articles about Randall's death on my phone.

A passerby found his body just after eleven on a Sunday night below the 606. That's an elevated trail that runs through part of Chicago's northwest side. People walk, ride bikes, and jog there. It includes parks, art exhibits, and event spaces, too. Police believed Randall was mugged because his wallet was missing. Stab wounds slashed across his palms, suggesting he tried to defend himself from a knife attack. The articles included no quotes from Julia, but noted that she'd been in California at a bar association conference when her husband was killed.

The barista handed me a paper cup so hot I shifted it from hand to hand as I hurried on to the Daley Center.

Julia waited on the twenty-fourth floor, holding open the glass door to the judges' chambers. Her head barely reached my shoulder when we hugged. Her hair, which normally fell in straight, silver sheets to her shoulders, straggled around her face. Makeup foundation caked in the fine lines around her eyes and lips. She was fifty-five but looked at least ten years older.

I sat in a leather visitor chair on the other side of her giant antique desk. After saying how sorry I was that all this happened, I asked about the cause of death. Julia's face paled as she told me it was a broken neck from hitting the ground beneath the 606 trail.

She must have finished her court call hours ago, but she hadn't taken off her judge's robe. Her arms, stick-thin, poked out of her rolled up sleeves. "The police say it was a random mugging. But I'm certain it's not."

"Why?"

"He was a magician."

"And that means....?" I took out the small notepad and pen I always carry in my shoulder bag.

"Forty years of sleight of hand. He'd never fight someone over his wallet. He'd hand it over after slipping the cash out."

I nodded. "Maybe. Still, staring at a knife is scary for anyone. No one knows how they'll react."

I had never met Randall. He and Julia married three years before his death. But he never joined us when Julia and I had dinner, and he didn't attend bar association events with her.

"Randall wasn't as short as I am." Julia's eyes became unfocused as she spoke, as if looking at the scene in her mind. "But close. Five-five. He was thinner than me, but stronger. Wiry. The police think he and the mugger scuffled. The mugger got the better of him and shoved him over the railing. Maybe so Randall couldn't identify them. But it doesn't fit." She shifted her gaze to me. "When I was a public defender I had that sense at times. I knew when the police were wrong."

"You felt it in your gut."

Gut instincts matter. I analyze everything. Yet sometimes the feeling in the pit of my stomach tells me a lot more a lot faster.

"Yes. Randall's not a fighter. He talked his way out of things. Ever since he was a kid."

"Anything else?" I said.

"His mom died the week after Randall did."

I stopped the note I was writing. "You think the deaths are connected?"

"No. No." Julia's straggly silver hair swung side to side as she shook her head. "It was pneumonia. And Alzheimer's. She was a lovely woman. And there's nothing—there's nothing I can do. Not about her illness. Not about her death. I took three weeks off after they found Randall. I could barely get out of bed. Except for the funerals. Then I started coming here just to…just to try and catch up. Today was my first day on the bench again. And I felt—better. Clearer. I don't know if that makes sense."

"It does," I said.

When things go wrong for me, my office feels like the safest place. The one place I can control at least some of the world around me. The one place I can get something done.

"And I thought, maybe I can do something about Randall's death. And I thought of you." She rolled her chair so its back rested against the shelves of worn law books behind her. "You'll turn over every stone. The same as you did for your sister's cold case. And for Marco."

Not many people who know me through my law practice know that I investigate crimes, too. It's not something I advertise. But when I started looking into my former boyfriend Marco's death, I asked Julia for her view of how the ethics rules for lawyers applied to that type of work. Later, she encouraged me to try to solve my sister's murder for the peace of mind it could bring my family.

Even if I could fit a new murder investigation into my workload, I wasn't sure I should raise Julia's hopes. It's hard to accept random events. But sometimes a mugging is just a mugging.

On the other hand, sometimes it's not.

"Is there someone who held a grudge against Randall?"

"Before I left for the conference he told me he was ruffling a lot of feathers." She stared out her floor-to-ceiling windows. She had a view of the silver bandshell at Millenium Park where summer concerts are held, and of Lake Michigan stretching to the horizon. "He worried it might reflect badly on me as a judge."

"Whose feathers?"

Clouds had formed outside as we talked. Gloom crept into the chambers. Julia turned on her desk lamp. The glow from her ruby red glass shade cast shadows the color of blood across her forehead. "He didn't give me any names."

"Any guesses about what Randall might have done to ruffle feathers?"

"Oh, that I know. He went after psychics and mediums he thought defrauded people."

CHAPTER 2
SOMEONE TO TRUST

Julia explained that Randall posted videos online showing techniques that anyone could use to make it look like they could channel the dead or read minds.

"But he went beyond that. He set up sting operations. Before I met him he broke a story about a so-called medium who claimed to free peoples' homes of bad energy evil spirits caused. He proved that she removed items like paintings and sculptures to 'cleanse' them, sold the originals, and replaced them with forgeries."

"You think that person might have killed Randall?"

"Not her." Bluish-green veins stood out on the backs of Julia's hands as she gripped her chair arms. "She died of a heart attack a year ago. I checked. But someone like her might hold a grudge. And he was working on a new project."

Unfortunately, Julia didn't know any details. While setting up a sting, Randall told no one anything unless they were helping him with it.

"You're his wife. He didn't trust you?"

"He did. But the fewer people who knew, the less likely word might leak accidentally."

I slipped my blazer off and draped it over the chair next to me. The chambers felt stifling. I hadn't heard the air conditioning cycle on since I entered the building. "And you felt okay with that?"

"It's the same reason I don't—didn't—tell him things about the court that were sensitive. I never thought he'd run around telling people. But this way neither of us had to waste mental energy making sure we didn't slip and say something."

"Did he keep records of his stings?"

"He must have. But I've been through his files at home and didn't find any. I started on his closet. He pared it down already because we were moving soon. To a loft in Logan Square. Not far from—" Julia squeezed her eyes shut.

"Take your time," I said.

"Down the street from where they found him. But I just can't go through any more of his things. Every photo I find sets me off. I finally calm down, and then I find something else." She cleared her throat. "Last night I came across a theater ticket from our first date. I'll lose my mind if I go through everything myself. Or miss something. Or both."

I asked if she knew why Randall was on the 606 that night.

She wiped her eyes. "He liked to jog there. But I think he was meeting someone."

Julia told me Randall's paper calendar, which he used for personal meetings, included a handwritten note with the number "830" on the night he was killed. That's how he listed appointments. The note didn't include a place or a name, only initials. But the police didn't believe her, or at least didn't feel certain, that 830 referred to a time.

Randall shared a separate online calendar with colleagues for work. He was a volunteer coordinator for a non-profit that he founded two decades before. He trained magicians to teach magic to kids in hospitals. Randall volunteered in the hospitals himself, too, and did magic shows to raise funds. Entries on the work calendar included names, phone numbers, and locations.

"Why was his home calendar different?" I said.

"Because no one else needed to read it. He liked using clues to prompt his memory. It was a way to keep his mind sharp," Julia said. "He thought about that a lot because of his mother's Alzheimer's. It's the same with phone numbers. It was. His phone saved the numbers but he never filled in the names. Just remembered who went with what number."

The sound of a vacuum cleaner filtered in from the hallway that ran along the inner walls of all the judges' chambers.

"And no one's admitted to meeting him that night?" I said.

"No. And the police interviewed, or say they interviewed, everyone close to him, including the only person we know with the initials PRG."

"PRG?"

"The initials written near the 830. That person was out of town, too, at the same judicial conference I was at. But who knows if the police contacted all the people on my list. You know how busy they are."

I did. I'm friends, of sorts, with a Detective Sergeant in the homicide division. A shortage of trained investigators plus the way the department is set up make his job, in his view, much harder than it ought to be. It's why he eventually decided to work with me instead of against me.

"I'm the last person to put a lot of faith in police." I wound my fingers into the edges of my hair and twirled it, then made myself stop. It's not a very professional-looking habit and I try to avoid it. "But they're not always wrong."

"No. But you and I know they can be."

Julia presides over a family law courtroom now. She respects police, but she retains some skepticism from her earlier work as a public defender.

I stayed silent to give her time to think about what she wanted and what else she might need to tell me. She drank some tea but tipped the cup too far and had to blot her lower lip with a paper tissue.

"There's money involved too. Maybe," Julia said. "Randall walked away from a family business his grandfather started. He still had a share of it and of the family trust. Now that he and his mother are gone, their shares are split among Randall's brother and father."

"Not you?"

"No. Randall and I don't even have life insurance policies on each other. We're both—we were both—pretty well set when it came to money. And neither of us has kids. All I inherit are some personal items."

"You think his family could commit murder for the money?"

Julia stared down at her desk. "I don't want to think that. Still, you can't be a lawyer or a judge and not know people do all kinds of things you'd never expect." She wound the tissue around the fingers of her left hand. "I always remind myself I only see people because something went wrong. That most people are good people. But the father and brother get more money because Randall's dead. I can't help thinking about that even if the police don't."

"You're sure they're not looking at Randall's relatives?"

"Sure? No. But they didn't seem interested in what I told them."

I closed my notepad. "If I do this, I'm sure you know investigating a crime isn't that different from bringing a lawsuit or defending one. I can do my best, but I can't promise results."

"But I'll know more than I do now."

"That's not always good. I learned things when I looked into my sister's murder that I wish now I didn't know. Things my whole family's still trying to deal with."

"Randall's gone. Nothing could be worse than that."

"Randall can't be worse off than dead. But some things could make you feel worse."

It felt strange to be more expert in this small area than Julia. From the time I started thinking about going to law school on, I went to her for advice, not the other way around.

"I understand. And if it really was a random mugging, I'd leave it to the police. But if the killer was someone who knew Randall, you're my best shot. Will you do it? Please. I'll pay your hourly rate, whatever you charge in your practice. But I'm guessing that's not why you're hesitating."

"It's not," I said.

Julia remained silent, taking her turn at giving me time to think. My mental list of open cases ran through my mind, including two that were headed for trial this fall if I couldn't settle them. But I needed to weigh that against something less concrete yet just as real. For the first time since Ty told me he planned to stay in Dubai for two years, I felt excited.

Plus there were all the times Julia guided me during law school, when I took my first job as a lawyer, and when I opened my own practice.

"My hourly rate is more than a private investigator's," I said. "It's the only way I can afford to take the time away from my law practice."

It was a lesson brought home to me during the last few months. I never dreamed of charging my parents for the Q.C. investigation. Which was why I'd been working almost non-stop since then yet was barely covering my bills. I couldn't handle the matter free anyway or give Julia a discount. The Illinois Rules of Professional Conduct prohibit a lawyer from giving a judge anything. Not gifts, not money, not time.

"Quille." Julia extended one arm across the desk and squeezed my hand. "I'm not looking for a bargain. I'm looking for someone who cares as much as I do about doing a job right. And who cares about me. Someone I trust. Will you do it?"

CHAPTER 3
WOMAN OF GOD

CHICAGO IS LITERALLY BUILT on swampland. Along with the chance to rebuild nearly an entire city after the Great Chicago Fire, the challenge of constructing skyscrapers on land with layers of jelly-like clay drew architects from all over the world in the late 1800s. One of the buildings constructed then was the historic Monadnock Building, where Randall Petrov had rented office space. At sixteen stories, it doesn't seem tall now. But it's considered an engineering marvel. It's one of the heaviest skyscrapers in the city and one of the tallest to be held up by its own walls rather than the steel skeletons used today.

When I stepped inside the afternoon after meeting Julia, a steaming cup of Chai tea in one hand, it felt like another world. My footsteps echoed on the marble floors. White marble walls and staircases surrounded me. The interior was cool and quiet. It shut out the traffic noise, sirens, and heat outside. Randall's office was on the eleventh floor. Like me, rather than renting a single office from building management, which can be very pricey, he sublet an office from a landlord who rented a whole office suite from the building.

The door to the suite had old-fashioned frosted glass windows and gold lettering. Inside, though, the carpet was tan, the walls beige, and the office doors plain dark wood. I was disappointed that it looked so ordinary. Four offices with windows were on one side of the suite and a windowless storage room with a kitchenette along the other. A desk and long table opposite each other at the end of the hallway probably belonged to an administrative support person, but no one sat there at the moment.

The nameplate on the wall outside the first office said Oscar Miller. That was the lawyer who rented the suite from the building and sublet an office to Randall. Oscar's light was on, but his office was empty. Randall's office was at the end of the hall. From Julia, I knew he rented it because the non-profit he started, Magic Works, never had a brick-and-mortar home. Long before remote work became common, Randall set things up so that everyone worked from home. They communicated by phone and fax, then later through email and video conferences. He paid for the office with his own money. It came with access to a building conference room where he could train volunteers.

Randall planned to move out soon, though. The new loft condo he and Julia bought was zoned so owners could both live and work there. Randall planned to donate what he saved on office rent to Magic Works. But it didn't look like he'd begun packing. I saw no boxes on the floor or credenza. The light wood shelves were still filled with books, mystical items like crystals and runes, and colorful boxes of tarot card decks.

I set my tea on the desk and unlocked Randall's laptop with a long, complex password Julia found in his estate documents. An icon took me to Randall's YouTube channel. It included nearly a hundred videos. Randall devoted them to behind-the-scenes looks at psychic phenomena. The first dozen I clicked through covered tarot reading, mentalism, contacting the dead, and astrology.

After checking the time—I had somewhere to be at 3:30—I scrolled through the hard drive. Most folder and file names were self-explanatory, except for one labeled Alchemy. The first PDF inside it was an email that had nothing to do with alchemy. But it did sound threatening.

> Randall Petrov. Yes, I found you. You should be ashamed. My wife is devastated. She believes you. I told her you are a terrible man to attack a woman of God. A woman who was our lifeline to our daughter.
>
> You must have no children. You know nothing of what it means to lose one. How dare you play tricks? Pretend to be righteous and expose a scam when you are the one scamming. You think you know more than the Krakow police? You are not smarter than them.
>
> You are nothing. You do not deserve to live. If you publish the video, if you expose everyone and shatter more people's hopes and dreams you will regret it.

The sending address began with AngryHusband. The email lacked any signature line but was dated two weeks before Randall's death. I found no response from Randall.

A "woman of God" who acted as a lifeline to the man's daughter sounded a lot like a medium or psychic. The video mentioned could relate to the sting Julia said Randall was working on exposing a psychic as a fraud. I looked at YouTube again. None of the video descriptions referred to a missing or dead child or Krakow. I didn't find any other videos on Randall's computer.

The Alchemy folder contained nothing else about AngryHusband. There was a series of photos and PDFs of what looked like hand-printed letters. Dated in the 1990s, they were all signed by someone named Nellie Havel. A few had coffee stains on them, as if Nellie wrote the originals at her breakfast table.

My tea was now only lukewarm. But I took a long swallow, wishing I liked coffee. I could use more caffeine. My workday had started at six-thirty in the morning. Over eight hours later, so far I'd had three cups of tea, a chocolate chip scone for breakfast, and a power bar and an orange for lunch. After making sure I had time, I read the first letter.

Dear Alice,

I don't know you, and I hope you'll forgive me taking the liberty of writing you. I was so moved when I read about your husband in the newspaper, and I felt I should get in touch. He sounds like a kind person. One others will miss, especially you.

Right now, I don't live in Monroe. But I did for a few years as a child. (That's why I know so much about Swiss cheese!) I still subscribe to the local newspaper. It takes me back. I was so happy in Monroe—as I hope you are, Alice, though I'm sure your loss makes it hard right now.

Since I read Your Harold's obituary, his name and yours keep coming into my mind. I feel sure he's trying to get in touch with you.

You might be tempted to stop reading now, but please don't. Please know I'm not asking for money or selling anything. And I'm not going to try to tell you I'm a psychic or medium.

I'm not! I'm just someone who gets feelings. If I feel like they can help someone who lost a loved one, I get in touch.

Where could feelings like that come from I bet you're asking. When I was eight (bear with me, there is a point to this story), I tripped while skipping rope. My head hit the stairs. My mother was hanging sheets on the clothesline. She ran to me. I had no pulse. I had stopped breathing. But a miracle happened. Right before an ambulance arrived, I started to breathe again. No one knows why or how.

Since then I get feelings, especially when I touch things that belonged to someone who passed on or I read about them. About six months after the fall, a neighbor showed my mother her father's dog tags from his years in the Marines. When I touched them I saw numbers in my mind. If you can believe it, they were the combination to a safe the neighbors tried to get into for over ten years! The poor man died without giving anyone the combination.

The family found savings bonds in the safe—over ten thousand dollars' worth. That was a lot of money at the time. (It still is to someone like me.) Of course the feelings I get don't usually lead to money. If they did everyone I met could get rich! But I can tell you they help people feel closer to the one they lost.

If you write back and tell me more about Your Harold, I feel sure I can sort out what he wants to share with you. To make it easier and show I'm not asking you for anything, I've included a stamped envelope addressed to me. Postage paid! Just write and send.

If you write me or not please know I am so sorry for your loss. My wish for you is that time, memories and good friends ease your pain.

Yours,

Nellie Havel

P.S. I hope to hear from you and hope we'll become friends. (Is it all right to say I already feel almost as if we are friends?) Yours with God's Grace.

A quick online search told me that Monroe probably meant Monroe, Wisconsin, known as the Swiss cheese capital of the United States. I found no listings for Nellie Havel of Monroe. But the letter was dated January 4, 1990, so I didn't expect to. The folder contained a couple dozen versions of the same letter with a few changes to personalize each. The peoples' names varied. So did the town or city and the comment about it. Two Chicago letters, one from 1997 and the other from 1999, mentioned the opening of Navy Pier to the public, which happened in the mid-1990s.

Another folder included a second letter to Alice. There were many versions of that one, too. The names and objects people sent Nellie changed, but the text was the same in each.

Dear Alice,

Thank you for sending Your Harold's pocket watch. When I held it in my hands I saw him in my mind. He was smiling. Did he have such a beautiful smile in life? Or is it the joy of Heaven showing through in his face? Either way, I know he was telling me he's at peace and he's always there if you need him. Just imagine his face and he'll be with you.

Harold wants you to know, too, that he's sorry for any time he took you for granted or let you down. And any time he forgot to tell you how very much you meant to him. If he could come back, he'd do more to be sure you know how special you are.

I hope this makes you feel closer to Harold. If you still feel sad, the St. Anthony medal I enclosed might help. It's my gift to you. Clasp it between your palms. Think of your loved one and you will be comforted.

Please write again and let me know if this helps. Through our letters, I've come to think of you as one of my dearest friends. Hearing from you means so much to me. I hope you feel the same.

Yours,

Nellie

P.S. I never sell these medals but only share them with my closest friends. If you want to help cover the cost you can send a donation in the enclosed envelope or with your next letter to me.

I felt tempted to research Nellie Havel. She might be the woman of God that AngryHusband's email talked about. If Nellie was in her twenties or thirties when the letters started, she could easily be alive now.

But I was running short on time. Better to dig in when I could spend an hour or two, making it less likely I'd lose track of search terms or results. I texted the Detective Sergeant I know and told him about the threatening email. The police hadn't searched the office. They didn't think it had anything to do with Randall's death, as Randall's body was found six or seven miles away beneath the 606 trail. I thought that was a mistake. But they had more resources than I did. If they could find the person who wrote a threatening email two weeks before Randall's death, I owed it to him and Julia to give them the chance to do it. Which didn't mean I planned to let the thread go myself.

I logged out of the laptop and, despite everything on my plate, tried calling my boyfriend Ty. It was nearly midnight in Dubai. But he was a night owl. He might still be awake. His voicemail answered.

After a last glance around Randall's office, which sadly still had no sign telling me who might want to kill him, I headed out, locking his office door behind me. On the way to the suite's exit I passed the office of the landlord, Oscar Miller, again. This time the door was open.

After a glance at the time on my phone, I veered toward the office.

CHAPTER 4
MEETING THE LANDLORD

As Randall's business landlord for a little over two years, Oscar Miller might be able to tell me about the man. Ideally, later in the week when my schedule was less intense.

The office was twice the size of Randall's, with heavy wood furniture. The man inside bent over a keyboard on his desk, a giant flat screen monitor in front of him. Judging by the gray wound through his sandy brown hair, Oscar was at least fifty. More than a decade older than me.

When I knocked on the open door he didn't look up. I knocked again, then stepped across the threshold. I caught a faint musty smell, probably from the scrunched towel poking out of a gym bag on the floor in the corner.

"Mr. Miller? Oscar? Sorry to interrupt. I'm Quille Davis. A friend of Judge Julia Lopez."

Julia had left it to me to decide whether to tell anyone I was investigating Randall's murder. Most people—no surprise— speak less freely if they think you view them as a murder suspect. On the other hand, if someone doesn't like talking, revealing the investigation sometimes intrigues them enough to draw them out.

I thought about doing that now, as Oscar typed on without pause. His starched white dress shirt and tan suit made me wonder if he'd had court earlier in the day. Most Chicago attorneys adopted business casual long ago for anytime outside of court. And we tend to stretch business casual to nice jeans with a blazer to throw on quickly if needed. That's what I did, though I drew the line at gym shoes in the office.

"Looks like you're busy." I raised my voice in case he might be hard of hearing. "I'll leave my card, and I'll email you. I'd really like to talk with you about Randall. Whenever you have time."

I was used to younger attorneys living online so much that they preferred texting or email over actual talking. But maybe Oscar just wasn't a people person. I turned on my heel.

"Just leave the check on the desk." His voice was deep, loud, and a little raspy.

"Sorry?"

"The rent check." Oscar lifted his hands from the keyboard at last. "That's what you're here about, isn't it?"

"Uh, no. I'm here to sort Randall's things and clear the office. Did he owe you rent?"

It was the middle of the month, an odd time to be paying. Plus I didn't know many people who paid anything by paper checks anymore. Though the three black metal file cabinets along the far wall and the framed photograph of a golden retriever sitting on top of them suggested Oscar was old school.

Oscar sat up straight, which made him seem taller and a bit

imposing. His shoulders looked broad under his suit jacket, though it was cut large. He might be smaller than he looked.

"Clear it out?" Oscar said. "Fine, if that's what you want. I don't care how the estate uses the office, or if they use it. But I need the rent paid."

He hadn't invited me, but I sat on one of the faux-leather chairs in front of the desk. Dull white showed through in spots where the coating had worn off. "For this month?"

Oscar tapped his pen—a thick one with a cartridge—on the blotter in the center of his desk. "Yes. I hadn't called Judge Lopez about it yet. I know she must have a lot on her mind. But Randall paid the first of every month, and he didn't—well, he died before that. And I need to know how she plans to pay for the remainder of the lease. Monthly checks? Automatic withdrawals?"

"When does the lease end?"

Oscar twisted toward his monitor, clicked his mouse, and a calendar appeared on screen. "Four years and, let me see, four months and one week from now."

Julia had told me Randall meant to move his office to their new home. She hadn't said he needed to break a lease to do it.

"Did Randall tell you he planned to move out?"

"I told him what I'll tell you. Move out, don't move out. Either way, rent is due through the end of the lease."

"But Randall died."

"Commercial leases don't end on death."

I doubted that was true across the board. But my law school property class focused on far less practical things. Like cases from the twelve hundreds about how many fowls one could shoot on a neighbor's estate. And so far I hadn't handled rent disputes in my practice.

"Could you send Julia or me a copy of the lease?" I slid my business card toward him. "It'll help her sort out what to do."

"Will do. And when can I expect this month's and next month's rent?"

"I need to ask Julia."

"Then why am I talking to you? I'm on trial tomorrow." He huffed and turned to his monitor again.

"I have a few questions. I'd like to talk later in the week." I expected at least a grunt in response, but I got nothing. "I'll email you about it."

On my way out, I swiped the key for the Women's Room from the rack hanging near the door. As I struggled to reshape my long, dark hair into waves rather than frizzy curls, I mentally estimated four and a quarter years of rent. It totaled over $90,000. It didn't seem like enough to be worth risking a life sentence for murder.

After returning the key I hurried outside. I was due at Petrov's Pizza in an hour and a half to talk with Randall's father. One of my friends was joining me, but I needed to do her a favor first.

My phone rang as I reached the corner of Wacker Drive and Clark Street. The call was forwarded from my office landline, so I couldn't see the number. I answered in case my boyfriend, Ty, mistakenly tried my office number.

"Quille C. Davis."

The voice of the man on the other end didn't sound happy.

"Who the hell are you and why are you asking questions about my brother?"

CHAPTER 5
FAMILY BUSINESS

An ambulance careened around the corner, its siren piercing the air. I put a hand over my free ear. "Can you hold for a moment, please? I'll get somewhere quieter."

"Don't bother."

The caller hung up. I stepped into the lobby of the closest office building anyway. My back to the guards, I dialed Julia and told her about the call.

"Oh, Quille, I'm sorry. I meant to let you know I talked to Max —Randall's brother—earlier. But I had such trouble concentrating on this stack of briefs. Then my one-thirty hearing ran late. And I forgot."

"Please. Don't worry about it. But I'm curious. Did you give him my number?"

"No. He must have looked it up."

So Max, brother of Randall, went to a bit of trouble to yell at me. "I'm meeting Ivan tonight at the original Petrov's Pizza."

Ivan was Randall's father and the head of the growing Petrov's Pizza chain, which began in Chicago.

"You're sure you have time today?" Julia said. "I don't expect you to drop everything else."

Two men peering at their phones headed straight for me from the elevator bank. I stepped aside but one nearly bumped into me before pushing through the revolving door.

"He's going on a two-week business trip in two days and it's the only time he could see me in person. I didn't want to miss the chance."

I left the building. There were no sirens now, only the usual sounds of car horns and motors running.

"I hope he'll be less rude than Max," Julia said.

I paused at a Don't Walk sign. "That'd be nice. But I wouldn't be much of an investigator if I couldn't talk to rude people."

"Or much of a lawyer."

"Sure, but that's usually my clients."

"The whole reason I'm a judge." She chuckled a little. It's an old joke in the legal profession that judges get all the fun of practicing law without having to deal with clients. I felt glad to hear her sound mildly amused. As I crossed the street I told her about the threatening email. She agreed it sounded like Randall carried out a sting of a psychic recently. And that AngryHusband threatened Randall to try to keep him from publishing the video of it. But she had no idea where the video might be stored other than Randall's computer or cloud accounts. She didn't think it had been published because at that point Randall would have told her about the sting.

With two minutes to spare, I met my friend Lauren on the upper floor of the Nordstrom Rack on State Street. It's an off price sister of the more upscale Nordstrom department store. I'm not a fan of clothes shopping, but when I need to do it, it's my first (and sometimes only) stop.

Lauren's straight, short blond hair shone despite the overhead fluorescent lights. Two shoeboxes at her feet, she rifled through a round rack of cocktail dresses. "There you are. I was afraid you were canceling. Which your new investigation is no excuse to do, so don't even think about it. And neither is Ty not making it in for the benefit."

"No chance I could just make an extra donation?"

"And leave another empty seat at my table? You totally could not."

Lauren is a real estate agent. Two or three times a year she commits to filling seats at a fundraiser for one or another of her best clients or referral sources. I try to attend any time she asks. This one stretched my budget. The Black Tie attire requirement meant a new dress on top of the five hundred dollars a seat I'd paid for Ty and me.

But Lauren helps with my investigations. She asks questions, eavesdrops on conversations, distracts others when I'm lurking somewhere I shouldn't be. She's great at it because she's naturally outgoing. And she's pretty and bubbly and most people who don't know her underestimate her. She's also fearless. Once she nearly broke an arm helping me chase down a suspect.

Attending her events is nowhere near enough to do in return. Plus, she's my unofficial fashion consultant, something I value more and more the longer I run my own firm. Like it or not, I am my own brand. When I started taking Lauren's advice on my wardrobe, people saw me as more successful. That made it easier to get more work.

I took a sheath-like black cocktail dress off the rack. "We've got twenty minutes at most." I peered inside the neck for the price tag.

"Right—pizza and intrigue at five in West Town. Don't worry, we'll find something fast." She took the dress and returned it to the rack. "But not this."

"It's pretty."

"The point of Black Tie is to wear something absolutely fabulous. And something fabulous is what you need to cheer you up with Ty canceling the visit. Not a boring black dress."

"Also known as classic and timeless."

"Only according to your Gram. This'll be awesome with your skin." Lauren held out an emerald green dress with a fitted top and flared skirt. I had to admit the color would set off my olive skin and nearly black hair nicely. She grabbed another like it in rose gold plus two more she'd set aside when I wasn't looking.

In the dressing room, Lauren said, "I'm sitting my client's niece next to you. She's thinking about law school. I want her to talk to someone who actually liked it."

Lauren and I met in law school. But she hated the whole experience. When on top of that she couldn't score all As, she left and got her real estate license instead.

I told her about Randall's death as I undressed and slipped on the emerald green dress. It fit perfectly. "This is it. I love it."

Lauren frowned, then sighed as she gave up on getting me to try on the other three. "Oh, fine. Now tell me about Randall's father while we look at shoes. You seriously think he might have killed his own son?"

———

Chicago is known for its deep dish or stuffed pizza. I'm a fan of Lou Malnati's, which opened in a near north suburb in the early 1970s and now has locations all over the city and in three other states. Its butter crust and tangy sauce appeal to me. Lauren prefers Giordano's, which started in the city's South Side neighborhood. Its stuffed pizza is heavy on cheese, with thick, almost bread-like crust, and sauce on the sweeter side. Neither of us are fans of the other iconic pizza places.

I love thin crust pizza, too, which Petrov's is known for. In Chicago, unlike in New York, thin crust is crispy and sturdy—never floppy. The first time I saw people in a movie fold pizza I was confused. Thin or stuffed, Chicago pizza, unless you buy it somewhere that sells by the slice out of a pizza warmer—which should only happen as a last resort—is a meal, not fast food.

The L rumbled beneath our feet as Lauren and I hurried across a six-corner intersection in West Town toward the original Petrov's. Old leafy trees and historic greystones and brownstones line a lot of the neighborhood streets. But Petrov's stands in a section of 1800s warehouses and factory buildings converted to other uses. Now most are loft apartment or condo buildings, boutiques, art galleries, or restaurants.

We passed lots of restaurants that serve the cuisines of the immigrants who settled the area in the 1900s. On the same block as Petrov's was an Italian restaurant I'd been to with Ty, a tavern where I tried Polish pierogis for the first time, and a Ukrainian restaurant. The café next door to it had a mural of rainbows behind the city skyline painted across its brick front wall. The hazelnut vanilla scent drifting out its open door almost made me rethink my dislike of coffee.

The Petrov's Restaurant and Pizzeria sign included the legend *Family Owned And Operated Since 1929*, the year the Great Depression started. Tough time to start a business.

The inside smelled of baking bread, fresh garlic, butter, and mozzarella. Maroon vinyl tablecloths covered the tables. All but two in the narrow main room were filled.

A bar ran along the back of a side room with about ten empty overflow tables. Colored string lights twinkled above the bar. One woman sat at the far end, a fountain soda with a plastic swizzle stick in front of her. Lauren took a seat in the middle.

The bartender wore a blue collared shirt with rolled up sleeves. Tattoos covered his arms. The largest was of the Picasso sculpture that stands in Chicago's Daley Plaza. I gave him my name and told him I was here to see Ivan Petrov. He waved me toward a set of metal double doors. I glanced at Lauren, who was already studying the menu.

"Take your time," she said. "They've got caviar. You don't see that at Lou Malnati's."

I'd never heard of caviar at a pizza restaurant. But I'd also never been to a pizza place with a Russian name. And leave it to Lauren to find the most upscale item the second she opened the menu.

Ivan Petrov's gray metal desk nearly filled his small office.

I held out my hand. "Mr. Petrov. I'm Quille Davis. And I'm so sorry for your loss."

When Ivan stood to shake my hand his chair slid back a few inches and bumped the brick wall behind him. An inch or so shorter than me, his hair was stark white but thick. Heavy lines etched into his forehead and neck. Research earlier in the day told me he was in his late seventies, but he moved quickly and gracefully. His tan business suit, plain but tailored, fit him well.

"Julia's detective lawyer." He jerked his head toward the single lumpy-looking armchair in front of the desk.

"Yes." I didn't describe myself that way, but it fit. The chair creaked when I sat and again when I moved to set my leather shoulder bag on the worn wood floor.

His top lip curled. "Bossy woman, Julia. But she's right. Someone should look at this. The police won't."

"Why do you say that? About the police?" I wondered why he saw Julia as bossy, too, but that mattered less for the moment.

"They're thugs. What do they know?"

"Anything in particular they said or did that makes you think that?"

"They've done nothing, that's the point. They assume my son was mugged by some stranger. Makes it easier for them. They do a half-hearted check of the area for witnesses or nearby cameras and they're done."

"I take it they found none of either?"

"You take it correctly. The cameras were out of service on that part of the 606. Our taxpayer dollars at work. And they claim none of the buildings with their own cameras cover the spot where my son was found. Or the trail above it."

As he spoke about the police, Ivan crisscrossed his fingers over one another, then opened them wide, then crisscrossed, then opened, over and over.

I took out a yellow legal pad. "It helps me narrow the investigation early if I can rule out people close to the crime victim. Where were you the night Randall was killed?"

"Really? His father? You want an alibi from his father?"

"I do."

"Hmph. Good. You should get one from everyone." He lifted one finger. "But before I give you mine, convince me you're the right person to do this."

"I've done it before. Multiple times, starting with my boyfriend's death a few years ago. And I solved my sister's murder over three decades after it happened."

"So. You might be a good investigator but your luck's bad," he said.

I blinked. "What do you mean?"

"People die around you."

"People come to me because someone died. Like Julia did. And my sister was killed before I was born. That had nothing to do with me."

My parents named me after her, which in some ways was bad luck I supposed. It led to me feeling as if I were in her shadow my whole life. But I suspected sharing her name was only part of that.

"And you think you can help Julia."

"I'll do my best."

Ivan scowled. "I didn't ask if you'll do your best. I asked if you can help."

"Julia and I discussed what I can and can't promise. The question is, are you willing to help?"

CHAPTER 6
IF YOU WERE TOUGHER

IVAN STOPPED CROSSING his fingers and formed them into a bridge instead. "I was visiting my wife. She was in a residential nursing facility. Alzheimer's. Until she died."

"Julia mentioned that. I'm sorry."

"Why? You didn't cause it."

This man was fun to talk with. "How long were you at the facility that night?"

"I didn't say I was there only at night. I arrived at four, just before the dinner hour. Dinner starts early there. I stayed until ten-fifteen, about half an hour after my wife fell asleep."

"Is that typical? To stay after she fell asleep?"

"Yes. She took a while to drift off. It helped if I was with her."

"How often did you visit?"

"Every Monday, Wednesday, Friday, and Sunday evening. Same schedule. The nurses can verify. And there are cameras all over. It helps keep track of the residents."

Ivan had no idea who Randall might have met that Sunday night. He couldn't confirm that the numbers in Randall's calendar referred to appointments. He didn't know who or what the initials PRG stood for. While he wasn't as sure as Julia that this hadn't been a random mugging, he believed Randall's killer was probably someone he knew. I asked why.

"Randall made poor life choices. They caught up with him. Lie down with dogs, and I lose my son."

He spoke almost as if Randall and his son were two separate people. It might just be a turn of phrase. But it could say something about their relationship.

The other phrase he shorthanded was one my Gram was fond of—lie down with dogs, you wake up with fleas.

"Who do you see as the fleas in Randall's life?"

His eyebrows lowered. "If you don't know you're not much of a detective."

"Your view of fleas might be different from mine."

Plus I only learned of Randall's death a day ago, giving me no time for the research I like doing before I talk to witnesses or suspects. But Ivan struck me as someone who viewed any attempt to explain as an excuse. It'd be more helpful to hear his insights about Randall rather than how he thought I ought to conduct business.

He huffed. "Vegas people. People who run casinos. They're dangerous. I told him that. But he had to keep pulling rabbits out of hats. He never listened to me. He listens to Julia—he did listen to her. But not me."

Randall met Julia a long time after he left Vegas, but I guessed

Ivan meant overall. I asked, but he didn't know the names of anyone Randall worked for or with in Las Vegas.

"Randall moved back to Chicago decades ago, correct?" I said.

"He could have kept in touch with people out there. Owed them favors. Money."

"Did he borrow money? I thought Randall was set financially. Due to your family's trust and the business."

"If you mean he got money for nothing, he did. I tried to change that, but I couldn't. And gamblers always borrow."

A clatter of plates, a crash, and a muffled curse came from the hallway alongside Ivan's office. Ivan grimaced but kept his eyes fixed on me.

"Did Randall gamble?"

"That's what Vegas people do."

After a few more questions, Ivan admitted he had no specific reason to believe Randall gambled or borrowed money.

"Why did he get money when he didn't work in the business?"

"His grandfather set it up that way. I told him no good comes of free money. What if we all decided not to work? No more Petrov's restaurants."

"How does the trust work?"

"Everyone in the family gets an income from the trust and a share of the business whether they work or not. If they work in the business, they also get a salary. And a vote on how it's run."

"Did Randall ever work in the business?"

"During high school. And summers during college. That was it. Never earned wages after that."

"From Petrov's."

"From anywhere. Everything he did was freelance. As far as I know. No salary, no benefits."

"He got benefits through the family, though, correct?"

Julia had explained to me that the family had what's sometimes called a paper company. They bought their vehicles at company fleet rates. They got better insurance benefits and rates because they could shop as a group. It's one of many ways the very rich skate around day-to-day hurdles the rest of us face. Lauren's family has the same type of company. She and I both work for ourselves, but unlike me she never needs to worry about, for example, being able to buy decent health insurance.

"But he should have worked for those benefits. Like I do. I came into this business and grew it. I took my income from the trust and grew it. Randall lived on his."

"And you think money, or the lack of it, caused his death?"

"You're the detective. You tell me."

"It's too early to tell. You're the first person I talked to other than Julia. Your son Max isn't eager to talk to me."

"Max isn't eager to do anything but strut around pretending to matter. Both my sons—worthless."

I bit back a comment about speaking ill of the dead. People handle grief in different ways. My parents turned my five-year-old sister, the original Q.C. Davis, into a legend. The perfect child. The most talented, the prettiest, the sweetest. Someone I must strive to—but could never— equal. Ivan was speaking of Randall just as he had, I guessed, when he was alive. Maybe a way to preserve his son's memory? Or he chose harsh words out of anger at his son for dying.

I asked when he last saw Randall.

"A month or so ago. Julia insisted the three of us get together for dinner every three or four weeks."

"Max didn't join you?"

"Now and then. But she made sure Randall and I were there. Before he met her, I saw him a couple times a year."

"You say she insisted, as if you didn't want to do it. You don't strike me as a man who does anything he doesn't want to do."

"You're right." His head bobbed almost imperceptibly. "I wanted to see my son. He didn't want to see me, but Julia insisted."

"Did Randall tell you he didn't want to see you?"

The dynamic between father and son might not relate to Randall's murder. But it could tell me a lot about both men.

"He didn't have to. He never invited me until he married bossy Julia."

I asked more questions but got few helpful answers. Ivan didn't know of anyone who held a grudge against Randall. He knew next to nothing about the non-profit Randall started, Magic Works, but it didn't impress him. He saw Randall as a layabout who never worked a day in his adult life. To Ivan, being a magician wasn't work. Neither was founding a charity or training volunteers, though he admitted that the only reason Randall didn't get paid was because he declined a salary. He felt he had enough money and the non-profit needed it more.

"I admire that," I said. "But it sounds like you might not."

Ivan pointed a finger at me. "A man works, he ought to get paid. Not give his time away."

"What about money? Do you donate to any charities?"

I couldn't help wondering where Randall got his bent toward volunteer work.

"My wife did. The accountant will make sure that keeps on."

"Did she donate to Magic Works?"

"Oh, yes, yes. She had a soft spot for Randall. And Max. Mama's boys, both of them. Probably why Julia could run right over Randall."

"And Max? Is he married?"

"Divorced. Two kids. Nine and eleven. Neither interested in the business. Another generation that'll get money for nothing."

The kids were preteens, a little early to know for sure if they were interested. Though I had started working at age ten as a stage actor. Maybe Ivan had a point.

I asked if Max and Randall got along.

Ivan brushed lint off his shoulder. "During high school they worked as bus boys here. But Max went out of state to college. By the time he got back, Randall moved to Las Vegas to waste time as a magician. Max, he insisted on working for me."

That word again. For a man with such strong opinions, Ivan appeared to see his relationships, and some of his business, as out of his control.

"You didn't want Max to work for you?"

"I told him he needed to get a job somewhere else first. Get some work experience. But he was too incompetent to get hired elsewhere. So what could I do? I took him in."

Despite that Max yelled at me over the phone, I felt bad for him. Feeling like your parent doesn't believe in you is tough enough. Having your parent say it to you must be far worse, and I had no doubt Ivan did. I had issues with my dad right now. But he always told me he admired my singing and acting and later my success in business and law. My mother, on the other hand, flipped between criticizing and ignoring me. But I felt sure that stemmed from her anger that I got to do so much while my sister's life was cut short.

And my Gram, who did the most to raise me, encouraged and believed in me every step of the way. Whatever else is wrong with my family, I'm grateful for that.

After a few more questions, I thanked Ivan for his time and put my legal pad away. "Is Max here today? If I approach him in person it might be harder for him to say No."

Ivan snorted. "Here? Max? That's way too close to real work for him. He presides over the corporate office downtown. But he'll contact you. I'll see to it."

I stood. "I'm happy to follow up with him myself."

"No need. You'll hear from him tonight." He put his hands on the desk and pushed himself to a standing position. "May I offer you some advice?"

"Feel free."

"You're too nice to be a detective. Or a lawyer. If you don't toughen up you'll never survive."

"You see a conflict between being kind and doing a good job?"

He shook his head and came around the desk. "You're young. You'll understand when you're older."

"How old do you think I'll need to be?"

"Older than you are."

"I'm thirty-seven."

He studied me. "Hmphf. You don't look it. But if you were tougher, you'd do better."

"I'll keep your advice in mind." I slipped my leather bag over my shoulder. "Before I go, is there anything else you can tell me about Randall? It doesn't need to be what you think of as evidence."

Ivan clamped his lips together and looked around the room as if answers might be written on the brick walls. "My son was kind. Too kind. But he never took anything at face value. He was the type of man who never misses the chance to tell people they're wrong. No one ever likes that man."

I wondered if that last comment reflected how people saw Ivan, not Randall. But there's a reason like-father-like-son is a cliche.

"Most victims aren't killed just because they're not liked."

"No. But if you publicly prove someone wrong, you've done a terrible thing. It might be the right thing. But it's a terrible thing. Someone might resent that enough to kill."

CHAPTER 7
PIZZA AND CAVIAR

I JOINED Lauren at the bar as she slipped her silver Visa card into her wallet.

"I got us a table," she said. "The pizza looks absolutely fabulous."

"How was the caviar?"

Her nose wrinkled. "Less caviar, more handful of potato chips, boatload of sour cream, and a tiny stray egg or two. But I learned a ton."

We settled at a table in a dark corner, away from the sunlight streaming through the wide windows in the main room. Normally I like sunny spots, but I didn't want to be overheard.

After we ordered, Lauren told me the bartender, Nico, was a longtime Petrov family friend. He started working at Petrov's Pizza over three decades ago, when this one was still the only location. He was an artist, too.

"I looked him up when he was helping someone else," Lauren said. "He does giant landscapes in oil paint. Giant like you could walk into them. They sell for tens of thousands of dollars. But he didn't start really selling until a few years ago."

"I'm surprised he still works here."

"He said he likes to get out around people to balance all his hours inside painting. Plus he paints during the day for the sunlight, so working evenings is perfect."

Nico had assumed Randall's death was a random mugging. But when Lauren told him Julia asked me to look into it, he said Julia might be right.

I spread butter on a chunk of black rye bread, one of three types in the basket at the center of the table. "Did he say why he thought that?"

"After I asked. And ordered a second glass of champagne."

"Which is why I'm buying dinner." I bit into the bread. It tasted faintly of sourdough but had a coarser texture.

"Seriously not. You shelled out enough today for my event. And this is fun for me."

"We'll decide later. Did Nico know of anyone with a grudge against Randall?"

"No. But he said Randall spoke his mind. If he thought someone was wrong, he pointed it out, thinking everyone wanted to learn the truth if they were mistaken."

It was a kinder spin than Ivan's take on his son. "I'm guessing others didn't always see it that way?"

"Probably not. Nico couldn't think of examples though."

"Did he remember when Randall and Max were busboys?"

Lauren frowned as she pulled a piece of ciabatta apart to butter it. "You knew about that? I thought I had a scoop. But did you know they fought about everything? And I mean fought. One night they had a fist fight and the police came."

"What started it?"

"Their dad, Ivan, let Randall do magic shows for the customers on some of the off nights. Right here in this room. One night Max came back from college—it was his first year—with a bunch of frat boys. They were all drunk, talking loud and banging into chairs when they came in during the middle of the show. Randall soldiered through. But he took it totally personally. When it was over, he punched Max out."

Odd that Ivan didn't mention that when I asked if the two got along. While it happened over thirty-five years before, it sounded like that was when the brothers spent the most time together.

"Julia told me Randall wasn't a fighter. And he wasn't a big guy."

Lauren finished the last piece of black bread. "Sounds like neither was Max at the time. Nico said he started working out and bulked up after that. I bet Randall was scrappy. You don't work a bunch of nightclubs and bars without learning to defend yourself."

The server appeared with a new basket of black rye, focaccia, and ciabatta. Lauren and I ordered a bottle of Chianti and a sausage pizza.

"Randall would've still been in high school then," I said after the server left. "Not working in nightclubs and bars."

"According to Nico, he was. He used to do his act in some of them, but he wasn't allowed to sit in the audience or drink alcohol."

"Really? He must have been good for them to take the trouble."

Lauren pushed the bread basket to the far end of the table, out of her reach. "It sounds like him being so young and such a good performer made him a novelty."

I made a note on my legal pad to research that. "What did Ivan do when he heard about the fight? Or was he there?"

"Not sure if he was there. But he fired Randall."

"What? He forgot to tell me that part of the family history."

Lauren had heard the same story of Randall's background that I knew from Julia. Randall moved to Las Vegas and started performing there as soon as he finished college. When he returned to Chicago, he started Magic Works. His mother donated some funds to help get it rolling and helped Randall connect with other donors.

When the pizza arrived it was so hot it steamed. The crust tasted buttery and crispy, but there was a little too much garlic in the sauce for both me and Lauren.

I slid a second slice onto my plate. "Ivan pretty much scoffed at the non-profit. And Randall's magic. I'm surprised he let him do shows here."

"I've got to think the only thing most parents want to hear less than that their kid wants to be an artist or musician is probably a magician," Lauren said.

"Except my mother." I sipped my wine, enjoying the smoky flavor with a slight hint of cherry.

"Sure but she's probably the only mother disappointed her kid became a lawyer instead of an actor," Lauren said.

"One of the few at least. What was Nico's view of Max?"

"He didn't like him. He didn't say it, but I could totally tell. He talked a lot about how hard Randall worked as a bus boy but said Max was marking time until he could come back after college and take over."

"And did he? Take over? My sense is old man Ivan still runs the show."

"That's the idea I got, too. But Max created a job for himself. Vice President, Marketing."

"Right out of college he ran the marketing department? Must be nice to be the boss's son."

"Right out of college he created the marketing department. The company didn't have one before."

"Huh. Really? If they wanted to expand, seems like they needed one."

"Yeah, Nico said the second Petrov's opened a year or two after Max came back. Then the third a year later. Nico sort of grudgingly said without Max that wouldn't have happened."

A slightly different picture than Ivan painted of his son, but that was no surprise. In every lawsuit or investigation, I hear many versions of what happened. Some get closer than others to what's probably the whole truth. But none of us can step back far enough from our lives to take ourselves out of the picture.

Sunset was over an hour away when Lauren and I left, so we hopped on the Blue Line subway. It was only a fifteen-minute ride, then a three-minute walk to get home. Alone, for safety I would have taken a taxi or an Uber. But Lauren and I live in the same condo building. We didn't need to part ways until the elevator.

Once home, I took my laptop onto my condo deck and researched the Petrovs. The restaurant website didn't mention Randall. It did feature his grandfather, long dead. But he was the founder.

I clicked on a company history video to see which family members it included. A deep-voiced narrator spoke over changing photos of Chicago streets from the 1920s on. Now and then photos of all types of food appeared, with more and more of the crisp thin crust pizza Petrov's later became famous for as the timeline neared today.

> In the early 1920s, the Petrov family arrived in the United States from Russia. They settled in the thriving Chicago neighborhood now known as West Town. Ivan Petrov Senior, a passionate cook and believer in the American dream, started a diner. Customers there enjoyed classic Russian dishes like savory pelmeni dumplings, beef stroganoff, and homemade borscht. Ivan made diners feel like part of the Petrov family. Russian immigrants viewed the diner as their home away from home.
>
> Ivan, though, fell in love with the thin crust pizza a nearby Italian restaurant served. Early tries at creating his own pizza recipe humbled Ivan. But after many attempts, he perfected the dish. Its distinct combination of rich tomato sauce, savory cheese, and unique Russian-influenced toppings set it apart from the crowd, yet still pleased diehard pizza enthusiasts. Thus, the diner became Petrov's Restaurant and Pizzeria, often simply called Petrov's Pizza by locals.
>
> Over time, Ivan's son Ivan Petrov Junior joined the business. By the late 20th century, Petrov's Pizza was a household name in Chicago. But it was Ivan's grandson Max Petrov who truly shaped the future of the family business. Born and raised in

Chicago, Max decided to open a second Petrov's Pizza in Albany Park and a third in Old Town.

Max then looked to Chicago's iconic pizzerias like Lou Malnati's and Giordano's for more inspiration. He began shipping pizzas all over the United States. By the early 2000s, the Petrovs opened pizzerias in nearby states as well, including Indiana and Wisconsin.

Alongside the famous thin crust pizzas, Petrov's offers side dishes and appetizers, including Russian caviar, that nod to the family's Russian heritage. The mix of Italian, American, and Russian cuisines continues to captivate pizza fans from all over the country and the world.

I noticed the video not only left out Randall but barely mentioned his father, Ivan Junior. At the same time, it credited Max with all the growth after the first restaurant. As head of the marketing department, Max likely influenced how the story was told. Skipping over Ivan might have resulted from the way Ivan treated his son.

A warm breeze drifted over the deck. I shut my eyes for a second, listening to the faint traffic sounds and the L trains rumbling across elevated tracks. My body longed for sleep. But I had far too much to do tomorrow to end my day now. Plus I hadn't jogged in days. The trainer I work with—a retired police academy instructor—stresses the need to stay in the best shape possible if I insist on doing things like investigating murders. That meant getting up half an hour early to jog to the lake and back.

Yet instead of getting ready for bed, I clicked on a video by Randall. It showed how to do an astrology reading that sounded personal yet fit anyone who listened to it. He talked about statements like, "You're dealing with some challenges in your relationships, but soon you'll hear from someone close to you....You feel good when you're able to help other people, but sometimes you feel you let down those close to you....That thing you're most hoping for is just over the horizon. If you keep heading toward it, you'll find success or discover an even more rewarding path...."

As the video ended, an email came in from Max Petrov. Unlike his phone call, the email was polite if not friendly. He copied Julia and said he could meet with her and me tomorrow evening around five. After that, he had no time open during the next three weeks. A meeting barely fit my schedule. I had a deposition the next afternoon that was likely to run until at least four-thirty. But I'd be only four blocks from the bar Max suggested, which would help.

Ivan's efforts likely caused Max's willingness to meet, such as it was. And despite being angry Julia hired me, Max included her in our meeting. I didn't know why, but I meant to find out.

CHAPTER 8
INTERVIEW WITH A
BROTHER

THUNDER CLAPPED. I ducked into the Starbucks vestibule as sheets of rain poured down. My afternoon deposition had run long. While I'd been stuck in a windowless conference room the weather shifted from sunny and cool to rainy and steamy.

I called Julia. I knew I was in the right general area—the corner of LaSalle and Monroe in the heart of downtown Chicago. But I didn't see a sign for Vol 39, the cocktail bar Max chose. Julia's voicemail kicked in, and an auto-reply text informed me she was on the phone. I noticed a missed call from Ty that must have come while I had my phone off during the deposition. But now it was nearly five. That was two in the morning in Dubai.

The Starbucks barista told me Vol. 39 was upstairs and pointed to a door at the end of the long counter. It led into a hotel entryway with a glass front. Lightning flashed as I headed up a wide marble staircase with ornate wrought iron railings. On the second floor, I saw what looked like an upscale library. Glass and antique brass shelves held rows of old books.

"Volume," I said under my breath, realizing what the "Vol" stood for.

A woman in a black cocktail dress led me to a grouping of armchairs and a velvet couch far from the rattling windows. A man twisted in his chair toward me as I approached.

The dark eyes and wide forehead reminded me of photos of Randall. But this man's shoulders looked broader. His short sleeved polo shirt showed muscled forearms. In contrast, all the recent photos I saw of Randall showed him as whippet thin. When Max stood to shake my hand I found he was shorter than me. I guessed him about five four, the same height as Randall.

His grip was firm. "Sorry we got off on the wrong foot. Julia drives me crazy, but I shouldn't have taken it out on you."

"It's a tough time for everyone."

I sat on the velvet couch, my laptop at my side. I looped the straps of its case over my elbow to guard against forgetting it or anyone swiping it. A server in black pants and a white buttoned down shirt brought over a large glass bottle of water.

"Julia's running late," Max said. "Something about a settlement conference. Typical."

"That she runs late?" I wasn't familiar with most of the drinks on the cocktail menu. Each had at least eight ingredients. There was nothing as simple as a whiskey sour, my mixed drink of choice.

"That whatever she's doing is more important than anything else."

I pulled out my legal pad and flipped to the first blank page after my deposition notes. "You two don't get along?"

Max's broad shoulders rose and fell in an exaggerated shrug.

"We do. More or less. But I don't see why she brought a stranger into this."

"I'm not a stranger to her. And my family history—one of my sisters was murdered before I was born. I think Julia felt she could talk to me. Trust me."

"But my brother wasn't murdered. Or, he was, but it was random."

"You're sure of that?"

"The police said so. It makes the most sense. No offense to you. I know you make your living making things complicated. If it's simple, there's no need to investigate."

"I don't make my living solving crimes. I do it to help people, and I've had some success at it. But my main work is as a lawyer."

"Like I said—making things complicated."

"Your father thinks someone who knew Randall killed him."

"My father thinks a lot of things."

Julia hurried in, water droplets scattered over the shoulders of her suit jacket. I suspect many judges wear casual clothes under their robes. But Julia's not one of them. She looked tired, but rushing up the stairs had given her face some color. Her silver hair looked damp but neatly combed. She brushed a few strands away from her face as she sat across from me and next to Max.

After the server took our drink orders, I asked Max about the number and initials written in Randall's paper calendar.

"Julia thinks that's an appointment." Max wiggled his hand back and forth. "But 830 could refer to a magic trick or the start of a zip code. Or how much money Randall needed to transfer to his checking account. He used all kinds of crazy codes for things."

Julia huffed. "The 30 is in small print, smaller than the 8. Like it's a time. Look." She opened a photo on her phone of Randall's weekly planner. The number was written as she said, and the initials PRG were hand printed a few lines below it. "And no dollar sign. It's not about his checking account. And he doesn't number his magic tricks."

"He did when we were kids."

"Could it be an area code? Texas uses 830." I had looked that up during a lull while my opponent at the deposition went over his notes.

"He didn't know anyone in Texas." Julia clicked some keys on her phone. "Or Wyoming. Zip codes in Wyoming start with 830."

"He could have," Max said. "You knew him, what, a year or two?"

"Five years."

"I knew him for fifty-five. Plus."

The server set our drinks on the table. Julia had a Chardonnay and Max drank Scotch neat. I had a whiskey sour. It tasted a bit too strong and was served with a lime slice for some reason. Whiskey sours are made with lemon.

I pointed to the letters. "What about PRG?"

Max shook his head. "Means nothing to me. But I didn't know Randall's friends."

"Any of your employees or family members have those initials?" I said.

"No."

"Tell me about the trust and the business." I glanced at Julia, then shifted my gaze to Max. "Julia told me she doesn't benefit financially from Randall's death. True?"

"More or less," Max said. "She gets his personal things. But I doubt he had much that was valuable. Randall wasn't about things. Maybe she'll take over for him on the board of his non-profit."

Under the table, my nails dug into my palms. I ought to have asked Julia about Randall's board position on Magic Works already. This investigation felt like it was flying forward without me. I'd been thrown into interviews fast, and I'd barely done any research. It was the opposite of how I like to work.

"Will you?" I asked Julia.

"I already did. I want to make sure Magic Works goes on. It's Randall's legacy."

"And the family business?" I said. "Who takes over Randall's interest?"

Max answered. "No one. When any one of us dies, our interests are split among the remaining family members. When Randall died, my dad, mom, and I became one-third owners of Petrov's Pizza instead of one-quarter owners. Now that my mother passed, Dad and I are fifty-fifty partners."

"No tie breaker," I said.

"No tie breaker," Max said. "Not great."

A lot of company owners think fifty-fifty is a good idea until they reach an issue they can't agree on. Sometimes it tanks the entire business. It sounded like Max grasped that.

"But Randall didn't have voting rights, correct?" I said.

"No. But my mother did. She was still on the books as an employee and owner."

"Despite her Alzheimer's?"

"Until recently—about six or seven months ago—she still looked over and commented on all the marketing copy and the monthly financials. Less and less every week, but she did. We never shifted her off the payroll."

"Could you have shown Randall as an employee so he got a vote?" I sipped more of my drink. It tasted less strong now that the giant ice cube at its center had melted part way.

Max frowned. "That was different. Mom didn't choose to stop working. She couldn't anymore. Randall never did anything beyond bus tables."

"And with him gone, you get a bigger share of the profits," I said.

"Yes. And so does my dad."

"And a bigger share of the trust fund," Julia said.

Max glared at her. "What, you think I killed my brother for the money?"

"I never said that. I'm giving Quille a clear picture." Julia squared her shoulders and looked across the table at me. "The trust works the same as the business. When Randall died it became a third, a third, a third. And now Max and his father share fifty-fifty."

"Not the grandchildren?" I said.

"They don't take from the trust until I die." Max held his hand out straight, then dropped it flat on the word "die."

"How much more money do you get with Randall gone?"

"Not much." Max held up a finger to get the server's attention and pointed to his empty glass. "Seven or eight thousand a month each."

That was between eighty-four and ninety-six thousand more dollars a year. All the Petrovs had to be quite well off if adding that per year meant little.

"So Randall was getting twice that before his death?"

Julia nodded. "It's why he never took a salary from Magic Works."

"Did he earn money as a magician, too?"

"Once he moved back to Chicago he only performed at fundraisers," Julia said. "But in Vegas he did birthday parties, corporate parties, that sort of thing, plus shows."

Randall's videos, Julia told me, didn't earn any money. He did them to inform people so they wouldn't get scammed.

"This is a waste of time." Max rubbed his chin. "The simplest answer is best. Randall jogged every night. This time he picked the wrong time and place, that's all."

"Did he always jog the same time and place?" I asked. If so, anyone who knew his schedule could intercept him.

"No." Julia drank a little more wine. "It depended what time he finished work and we had dinner. He ran anywhere from four-thirty to nine-thirty. He liked the 606 trail, but he only jogged there if he was at the new loft. Most of the time, he jogged lake-front trails."

"Why would Randall jog on the 606 after dark? Are there a lot of people out there?"

I'd never run on the trail myself.

Max sipped the fresh glass of Scotch the server set on the table. "Not enough to make it safe. But Randall didn't have the sense God gave a horse."

Ivan thought Randall was lazy, and Max called him senseless. A wonderful family.

"No sense?" Julia said. "How dare—"

"Oh, please. Like he wasn't just as awful about me. He thought I was boring. A mama's boy with no original thought in my head. Direct quotes, by the way."

Julia stayed silent, pressing her lips together.

"Randall said those things to you?" I asked Max.

"To my dad. Who didn't hesitate to pass them on."

"And why do you say Randall had no sense?" I said.

"Who pulls rabbits out of a hat rather than go into the family business? Randall turned up his nose at the business our grand-father founded and left me to be the only one to help Dad."

"He never asked for your help," Julia said.

Based on Ivan's comments, I agreed, though I didn't feel a need to point that out to Max. Ivan Petrov might think I needed to act tough to be a better lawyer or investigator. But I find people open up more when they feel understood and listened to. Once

I had a case that dragged on for three years before I got involved. The woman on the other side hugged me after the settlement meeting. She told me I was the only one, including her own lawyer, who listened to her. That's why she finally accepted my client's thousand dollar offer to go away.

Max's jaw tightened. "Dad might not want my help, but he needed it. Without me, the original Petrov's Pizza would be the only Petrov's Pizza. And there'd be no online business. It'd be a neighborhood pizza joint. If it survived at all."

"Did you want Randall to join you in the business?" I asked.

Julia pointed at Max. "Good question. You always make it sound like your father preferred Randall over you, so why complain that he stayed out of your way?"

I wrote *Ivan preferred Randall?* on my legal pad. Ivan didn't strike me as fond of either son, but there's only so much you can learn in one conversation.

"Hah. If you heard Dad scream at me you'd know Randall was the favorite. He's always sure Randall would have done a better job."

"The sibling who's not there is the hardest to compete with," I said. For my mother, nothing I did or could do matched what Q.C. would have done had she lived.

Max glanced at me in surprise. "Yes. The Great Randall was perfect. But he never did the job. Never took the responsibility. He did what he wanted."

"He had fun while you worked hard," I said.

"You got it."

"When I talked to your father, he didn't seem thrilled with Randall. I was a little surprised because a lot of people remember only the good things about someone after they're gone."

Julia nodded, but Max folded his arms over his chest and glared at her. "Ivan ever tell you how amazing I was? How I was a better son than Randall?"

"What? No. Why would he say that to me?"

"He wouldn't. But he told me how amazing Randall was, how Randall was the better son. And he says it to my ex-wife. Over and over. And to my kids. My kids."

"I—I'm sorry." Julia rested her hand on Max's upper arm for a moment. "I didn't know."

Max squeezed his elbows tight against his sides, shrinking from her touch. "No big deal. I'm used to it."

I drank a little more of the watered down whiskey sour to give Max a moment. Then I turned a page on my legal pad. "More than one person told me Randall had a knack for pissing people off. True?"

He cleared his throat. "Very true."

"So someone could have had a grudge against him?"

"Probably more than one someone."

"Who are the someones? Who should I talk to?"

Max answered with no pause to think. "Start with Magic Works."

"What?" Julia's eyes widened. "Everyone there loved him."

"Not everyone," Max said.

CHAPTER 9
STORMING OUT

THE SERVER OFFERED DRINK REFILLS. Julia and Max hesitated. I asked for a ginger ale, hoping to extend the evening but not wanting more alcohol. My head already felt a bit fuzzy. Julia decided on a second Chardonnay and Max a third Scotch.

Max gulped the rest of his second drink and tapped his index finger on the table between us. "Magic Works stood to gain from Randall's death."

"How?"

"The money in Randall's personal investment accounts goes to Magic Works. Big payday for them."

Julia banged her wine glass on the table, hard enough that I was surprised it didn't break the stem. "No one there would kill Randall for the money. Magic Works was his mission. It mattered more to him than anything he'd ever done."

"I know, I know. It was his raison d'être. Settle down," Max said.

Julia glared at him. "Settle down?"

The server brought the next round and whisked away our empty glasses.

"Just because Randall loved Magic Works," Max said, "doesn't mean everyone there is above board."

"Who's not?" I tore out the last page of my legal pad, covered in writing already, and turned it over to use the back.

"There was an issue with the woman he started Magic Works with."

"Ridiculous. Colleen's lovely." Julia turned to me. "Randall met her in Vegas. She worked as a magician's assistant. Not Randall's. Someone else's."

Max took a long drink. "She might be 'lovely.' But when she became Executive Director, there was some sort of dust up. Half the board quit."

I glanced at Julia. "Did Randall ever mention that to you?"

"No. How long ago was this?"

Max shrugged. "Not long after he started it. Twenty years ago? Randall had to stay on the board and it pissed him off. He wanted Colleen and the board to run things and fundraise. Then he could find and train volunteers and get into more hospitals. Instead, he had to hassle with board members. He was not happy."

"So I should start with Magic Works because of a twenty-year-old board dispute?"

"Not just that," Max said. "Randall was aggravated with the board until the day he died. It made no sense. He could've been aggravated at Petrov's Pizza and earned money."

"But not helped sick kids," I said.

"Depends how you look at it. Petrov's and plenty of other companies donate to Magic Works. That helps a lot of sick kids."

Julia still felt sure no one at Magic Works had reason to be angry at Randall.

"Did Colleen and Randall ever clash over how to run Magic Works?" I said.

"If they did, I didn't see it," Julia said. "She and Randall were good friends. We had her over for dinner all the time. Her husband, too, when she was married."

I nodded toward Max. "What's your view of Colleen?"

"Schemer."

"Based on exactly what?" Julia said.

"Based on exactly instinct. You've got to have some in business."

"Judges have to have instincts too. Mine say there's nothing wrong with Colleen."

"Because Randall told you nothing but good things about her, no doubt. He bought anything she was selling." His eyes darted toward me. "Like I said, no common sense."

A man dedicated to exposing fraud didn't seem likely to be taken in by a scam, even by someone close to him. But everyone has blind spots. Colleen might have been Randall's.

"Are you saying he had feelings for Colleen?" I said.

Julia didn't look troubled by my question. I felt relieved. I didn't want to upset her. But I needed to ask about sensitive things to find the truth.

Max shook his head. "What, like an affair? Didn't get that vibe. But Colleen was there for him when he moved to Vegas. She helped him launch his quote-unquote career."

"As a magician," I said.

"Right," Max said.

Julia frowned. "Randall was a good judge of character. He trusted Colleen."

"It does sound like Randall wouldn't be easily fooled," I said. "At the same time, if someone Randall agreed to meet killed him, that person took him by surprise. Maybe played on his trust. I'll talk to Colleen. But the sting operation might be a better place to start."

Max stared at me. "The what?"

"Randall exposed psychics and mediums who defrauded people."

"Really?" Max snorted. "That's rich."

"Meaning?" I said.

"Randall worked as a psychic for decades in Vegas. Corporate events, bachelorette parties, psychic fairs. All woo-woo and scary." Max waved his fingers in the air. "Then he turns on people who do the same thing?"

"He did readings as entertainment," Julia said. "He made that clear. He never claimed he could really contact the dead."

Max shoved his chair back and threw his napkin down. His water spilled over as he stood and bumped the table. "Right. I'm sure he explained it perfectly. Because he is Randall the Great, Randall the Perfect. No hypocrisy there."

He stalked out of the room.

"I didn't see that coming," I said.

Julia wiped the table. "That's Max. You never know what'll set off that temper."

"So that wasn't unusual?"

"It didn't happen all the time. But maybe two, three times a year."

"Are you surprised Randall didn't tell him about doing stings?"

"No. I told you, he kept that quiet. And it wasn't as if Max could help him with it."

I shared what I found on Randall's computer about the psychic Nellie Havel. Julia had never heard of her.

"I will need to look into Magic Works," I said.

"I don't think you'll find anything off about it But you're right. Randall probably trusted whoever killed him. That's how they got so close. I stand by my faith in his instincts, but no one's perfect."

"And Max—ever seen him become violent?"

Julia shook her head.

I finished my ginger ale. "I hear he and Randall got into fights when they worked together. Including a fist fight that led to Randall getting fired."

"Randall got in a fist fight? Max must have started it, with that temper of his."

"Randall didn't have a temper?"

"You had to push him pretty far before he'd explode. And then it was yelling only. Never anything physical."

"As a teenager he might have been different."

"Maybe. But he didn't get fired from Petrov's. He quit to go to college."

Both stories could be true. Ivan Petrov might have fired his son in front of other employees, then walked it back. Randall might then have quit since he was leaving for college soon. Or Nico the bartender got it all wrong. But if the fist fight happened, it lent some weight to Max's point that there were sides of Randall Julia didn't know.

Something that could be said of all of us.

Max never returned. Julia paid the bill and we headed down the marble stairs together. In typical Chicago fashion, the weather had changed completely. The late evening air felt warm. The sidewalks were nearly dry. Julia ordered a ride from the Uber app.

"Did Oscar Miller—Randall's office landlord—send you the lease between him and Randall yet?" I said.

"No. Just his lease for the whole office suite with the Monadnock Building management company. Randall's not listed on it at all."

"Hm," I said. "So either Oscar Miller sent the wrong lease by mistake or there is no written sublease between him and Randall for that office."

"I'm thinking the latter." Julia's phone dinged. She glanced down the road, looking for her ride. "Randall would never have signed a long-term lease. We always planned to find a live/work loft space with enough room for him to train volunteers. That way he could work from home."

It was still light out and there were lots of people around, so I walked home. I stopped at Potbellies for a meatball sub. While I waited for it, I updated my task lists for the investigation and my law firm on my phone. And discovered I needed to work all day the next day, which was Friday, all day Saturday, and all day Sunday to have the faintest hope of keeping up with everything.

As if the talk about siblings earlier in the evening conjured her, my sister Kendra called when I walked in my door. I had a pretty good idea what she was going to say, which was why I'd been ignoring her voicemails. But I answered. Might as well get it over with.

She got right to it. "Dad says you've barely talked to him all summer."

"We talk every Sunday." I call my parents on Sunday mornings because, except in the most extreme weeks, I don't work then.

"You say Hello every Sunday. But he says you've talked to Mom about twenty times longer than him."

"I think he means I've listened to Mom." I dropped my keys on the small wood table right inside my door, put the phone on speaker, and headed for the kitchen area.

"I thought things were a little better. With you and Mom."

"Emphasis on little."

"You know what I mean. Why are you barely talking to Dad?"

At the kitchen island I unwrapped my sandwich and got myself a glass of water. "I need time. The things I learned about him are still sinking in. I'm not sure how I feel about it."

When I told Julia she might learn things she didn't want to know if I investigated for her, I spoke from experience.

Kendra's sigh came through the phone. "I guess it's easier for me. I didn't have a relationship with Dad to ruin."

"You had a relationship. Just not a close one. And I seem to remember you not talking to me back when I looked into your husband's life. At your request."

"I know, I know. I'm sorry. It's just…Dad feels awful. You kind of had him up on a pedestal and now the secret's out that he's human after all."

"I never thought he was perfect." My stomach rumbled as I eyed my sandwich. "Let's talk about this another time. It's been a long day and I'm starving."

And a little buzzed from the alcohol with no dinner.

"Sure. The kids and I are driving in to see Gram tomorrow. Will you be around Saturday morning?"

"Uh, yeah." My mind raced as I thought of everything on my task lists. It was impossible. But I never saw my niece and nephew as much as I wanted. And Kendra rarely came along when they visited. I couldn't pass it up.

"Great. I'll text you about plans."

I bit into my sandwich as soon as we hung up, getting tomato sauce on my blazer. As I wiped it away, I thought about how I might combine things.

One idea came to me right away. It was a long shot, but there was no downside if it didn't work. After checking with Julia, I texted Lauren.

Still have that empty seat at Saturday's benefit?

CHAPTER 10
CARDS AND MAGIC

CHICAGO'S SUBWAY and elevated train system is color coded and runs throughout the city. The Blue Line, the same one that reaches West Town where the first Petrov's Pizza stands, also goes to Logan Square. Randall and Julia's loft condo was in a building in that neighborhood.

Before I went there, though, I took a railroad line to LaGrange, the suburb where my Gram lives. After a morning visit with her, Kendra, and my niece and nephew, I took the railroad line back downtown, walked about eight blocks, and got on the Blue Line. I arrived at Randall's building by two.

Randall and Julia's loft was on the ninth of ten floors. The common area hall smelled of sawdust and the sounds of hammering and sawing filtered into it. Inside the loft, though, I didn't hear any construction noise.

Morning sun streamed through large windows into the open plan kitchen, living, and dining area. There were no rugs or window treatments. My flats echoed on the hardwood floors. Other than a few paint cans under the sink, the kitchen cabinets were empty.

The second largest of four bedrooms was the only room that was furnished. A rectangular table with two removable leaves stood at its center. Padded conference room chairs surrounded it. A large flatscreen monitor was mounted on the wall, though I didn't see a computer or laptop anywhere. A shelving unit on one of the long walls held props for magic tricks. This must be where Randall planned to work with Magic Works volunteers.

The only trace of recent human activity was from the police—fingerprint dust across all the surfaces. Detective Sergeant Beckwell, my friend at the Chicago PD, wasn't handling the case. But he was a supervisor and had access to the file. He was willing to share information given our work together on past cases, including one where he asked me to investigate a matter involving his son.

He'd told me that only Randall's and the realtor's fingerprints had been recovered. Julia confirmed that she had a cleaning service come in right after they closed on the unit. If Randall's killer met him here, that person had been very careful about touching anything.

Beckwell told me, too, that no neighbor saw or heard Randall the night he was killed. But concrete floors beneath hardwood or carpet and brick interior walls made the building fairly soundproof, at least from one condo to another, as the lack of construction noise showed.

I only had an hour or two before I needed to get home and change for the benefit tonight. But I went through each item in the shelving unit. I found it only held magic props. After I took photos of the entire loft, I headed for the spot where Randall was killed. His building's main entrance was about three blocks from an outdoor metal stairway that led up to the 606 elevated trail. Randall's body was found on the sidewalk about a block from the stairway. Assuming Randall knew his killer, that person might have met Randall at the loft and taken a walk with him. Or the killer might never have gone to the loft at all but made an appointment to meet Randall on the 606. Or simply knew enough to wait there to ambush him. A last option was that the killer just happened to run into Randall, the two argued, and it escalated.

Using the photos and police report as a guide, I found the section above where Randall had been found. I gripped the railing and stared down at the sidewalk below. It was a nearly two-story drop, making it unlikely anyone could survive the fall.

There was a pole with a camera about thirty feet away. But according to police, as Randall's father complained of, it hadn't been working. No huge surprise. Safety matters, but so do hundreds of other expenses the city can't keep up with. Despite an extra sales tax on anything bought downtown, real estate transfer fees for buying or selling property in the city, and any number of other fees and taxes, Chicago is deep in debt. Many Chicagoans talk up the second Mayor Daley—son of the mayor for whom the Daley Center was named—but he kicked a lot of cans down the road when it came to costs.

Which means some things don't work so well in the city that works.

The flared skirt of my emerald cocktail dress brushed against an array of magnets with photos of Chicago skylines. It knocked five or six of them onto the off-white, scuffed tile floor. I needed to be at the Cultural Center for the benefit in twenty minutes. But the Walgreens was just across the street, so I had plenty of time.

I squatted to collect the magnets from the floor, not wanting to bend over and risk giving anyone nearby a peek at my underwear.

As I stood, a slim man with sandy brown hair and dressed in a tux headed for me. His lips quirked into the half-smile I remembered well. And I was struck, as always, by the black lashes around his pale blue eyes.

Dylan Sabatini nodded at my outfit. "At last, someone else who gets the importance of formalwear for souvenir shopping."

I met Dylan when I investigated the original Q.C.'s murder. He was a childhood friend of both my sisters. He moved back to Edwardsville, where my parents still live, temporarily. A musician and high school teacher, early this summer he'd moved to Chicago to enter a graduate school program. I sent him to Lauren for help finding an apartment. I hadn't seen him since.

"You're going to the benefit?" I said.

"Absolutely, as your friend Lauren might say. But I was early so I'm getting a little shopping in." He held a box of Tylenol in his hand.

"She put the arm on you to help fill her table."

"That she did."

"Okay, I owe her for helping me with my investigations. But you earned her a commission by taking that apartment. How'd she get you to buy a ticket?"

"Told me you'd be here."

Dylan's an admitted flirt, so I didn't take what he said at face value.

"Right." I held up my phone. "Because a text or a phone call costs way more than that."

"We couldn't see each other in Black Tie over the phone." He glanced at the magnets, T-shirts, and mugs with Chicago scenes on them. "Low on Chicago memorabilia?"

I pointed at a rack of greeting cards. "I need a birthday card for my mother. If I don't mail it first thing Monday, there's a good chance it'll get there late."

"I thought your parents didn't celebrate birthdays."

The original Q.C. Davis was kidnapped from her own birthday party when she was five. Since then, no one in my family really celebrates birthdays.

"They don't. But that doesn't stop my mother from being upset if she thinks I forgot hers."

Dylan spun the rack and took out a few cards. "To the sweetest mother in the world…You're more than a mom, you're my best friend…Another word for 'kindness' is 'Mom'….Hm."

"You see the challenge."

Dylan's relationship with his father is much like mine with my mother, so he understands.

"You want to be honest, but you want to say something nice, and nothing here walks that line." He spun the rack. "Have you tried blank ones?"

"That's worse. What do I write? 'You're my mom, thanks for not raising me, Happy Birthday'? It's honest. I was better off with my Gram taking over. But it doesn't quite feel like a Happy Birthday message."

"I thought things might be better with you two. You solving your sister's murder and all."

"A little better. But what I learned stirred up things between her and my dad once she really thought about it. So now she calls to tell me all the ways he's driving her crazy. And sort of blames me because I'm the one who set it off."

"Well, sure." Dylan flipped through a few more cards. "Very careless of you to uncover some family secrets while you solved a decades-old murder. You are so thoughtless, Quille."

"That's me. Though to be fair, she did ask how I was last Sunday for the first time in—for the first time."

I didn't say it to Dylan, but I choked up when my mother asked me that. She moved on to talk about something else before I could answer. But at least she inquired in the first place. My mother was so depressed or filled with anxiety, or both, most of my life that there was little room in her crowded mind or heart for anything else. All my life, my job had been to take care of her and be considerate of her feelings, not the other way around.

"That's progress." Dylan shuffled through a few more cards. "And my take on the card thing, if you want it? Write about the day."

"What?"

He chose a card with a photo of one of the prettiest parts of the Chicago Riverwalk. "The day you want her to have. That's what I do. 'Dear Dad. Wishing you a birthday filled with peace and joy, and all the best things life can bring. Love, Dylan.' It's sincere. I do wish him all those things. At least for a day. And whether or not I feel like I love him, I do love him because he's my father."

I nodded. "Perfect."

He handed me the card. "Feel free to steal it. Unless you think our parents are going to compare notes."

"Last I checked, Mom was avoiding all things relating to my investigation. Almost all things." I glanced at the time on my phone. "Ugh. I was hoping for one more errand before I headed upstairs."

"Cocktail hour's barely started. You've got time."

"Can't. I'm meeting someone there."

"Oh. Is Ty in for a visit?"

I headed for the cashier, the expensive heels I bought at Lauren's urging clacking on the tiles. I had to admit, though I balked at the price, they were far easier to walk in than my usual brand. "No. He had to cancel. I'm meeting someone for an investigation."

"And Lauren approved? She told me you need to have fun. And I'm required to make sure you do."

I tapped my credit card, feeling foolish putting such a small amount on it. But the only open checkout line didn't take cash. "Really? She took your money and gave you an assignment?"

"More or less."

I tucked the blank card, grateful it was small, into my evening bag. "So I'm a charity case."

"I did donate five hundred dollars to charity to see you."

"Texting—still free."

The Cultural Center, right across the street, was built over a hundred years ago as Chicago's first central public library. Now it hosts art and history exhibits, concerts, dances, and lectures, most of them free. The mosaic tiled entryway on the Washington Street side is breathtaking. Two of the Center's largest rooms can be rented for events and feature soaring glass domes.

On the elevator ride up to one of them I turned to Dylan. "You weren't serious about donating the five hundred because I'd be here, were you? I haven't heard from you since you got to town."

He gave a slight shrug. "You didn't look all that thrilled when I showed up on your doorstep. So I didn't text. I didn't want to seem like I was hanging around hoping things didn't work out with your long-distance boyfriend."

"And now?" We stepped out on the third floor and I glanced around for a sign directing us to the event.

"One, I figure by now things are working or they're not. You'll tell me. Two, Lauren's hard to say No to. And three, your mother—"

"My mother?"

Before Dylan could answer, the second elevator dinged and an older woman in a long blue evening gown stepped out and stared at me. "Quille?"

She looked about five years older and twenty or thirty pounds heavier than her profile photo. But the curly dark brown hair and heart-shaped face were the same. This was Colleen Cahill, Executive Director of Magic Works.

CHAPTER 11
CAREER CHANGE

I HAD CALLED Colleen Thursday and explained who I was. After answering her questions about why and how I planned to look into Randall's death, I offered her a free ticket to Lauren's event. Julia was paying, but Colleen didn't need to know that. It gave me the chance to talk to her in a relaxed social setting. And I could multi-task by attending the event myself as promised.

I told Colleen it was Black Tie and that she might meet more people willing to spend to support Magic Works. Colleen already had plans for the night. But she'd been trying to grow her donor base, so she said she was tempted.

"I'm guessing you want to talk about Randall's death, too?" she said. "I'm so glad Julia is having someone look into it."

"Yes. Let's try to talk before dinner. Then you can relax and enjoy the rest of the evening."

"Well, why not? I never get to dress up anymore. I'll see you there."

The air in the Preston Bradley Hall on the third floor of the Cultural Center buzzed with excitement. Well-dressed guests talked and drank under the vaulted Tiffany glass dome. Art deco wall sconces and crystal chandeliers cast a warm glow over the space.

Lauren stood under an archway in a sleek but sparkly cocktail dress. When I introduced Colleen, Lauren gushed over her Thred Up webpage. She'd researched Colleen and discovered a fellow fan of designer clothes. I kept an eye on them while I grilled Dylan about his conversation with my mother. Based on what he told me, I was tempted to slip into a quiet photo exhibition hallway to call her. Instead, I got a drink at the bar, then approached Colleen and Lauren.

I smiled at Colleen. "Do you mind if we get some questions out of the way now?"

"Of course, of course. Whatever I can do. I still can't get over it. Randall. Murdered. It's devastating. For me. For Magic Works. For everyone."

"I'll go say Hello to my client." Lauren squeezed my arm. "Remember, you're supposed to have fun. No working all night."

Colleen and I moved to the other side of the room, far from the four-piece quartet so we could hear each other. We snagged a tall table as two other guests left. It was draped in black cloth with tiny rhinestone roses strewn across it.

I opened the Notes app on my phone. "You knew Randall before Magic Works, didn't you? From your Las Vegas days?"

"Yes, yes." Colleen pushed aside the empty glasses the other guests left and set her champagne flute down. "He opened for the two illusionists I worked with in Vegas. They were like Penn and Teller but a little less well known." She bent her head toward me and half-whispered as if the famous illusionists might hear her. "Better looking, though."

Colleen told me she'd worked as a dealer in Vegas, too. When Randall moved back to Chicago and decided to start Magic Works, he called to beg her to help out.

"Why you?" I said.

"I made the mistake of telling him once that I was getting tired of Vegas and wished I had something more stable."

I shifted to allow a white-haired woman to squeeze past me. "And more stable was starting a brand new non-profit?"

Colleen touched my arm just below the elbow. "The exact point I made to Randall. But he promised to match what I was earning if he had to pay me out of his own pocket to do it."

"And he did that?"

"Just for a while. With his income from the family trust. He said he was putting in seed money for other things so why not to pay the salary of someone he trusted."

I typed a few notes, then looked at Colleen again. "Had you run a business before?"

The Magic Works website included one-sentence bios of Colleen and the current and past board members. It said nothing about her work before becoming the non-profit's Executive Director.

"I basically ran the illusionists' business. Before me, they were popular on the Strip, but they struggled financially. I whipped them into shape. My college major was business, but I never wanted to work in a corporation."

"That was my major, too," I said. "I did it to help my career as an actress. But I ended up liking the world of accounting. And later law."

"And now murder investigations?"

"It's an odd combination I know. But yes. You handle fundraising, too?"

"Yes, yes. That's what Randall really wanted me to do. I've got no problem asking people for money. He hates it. Hated it." She shivered and looked down at her hands for a second. "I still can't believe this happened."

The more people joined the throng, the warmer and louder the room became. I pressed my glass against the inside of my wrist, enjoying the coolness for a moment. Then I asked Colleen how the fundraising worked when she started at Magic Works.

"If Randall wanted to approach someone he or his family knew, we worked as a team. Met them for cocktails, told them about Magic Works. Invited them to events. For new people, it was all me. Within a few months we had regular donations coming in and started applying for grants. By six months in, my salary came from the non-profit, not Randall."

"That was a big career change for you." I drank a little of my whiskey sour, which I'd asked the bartender to make with very little whiskey. It was more like a fresh squeezed lemonade on ice.

"It came at the perfect time. I just met a guy, not a huge gambler thank God. He was from Wisconsin. I wasn't sure where it was going, but I moved to Woodstock. We got married and had kids. Then divorced. That part's not great. But I'm glad I came here."

Woodstock is a far northwest Chicago suburb, closer to the Wisconsin state line than to Chicago.

"You've got a long drive home."

"Oh, I'm staying with a friend in the city." She set her empty champagne flute on the tray of a passing waiter and took a full glass. "No worries about driving home."

I thought about the timeline. "A recession hit not long after you moved here. That must have been tough."

"You have no idea. We bought our house right before it all tanked. Got one of those balloon payment mortgages. I was so afraid I wouldn't be able to manage when it came due. But things calmed down and I refinanced."

"It probably has nothing to do with Randall's death, but can you tell me about the board members who resigned?"

Colleen put her hand to her throat, just above where her vintage string of pearls draped across her chest. "Oh, that was embarrassing. It happened a few years ago. We all thought this new board member, a lawyer, would be fantastic. Then his wife messed up this golf tournament fundraiser."

This didn't sound like what Max talked about. But it might be more important since it was more recent. "Messed up how?"

"Something with the sponsors. Some paid cash for their holes and it didn't get written down right."

I knew nothing about golf or golf outings. But Lauren's boyfriend, who was also my longtime friend and was here tonight, did. I'd need to ask him a few questions later.

"How did you find the problem?"

"Randall caught it. Luckily before there was any bad press. We had to ask the lawyer to step down so the donors knew we took it seriously."

Another server came by with a tray of crab puffs and tiny lobster rolls. I took one of each, as did Colleen.

I ate my appetizers in two quick bites and wished there were more. I hadn't had time to eat more than half a sandwich for lunch. "You said a few years ago. How many?"

"Two or three? He was a collections lawyer."

"Had you had lawyers on the board before?"

"Oh, yes, that's why I thought it'd be so good. I thought Mario—that's his name, Mario Orvino—would invite a lot of other lawyers to the events. Well, he did, but most of them barely bid on anything at the silent auctions. And boy did they suck up the booze. All that money lawyers make, you'd think they'd donate more."

Not all lawyers make a lot of money. But that sounded like the least of the problems the board had with this one. I made a note of his name.

"Anything else wrong with the fundraiser?"

Colleen drained her second champagne, set the empty glass on the table, and took a lipstick from her evening bag. She reapplied it to her lower lip, then rubbed her lips together before she spoke. "When Mario submitted receipts for prizes and the golf course fees, Randall thought some were fake."

"You could check with the golf course, couldn't you?"

"We did. But Mario's friend owned the course. Randall didn't trust him."

"Was there a police report?"

"Oh, no, nothing like that. But you've got to keep good records. No one's going to attend your fundraisers if they don't feel sure about where the money's going."

"Was Mario angry at Randall?"

"No, no. He didn't know Randall was behind the questions."

"Who invited Mario to join the board?"

"To tell you the truth, I did." Colleen ran a hand through her curls and glanced around the crowded hall. "I went to a board development seminar. They said to reach out to all the professionals and businesspeople you know. They can afford to donate or know people who can."

"And you knew Mario Orvino?"

"He's my mother's cousin. I still think Randall overreacted to what he did. It was an innocent mistake. But maybe I'm biased because Mario's sort of family."

A chime sounded to let everyone know there was only half an hour left of the cocktail hour. Colleen texted me the last contact information she had for Mario Orvino. She claimed there were no other problems during the time she was on the board. Everyone got along well.

"Is there anything else?" Colleen pointed toward the main entrance. "I want to talk to that man near all the silver and black balloons. Your friend told me he's high up in American Airlines."

I swallowed the last of my drink. "Just one more question. Anyone else you can think of who might have a grudge against Randall? His brother said he had a way of setting people on edge."

Colleen waved a hand. "Oh, of course Max said that. He's the one who sets people on edge. To be honest, I can't see anyone going after Randall. It really was probably a random mugging."

As Colleen wound her way through a sea of evening gowns and tuxes toward the airline executive, I opened my phone for some quick research on Mario Orvino. And questioned whether Colleen was being honest with me about anything.

CHAPTER 12
HAVE A LITTLE FUN

Mario Orvino wasn't a lawyer. Not anymore. He got disbarred three months before Randall's death.

The Illinois Attorney Registration and Disciplinary Commission—known as the ARDC—investigates complaints against attorneys. Anyone can search the ARDC website to find out if an attorney has a valid Illinois law license or has ever been disciplined. Discipline includes censure, which is more or less strongly worded public criticism, suspending an attorney's license for a stretch of time, or disbarment, meaning the attorney can no longer practice law.

It's not easy to get disbarred in Illinois. If the ARDC believes there's a chance the attorney can be rehabilitated, the law license is suspended. The attorney is urged to get help and reapply to practice law again. Stealing money from clients is the main reason an attorney gets suspended. If the Magic Works fundraiser issues prompted Orvino's disbarment, whatever happened was a lot more serious than what Colleen told me. I decided not to ask her anything else until I knew more myself, though. I'd already done more interviews for this case blind than I wanted to.

I headed for our table after getting a ginger ale with lime from the bar. My friend Joe, who is now Lauren's boyfriend, stood with Lauren. His tux fit him well, highlighting how trim and tall he is. I suspected Lauren insisted he get a new one and have it tailored. Joe's a financial advisor and always dresses well. But since dating Lauren he's stepped it up a notch.

He gave me a one-armed hug.

Lauren glanced around. "Where's Hot Teacher Guy?"

Joe grimaced. "Do you have to call him that?"

Hot Teacher Guy was Lauren's nickname for Dylan. She met him when she traveled to Edwardsville to help with the Q.C. murder investigation. And to help me deal with my mother.

"Seriously good point," Lauren said. "Dylan doesn't teach anymore. Maybe it should be Hot Grad Student Guy, though that sounds like he's a kid and he's not. I know, Hot Guitar Player Guy. When are you two going to sing together again, Quille?"

Joe rolled his eyes.

Lauren elbowed him. "You hardly sing with Quille anymore. Is she supposed to quit?"

"We haven't talked about it," I said, though Lauren wasn't wrong. Joe, our friend Danielle, and I for years sang as an a cappella trio. But Joe had been too busy over the last few years.

"Quille," Joe said. "Want to dance?"

"Uh, sure. If Lauren doesn't want to."

Though he's a musician himself, Joe's skills on the dance floor are limited to swaying back and forth to the rhythm of One-Two, One-Two. We met decades ago when I was ten and acting professionally for the first time. Joe was eighteen and playing the lead in the same play. In all that time, I'd never known him to head out onto a dance floor other than under protest.

"You two go." Lauren grabbed her Louis Vuitton clutch. "I promised my client I'd talk up the silent auction."

Joe led me to the edge of the dance floor, directly under the translucent Tiffany glass dome. "She's driving me crazy with the Hot Guy thing. Why does Dylan have to be Hot anything?"

"She just enjoys tweaking you," I said. "You're the only guy she cares about."

"She's tweaking me a lot lately."

"More than usual?"

"Much more." He did a quarter turn, surprising me. We both stumbled a bit, but quickly regained our footing.

"Did you ask her what's wrong?" I said.

"She says work."

"Really."

"Yeah."

Joe sounded as doubtful as I felt. When things don't go Lauren's way, she sorts out what to change and charges forward, much as she did when she discovered she hated law school and left to get a real estate license.

"I don't see why she's pushing Dylan on you," Joe said. "It's weird he didn't tell you ahead of time he'd be moving to Chicago or that he applied to the UChicago grad program."

We inched sideways as another couple veered a little too near. It took a moment to get into rhythm again.

"Dylan didn't know he'd gotten into UChicago when I saw him the last time in Edwardsville," I said. "Plus I told him I was trying to make things work long distance with Ty. He figured he should back off."

"Then showed up mid-summer and surprised you? That's not backing off."

"My mother helpfully told him she didn't think Ty was serious about me. Which, thanks Mom."

"Your mother? Since when has she paid attention to your love life?"

"I think she thinks she's making up for lost time. Which is sort of nice but weird. Especially when she doesn't know anything about me and Ty."

Joe started to speak, but closed his mouth.

"What?" I said.

"I'm not sure your mom's wrong. If I loved someone, I'd never take a two-year work assignment on the other side of the world. Especially without promising to move straight back to Chicago when it's done."

"Plus Lauren would seriously kill you," I said.

"That too."

"I understand why Ty's career matters so much to him."

Over Joe's shoulder I saw Dylan and Lauren step onto the dance floor. Dylan twirled her effortlessly.

"It should matter," Joe said. "But he's a real estate developer. He can develop here. And why wait for him if he's not sure he'll be back?"

"So you think I ought to go out with Dylan? Who hasn't asked me, by the way."

Between the string quartet and the buzz of conversation around us, I felt sure Lauren and Dylan were too far away to hear us.

"He will. And no, not Dylan. Or yes, Dylan if it'll make you happy. And help you have a little fun."

"I don't have to have a guy around to enjoy life."

"Far be it from me to call you out for working too much, but it's all you seem to do lately."

"I've got all the cases I put on hold while I worked on Q.C.'s murder. I'm catching up."

"And avoiding your feelings."

"Spoken like one who knows."

"Guilty," Joe said. "And I can tell you, it doesn't usually end well."

"I think you really do want me to go out with Hot Teacher Guy."

"Please. I do not need to hear that again."

We stepped apart as the song ended. Lauren and Dylan appeared at our sides.

Dylan extended his hand to me as the quartet began a waltz. "May I? This is probably the last one before dinner."

"I'm done." Joe headed for the table. Lauren shot me a mischievous look and followed.

The music swirled around us as Dylan guided us toward the center of the dance floor, his hand on my waist. The crowd noise faded into the background and I felt myself relaxing.

"Dance classes?" I said.

"Far too many." Dylan twirled me with a smooth motion. "My mother believed it was important for a pastor's son. She was kind of still living in the 1960s. Or possibly fifties."

I laughed. We glided in perfect harmony across the dance floor. I let my mind drift, swept away by the enchantment of the sparkling tables, the string music, and Dylan's unexpected skill as a dancer.

"What was the other stop you wanted to make before the event?" Dylan said. "Unless you think Lauren would kill us if we ducked out."

"What? Oh. There's a games shop two blocks away. I wanted to see if they sell tarot cards. But it's a long shot, and I'm sure it's closed now."

The slight pressure of his hand in mine signaled me to twirl again. I spun, returning gracefully to his arms.

"You're hoping tarot cards will reveal a murderer?" He said.

"The victim, Randall, debunked a supposed medium. With all the tarot decks on his bookshelves, I'm wondering if there's a connection. I figure it can't hurt to learn more about people who use them."

"I know one place you can learn a ton. There's a magic store in Andersonville that sells lots of decks. And sometimes has tarot readers on site."

Andersonville is an artsy Chicago neighborhood about eight miles north of where I live. It's known for bookstores, art galleries, and antique stores as well as bars and restaurants. I'd never noticed a magic store there, though.

"You've lived here five minutes," I said. "How do you know this place and I don't?"

"The drummer from one of my bands in New York is an artist, too. He designs tarot cards and other things. When I moved here, he told me about the store. Wanted me to stop in and see whether his decks are displayed there. I haven't gotten to it yet, though."

"Are they open Sundays?"

"Yep. I could meet you for an early breakfast tomorrow and we could head over. Maybe the owner can answer your questions."

My shoulders tensed as I mentally ran through all the work I needed to do. But it could be a fun break that helped my investigation, too. "Nine-thirty? For breakfast?"

"Mmm. Okay, our ideas of what's early on a Sunday morning are very different. Eleven?"

"Perfect," I said. "I can work a few hours before I meet you and finish after."

"You really do need to have a little fun," he said, making me wonder if somehow he'd overheard Joe's and my entire conversation.

CHAPTER 13
AFTERLIFE AND DEATH

A LITTLE BEFORE seven the next morning, my neck and shoulders aching from too much computer time over the last week, I headed for my office. The door to the suite where I rented stuck. I yanked on it. On the third try I saw the problem. A folded over brown envelope was wedged between the door and the jamb an inch or so above the floor. I hoped it was for one of the other tenants of the office suite, but it was addressed to me.

I opened it as I waited for a mug of hot water to heat in the microwave. The five-page brief inside raised new arguments relating to a hearing set for tomorrow morning. By putting it in my door over the weekend instead of emailing a copy when he sent it to the judge Friday, my opponent gave me less time to look it over. He probably thought I wouldn't be in until Monday and might not see it at all if I went straight to court.

Little did he know what my schedule was like lately.

My head started throbbing. I should have eaten before my morning jog. I dropped a Chai teabag into the boiling water and sat at the table under the window to eat a power bar and read. Under the court rules, the brief was too late for the court to consider. But judges vary in how they enforce the rules, and I didn't know this one well enough yet to be sure.

After taking three Ibuprofen to stave off a migraine, I researched the new cases the brief cited. None of them said what the plaintiff claimed they did. But it took me over an hour to be sure of that. Then I turned to other work. The most pressing was a case where the plaintiff claimed my client committed fraud by advertising her brownies as the chocolatiest in Chicago. An arbitration, which is like a mini-trial, was going forward this month. If only I could manufacture an extra few hours in every day. Or, better yet, an extra day a week.

Another hour and a half and two mugs of tea later, I got to what interested me most: Randall's murder.

I read the ARDC's full report on Mario Orvino. The disciplinary commission isn't a trial court, but its hearings run pretty much the same way. The prosecutor has to prove it's more likely than not that the defendant violated the ethics rules. After hearing evidence about the golf outing, the ARDC found it more likely than not that Orvino created inflated fake receipts for expenses and prizes and pocketed the difference. Plus a golf club salesperson testified she gave Orvino a thousand dollars to sponsor a hole. He told her it cost five hundred, but that for an extra five hundred she would get extra signs about her company. Orvino didn't tell Magic Works about the extra fee he collected, keeping that for himself, too. He did the same with four other sponsors, all of whom paid by cash or Venmo to his personal account.

I couldn't tell who reported it to the ARDC. Lawyers are required to report when colleagues break ethical rules. If they don't, they can be disbarred themselves. Not that many non-lawyers, on the other hand, know about the ARDC.

Randall likely knew from Julia. If he made the complaint, Orvino might have held a grudge. The timing fit, too. While the fundraiser occurred over two years ago, the ARDC made its final decision only a few months ago.

None of it fit Colleen's view of an innocent mistake. And it surprised me she didn't tell me Orvino was disbarred. But if they didn't keep in touch, she might not have known. The local news rarely covers disbarments unless the lawyer was a politician, too, or well known.

My email dinged with a question from another lawyer lucky enough to be working on a Sunday morning. I shot off a quick answer and returned to my Magic Works research.

I found no criminal case pending against Orvino. The ARDC listed what looked like a home address and phone number. When I called it I got voicemail and hung up. I wanted to talk directly to him if I could, not explain myself in a message and hope he'd call back.

I turned to my copy of the Alchemy folder from Randall's computer and the letters from the psychic Nellie Havel. Online searches for her brought me to a website about psychic phenomena. It warned the unwary about fraud. A photo of Nellie Havel appeared there. It was a head shot, so I couldn't judge her height. She looked to be in her thirties and had shoulder-length brown hair that curled under at her shoulders, walnut-shaped eyes, and thick, heavy eyebrows. I enlarged the text below it.

Photo of Nellie Havel from brochure for tarot card reading at a 1989 New York City psychic fair. Havel found victims in obituary columns and gained their trust through heartfelt letters of sympathy. Investigators discovered a trove of costume jewelry, handkerchiefs, anniversary cards, photos and similar items in a dumpster near one of over a dozen mailbox centers she used. It appears Nellie Havel kept or sold any valuable items that belonged to deceased persons, as well as monetary donations. The "psychic" herself was never located.

The website hadn't been updated in over four years. Its Contact Us screens errored out.

I did more searches based on the email to Randall from AngryHusband about a "woman of God" and the Krakow police. That led me to a website that mentioned a medium named Nova Moon. Five years ago, Nova Moon volunteered to help police in Krakow find a missing twelve-year-old boy. While she didn't locate him, Nova claimed spirits told her the boy was still alive. She described him, including what he wore when last seen. The description included the color of the laces on the gym shoes the boy wore, a detail never disclosed in the press. The boy's mother was quoted. "I can't express how grateful I am to Nova. Now we know our son's alive. We're sure he'll be found soon."

I couldn't find anything else about the case. If articles about it were in Polish, though, my English search terms might not translate well enough to uncover them. I did find a photo of Nova with the Krakow police. She was nearly as tall as the two officers on either side of her, with dark gray hair and a rounded face that narrowed at her chin, wide walnut-shaped eyes, and thin eyebrows that arched gracefully above them. I guessed her in her sixties when the photo was taken. She could be Nellie Havel aged a few decades with very plucked eyebrows.

After trying again to call Mario Orvino with no luck, I searched for Nova Moon with the word Alchemy based on the title of Randall's folder. That brought me to a Facebook page called Afterlife, Alchemy and More.

People there posted about grief and loss. A few members offered words of comfort. So did Nova Moon. Her profile included no photo. Instead there was a drawing of a circle with curved lines emitting from it so it looked like a sun. An image search brought me to an alchemy symbol for the sun.

All I knew about alchemy was something about turning other metals into gold. I had no idea how it related to grief. The style of Nova's comments, though, reminded me of Nellie Havel's letters. Many psychics might write that same way. But it added weight to the idea that Randall believed them to be the same person.

Nova offered readings to help grieving people process their feelings. Individual and group sessions were available. Some members posted to say that Nova conveyed messages to them from their loved ones. It helped the members feel better and closer to those they lost.

There was also a private Facebook Group where users could share with each other. You had to apply to join. I wanted to, but I don't like sharing a lot online. I have social media pages for my law firm. But my personal Facebook page is under Cathy Dearborn—a combination of a short form of my middle name and the street where my law office is located. I don't include a photo or details. I started it mostly to keep in touch with my niece and nephew, who've since dropped off Facebook, and for occasional research.

As Cathy Dearborn, I asked to join the Afterlife, Alchemy and More Facebook Group. A questionnaire popped up. I took a few moments to decide how to answer. Attorneys aren't allowed to lie when pursuing their cases, and I felt sure that applied to investigations as well. And, ethics aside, I find most people, including those who engage in crime, are most apt to open up to me when I speak from the heart. Nova Moon, if that was a real person, might look at my answers, so sharing more might be useful.

On the other hand, if she or the others in the group had anything to do with Randall's murder, I preferred to keep my identity to myself. And the form might be there only to weed out bots, not people, in which case I'd be taking the risk for no reason.

I finally decided on honest but brief and vague.

> How did you hear about the Afterlife, Alchemy and More Facebook page:
>
> *Through an Internet search for psychics and mediums.*
>
> What do you know about psychic phenomena?
>
> *I did a research paper on them in college for a Psych 101 course.*
>
> Why are you interested in joining the private group?
>
> *One of my sisters died before I was born. I've always felt like I live in her shadow and wish I knew more about her as a person.*

An automatic message dashed my hopes for a quick entry to the group. It took at least seven days to process requests. I did what I do whenever I'm stymied in one part of my work life. I turned to another part and dialed Mario Orvino's number again.

This time a man answered.

"Mr. Orvino? Mario Orvino?"

"Yes. Who are you and why do you keep calling me?"

The gruff voice fit the two profile photos I'd found. They showed a man with a fleshy nose, age spots under his eyes, and deep-set wrinkles around his mouth though according to his ARDC listing he was only in his mid-fifties.

I clicked over to that listing now as I spoke. "My name is Quille Davis. I'm a friend of Randall Petrov's wife. And a lawyer. I'm hoping we can talk."

"Well, Quille, friend of Randall and lawyer, you're too late. The well is dry."

"I'm not sure what you mean."

"There's nothing left. Sue me if you want. All my money went to the lawyers. A bit of irony you can feel free to enjoy."

"I'm not calling to try to get money from you. I want to ask about Randall's death."

"What? Randall died?"

CHAPTER 14
SUSPICIOUS MEN

Mario Orvino sounded genuinely surprised to hear of Randall's death. But I wished I could see his expression.

"You didn't know Randall was murdered?"

"Was it on the news?"

"Maybe the local news." I filled him in on the mugging theory and that Julia hired me to look into the death.

"And you're, what, some sort of detective?"

I decided to ignore the sarcastic tone. "Yes. Of a sort. I heard Randall had a way of getting on people's bad sides. Do you agree?"

"I wouldn't put it that way."

"How would you put it?"

"He was thorough. Determined. Like a detail-oriented pit bull."

"Is that how he approached the golf tournament issues?"

"You heard about that. As a fellow—or do I say sister?—lawyer I'm sure you understand why I'm not going to comment on it."

Tired of sitting in front of the computer all morning, I stood and paced a small circle in the open area of the office. The cord trailed behind me. "Were criminal charges filed against you?"

"No. And I'm still not talking about it."

"No one asked me to look into the tournament. I don't need to know about anything you did. I'm interested in your impression of Randall. I'm Julia's friend, but I barely knew him."

"Look, I'll save you some time. You think I held a grudge and killed Randall because he's the one who started questioning the receipts. I didn't."

So Mario knew Randall raised the first questions about the fundraiser.

"I suspect you wouldn't have answered this many questions if you had. But if you can share an alibi for when he was killed I can cross you off my list."

Mario asked for a date and time of death. I gave him the rough timeframe. After a little more sparring, he checked his calendar and told me he'd been in Traverse City, Michigan, to visit his daughter. He refused to give me her contact information, but I figured I could find it with a little digging.

"Now that's out of the way," Mario said, "did you ask Colleen Cahill for her alibi?"

With a start, I realized I hadn't. And I hadn't created a chart of suspects yet, something I do to help me track what questions I ask whom and their answers. I could easily fix both things, though.

"Is there a reason I should?"

"If you're looking at the golf fundraiser as a motive, there's a reason. Colleen was the Executive Director. She had her fingers in all the pies."

My phone dinged. It was Dylan. It was 10:55 and he was in the café downstairs. I texted him asking if he could wait. He sent an OK sign.

"Are you saying she knew something was wrong with that fundraiser?"

"I'm saying she signed off on everything. That's all. Good luck."

"Wait, please."

I couldn't expect Mario to admit to stealing funds. Just because no one charged him yet didn't mean he'd never be arrested. But he'd come as close as he could to saying Colleen was in on it. While I wasn't about to trust the word of someone who lost his law license for scamming a charity, I wasn't going to ignore it.

"Colleen and Randall were close. Setting aside the golf outing, if Colleen was involved in anything shady, why would Randall blow the whistle and risk exposing her?"

"They were close. Thick as thieves, if you will."

I wondered if he chose the thief comparison purposely. For someone who stole money, it clearly irked him when anyone else got too much of it. But that might explain why he talked to me at all. He'd been waiting to air his grievances.

"So?" I said.

"Randall was a—what's that term he always used? Shut Eye. When it came to Colleen, he was a Shut Eye."

"I don't know that phrase."

"He didn't see, or chose not to see, anything about Colleen that wasn't right."

"Sort of a Don't Ask, Don't Tell approach?"

"More like, Don't Ask, Don't Tell, Don't Even Think."

This sounded like a way to divert me from Mario's own wrong-doing, but I planned to follow up.

"Did you tell the ARDC your suspicions about Colleen?"

"Yes. But they didn't care what anyone else did. Only me."

"What about the police?"

"Sure, that'd be smart. Colleen and the board didn't go to the police. I wasn't about to."

I touched my mouse to wake up my computer. "Didn't the other board members ask any questions about fundraisers?"

"It's not an active board. Most of them got on because MW helped their children. They like eating pizza at the meetings. They glance at the financial reports, ask a question once in a blue moon, and rubber stamp whatever Colleen wants. The current Chairman hardly ever attends meetings."

If true, it was a great set up for Colleen to skim money.

"But you've no evidence Colleen knew anything was wrong?"

He sighed. "No evidence. Just common sense. And that's all I've got to say."

The phone clicked and he was gone.

I typed a few quick notes and headed out to meet Dylan. On the way down in the elevator, though, a text came through from Lauren.

At open house. Need help.

CHAPTER 15
FAVORS

Café des Livres, my favorite place to get tea, dark hot cocoa, or breakfast, is on the ground floor of the building where I rent my office. I paused in the lobby to call Lauren. Through the glass inner door to the café, I saw Dylan sitting in an armchair near the fireplace. He wore faded jeans and a fitted navy blue T-shirt and had on headphones. His fingers hovered over a tablet.

"Quille, thank God." Lauren's voice was hushed. "Where are you?"

"Just left my office."

"Perfect. There's this seriously odd guy at my open house and he is not leaving. I don't want to be alone with him."

Lauren handles a lot of properties in or near our neighborhood. She texted me the address. It was only five blocks away.

"Be right there. Are you calling the cops?"

"He hasn't done anything exactly. It's just—I'll tell you when you get here. But hurry. I'm staying near the door."

"I might bring Dylan."

"Totally better. You can pretend to be potential buyers and the guy won't think I'm creeped out. Just in case he's some sort of millionaire who's actually thinking of buying."

Dylan stood when I stepped inside. I still had Lauren on the phone, on speaker, so I'd know right off if anything happened to her.

"I hope you're not hungry," I said to Dylan. The blue in the shirt set off his eyes.

He glanced at my phone. "Trouble?"

"I'll explain on the way. If you want to come with."

"To an unknown destination for some unknown yet seemingly urgent reason? Why not?"

The Printers Row neighborhood consists mostly of hundred-year-old paper warehouses and printing factories converted into lofts, condos, and businesses. A big brick former railroad station turned into retail and office space stands at the south edge of the neighborhood. Beyond it is Dearborn Park. Cut off from most vehicle traffic and filled with old leafy trees and townhomes with stone patios, that area feels much more suburban than urban. It ends at a pedestrian underpass beneath Roosevelt Road, a busy street that runs through the city and far into the suburbs.

Today Lauren was showing a newer, pricier three-story town-home near the underpass. The two main neighborhood streets dead end at the park on one side and the underpass on the other. Because of that, it was faster to walk there than drive.

Dylan kept pace with me, which couldn't have been easy. A fast walker already, when I started training to up my endurance and speed I increased to just over four miles per hour. I filled him in on Lauren's concerns.

"Joe not around today?" he said. "I don't mind joining you but he seems like he's the protective type."

"He seriously is." Lauren said over the speakerphone, her voice quiet. "But he's at the home office in Cincinnati. Left early this morning on the cheaper flight."

Like me, Joe started working and paying his own way early. Despite that he earns a good salary and his firm pays his travel, he still searches for the least expensive options.

We reached the townhome in less than ten minutes. Lauren opened the side door for us. We stepped into a granite and marble kitchen that smelled of fresh-baked sugar cookies. I asked in a quiet voice where the man was.

"Rooftop deck. I sent him up alone."

"What did he do that creeped you out?"

"He keeps circling through the rooms. Literally circling. One direction, then the other, retracing his steps and pausing at the same spot each time. It's been forty-five minutes."

"Sounds a little OCD," Dylan said.

"Possibly," Lauren said. "But I have a bad feeling."

Lauren doesn't scare easily. And she does all the things realtors, especially ones who aren't male, are advised to do. She never walks first into a room or building. Instead, she follows behind, keeping all doors open. She asks for names and contact information for every visitor to an open house. And since a sexual assault last year on a real estate agent in the north suburbs, she takes a quick photo on her phone when anyone arrives and saves it in a shared drive Joe and I can access in case anything happens to her.

While all that won't protect her against someone set on hurting her, it helps avoid issues. If she still felt uneasy, that made me uneasy, too.

Lauren stepped into the hallway for a moment, cocked her ear near the stairway, and returned. "Footsteps."

She raised her voice and moved to the granite breakfast counter beneath the front windows. "This kitchen was remodeled last year. All top of the line. Subzero appliances."

"Beautiful," I said, meaning it.

A man about six feet tall with broad shoulders entered the doorway between the kitchen and the hall. A small, curved scar the size of a dime marked his right cheekbone. He stared at Lauren, unblinking and silent.

"Seen all that you need to?" Lauren said.

"For now." He tapped his fingers against the door jamb, then circled the perimeter of the room, edging around the three of us. Then he retraced his steps, ending in the doorway where he began. He tapped his fingers again, eyes fixed on Lauren again.

She handed him a glossy fact sheet with a QR code at the bottom. "Call or email my office if you have questions."

He folded the sheet, put it in his shirt pocket, then patted the pocket with one hand and then the other.

After studying the floor for a long moment, he headed out the side door. I watched through the window over the breakfast counter as he strode along the side path to the street and turned right.

I exited the townhome and Dylan followed. We crouched behind the bushes near the side path. A few seconds later a blue Toyota sedan drove past. I took a series of photos, hoping one might capture the license plate. Not very subtle. If he were a real potential client he might be offended if he saw me. But I cared more about Lauren's life than her bank account.

Dylan's phone clicked away, too. "He didn't look back. I doubt he saw us."

We compared photos. Neither of us got the full license plate, but we got some of it. I didn't know if my friend the Detective Sergeant was allowed to check license plates based on Lauren's bad feeling about the man. But I texted him to ask. If he couldn't, at least we had the information if the man returned.

We ordered a pizza for lunch since Dylan and I had missed ours. He waited outside for the delivery, listening to his headphones on the front patio. I suspected he did it to give Lauren and me time to talk alone if she had something to say that she didn't want to share with him. But she didn't. At least, not about the visitor.

"You sure you don't need to leave? I know you've got a lot to do." Lauren perched on the breakfast counter stool next to me.

"I'll get to the magic shop eventually. And I've got time tonight to work."

"On Sunday night? That's too sad. I can ask Dylan if he'll stay if you'd rather go back to the office."

"Joe will love me leaving you alone with the guy you always call 'Hot' something or other."

"I just like to get a rise out of him. Joe, I mean. Not Dylan. Obviously."

"And obviously that can be fun because Joe's so uptight," I said. "But you seem like you have a purpose."

"I don't want to put you in the middle."

"Already there." I shifted the counter stool to face her more directly. "You're my friend, Joe's my friend. The tension's getting thick."

Joe's been my friend forever. But Lauren and I bonded that first year of law school and became closer every year after. I couldn't lose either of them. Which was why from the moment they started dating part of me dreaded what might happen if things didn't work out. Lauren was on a friendly basis with a couple of her ex-boyfriends, but it took time. Joe never said anything bad about an ex. But he never mentioned one either unless I directly asked.

Lauren glanced out the window. "I want to know if he and I have a future. But he broke up with his last girlfriend after she pushed him to propose."

"If she pushed it wasn't very hard. They were seeing each other for years."

The screen door rattled. Lauren's head jerked toward it. But it was only the wind. "He proposed because he thought he'd lose her if he didn't. But she realized he wasn't that in love with her, said No, and that was it. That's what he told me."

"Sounds about right." I thought back to the fallout from the break up. "He ran around the city to find the right ring. Heather thought the one he finally chose showed he didn't really know her."

Lauren's eyebrows raised. "Seriously? You never trust a man to pick a ring—or anything—that suits you. That's what returns are for."

I heard a car approaching and peered out the window. A sedan cruised out of my line of sight. "She must have felt it was symbolic."

"Or she was super-shallow."

"Could be."

Heather and I had never gotten close. She rarely attended when Joe and I sang with our friend Danielle at local bars or folk clubs, something we did pretty often back then. And I wasn't seeing anyone for most of the time he dated Heather. In Heather's view, to socialize with her and Joe as a couple I needed my own date.

"I know it's absolutely ridiculous to try to make Joe jealous," Lauren said. "But I'm not good at being diplomatic and strategic. I'm good at saying what I think."

The sedan reappeared going the opposite direction. The driver probably reached the dead end at the underpass without finding a parking spot and turned around. But I felt glad Dylan sat in front keeping an eye out, too.

"Which is part of what he loves about you," I said. "You did tell me he said he loves you. Big step for him. Why not just talk to him?"

"He probably told Heather he loved her, too. And it's only been a year. What if he feels pressured?"

"So it's better to wait two or three or four years and then have him do what he did with Heather?"

"I totally don't want that. That's why I need your help."

I studied her face, ignoring the street outside. I didn't like where this was going. "Me? How?"

"By doing what you do. Investigate. Find out what really happened."

"Lauren, I love you, but remember not wanting me in the middle? You should ask Joe whatever you want to know."

"No, I mean literally investigate. Track down Heather. Talk to her."

"You want me to question his ex-girlfriend behind Joe's back."

"It's not behind his back. He never said no one should talk to Heather after they broke up, did he?"

"Talking is different from investigating."

"Then just talk. Run into her somewhere, start a conversation, and see where it leads."

"Like I do when I investigate."

"You do it for your clients. Why not me, your friend?"

"Joe's my friend, too. My oldest friend."

"A friend who's never nearly broken an arm helping you chase a murderer. Or risked confronting a crazed gunman. Or climbed up—"

I held up a hand. "I get your point."

I couldn't argue with all Lauren had done for me. Joe was a good friend, but he stayed out of the fray when I investigated murders. Not because he didn't want to help but because he didn't want to encourage me to keep doing it. Lauren dove in.

Lauren squeezed my arm. "I'll explain it all to Joe if it comes to that. He'll understand why you agreed. He knows how totally persuasive I can be. And I'll dial back my Hot Teacher comments in the meantime."

I felt less sure Joe would understand. But he'd probably forgive me given our long history. I hoped.

"I'll look into where she lives and works these days and think about the best way to approach her. But that's all I'm promising for now."

"Awesome, awesome, awesome. Thank you."

"I hope you'll feel that way after I talk to her."

CHAPTER 16
PSYCHICS AND LEASES

DYLAN INSISTED he could work on a piece he was composing on his tablet here as easily as in his apartment. He set up in the living room where he had a view of the kitchen through the hallway. I practically inhaled three pieces of thin crust sausage and black olive pizza. Then I climbed the stairs to the town-home's third floor. Its dark hardwood floor gleamed with polish. The en suite bathroom had a sunken tub and separate shower. A wrought iron spiral staircase near the windows led to the rooftop deck.

But there was no furniture. I stood near the window, looking at the tree-lined road below. I texted Ty but got no answer. Then, pacing as I talked, I answered emails on my phone. In between, I texted Julia to ask if she knew what the term Shut Eye meant. She called me.

"Randall used that for the people who convince themselves they really have psychic powers. He said a lot of so-called psychics research people on the Internet or, if it's an event with an audience, have a helper who chats with people beforehand to learn about them. Then the psychic acts like they picked up things about supposedly random persons though their powers."

"And people buy that?"

"If they're not very social media savvy they don't always realize how much is out there. And most people who come to events want to believe. Randall said that's especially true if they're pretty honest themselves. It doesn't occur to them that the other audience member in line is working for the psychic. The other way it works is the psychic uses vague phrases. Like 'you lost someone you love very much and sometimes you still think about them.' If a person's over forty-five the odds are good they've experienced the death of a grandparent or someone else they love."

"But not everyone who sees a psychic is over forty-five."

"No, but to be human is to suffer loss. If there's no person who died, the psychic suggests it could be a pet. If that's a miss, they double down on how they're sensing loss, and say maybe it's metaphorical. A best friend moved away. You got divorced. Your adult child went off to college."

I paused near the bathroom with its sunken tub and granite sink counter. "You lost your job."

"Exactly. If the psychic keeps trying, something eventually hits. The audience remembers the hit, not the three or five or ten misses before it."

"I can see Shut Eye referring to audience members or customers who want to believe. But psychics?"

"Randall said there are three kinds of psychics. Those who know how it works and see themselves as entertainers, like he did. They give disclaimers. The second group knows, too, and just doesn't mind tricking people for a living. They might justify it by saying they help people work through emotional issues. Then there are Shut Eyes. A Shut Eye uses the same techniques but starts to think they're tapping into psychic power. They view the advance research or the vague questions as warming up. Getting their intuition in tune. Or being 'open to the spirits' if they're mediums."

"There's no fourth category? A real psychic?"

"Randall said he never saw anyone do anything he couldn't do himself without any supernatural powers. But he wished sometimes he could find a real psychic. He liked the idea of a world with magic. And he was angry at people who took money by claiming to be psychic."

A text came in from Ty.

Sorry. Crazy day. Tomorrow?

I asked Julia to hold for a moment and texted Ty to suggest 7 a.m. my time.

I hit Send. "Was he angry at psychics who really believed in their own powers?"

"I think he was angriest at them. They were lying to themselves, too, which made them more convincing. Meaning they could steal more money."

Stealing was a strong word. And it reminded me of the Magic Works issues.

"I talked to someone today who hinted Colleen might know about some fundraising problems. But he had no evidence. He might have been trying to deflect attention from himself."

"I'm sure that's the case," Julia said. "Randall never hinted at any concerns about Colleen or Magic Works."

Before we hung up I asked if she'd heard from Oscar, Randall's landlord, about the supposed lease between them for Randall's office. She hadn't but said she'd follow up.

Lauren texted me that a couple arrived and would be heading up to the third floor office soon. Dylan still worked away, headphones on, in a leather armchair—the living room was still furnished. After checking in with Lauren, who knew the couple from the neighborhood, I went outside and over to Roosevelt Park. It was right down the path from the townhome. I sat on a bench near the gates of two more townhome complexes with a view of the play areas and tennis courts. It was quiet, other than birds chirping and a rush of traffic from Roosevelt Road.

I took a few minutes to enjoy the sun on my face and the smell of fresh cut grass. I listened to kids laugh as they jumped off the swings. It was a small slice of summer, but at least I wasn't spending all of it indoors. Then I tried calling Colleen to ask about her alibi. She didn't answer, but she returned the call ten minutes later. At the same time I got a text from Ty saying 8:30 a.m. central time might work tomorrow if he could get out of a meeting in time.

"Thanks again for including me in the benefit," Colleen said. "I met a board member who told me about another grant we might qualify for."

"That's terrific." The breeze blew my long hair into my eyes. I brushed it away. "In all the rush, I forgot something. I'm asking everyone Randall cared about this question, not just you, so that I can rule them out as far as his death goes."

"No worries. You need to know where I was the night he was killed."

"It would help." I kept an eye on the walkway that ran past the townhome. If anyone else went in to browse, I could be back there in a couple minutes.

Colleen texted me a website link to a high school fundraiser she attended that evening. It included photos of her with other people. She sent me their names and contact information. After thanking her, I asked about the Board Chairman.

"Did he know Randall? I heard he often can't be at meetings. The Chairman, I mean, not Randall."

"That's true. Theo's work takes him all over the world. It was funny. He wasn't even at the meeting where he got elected."

I didn't quite see the humor. In my world, judges and clients get pretty irked if you don't show up for an important meeting. Or an unimportant one. My steady stream of work would dry up fast if I behaved that way.

"But people voted him in anyway?"

"Oh, everyone loves Theo. He's so dedicated to Magic Works."

"How so? If he doesn't come to meetings." A pink and green bouncy ball rolled toward me. I stopped it with my foot and tossed it toward two kids on a wide open grassy area.

"He runs an annual teddy bear picnic—they call it the Theo Bear Picnic—at his local hospital. It helps raise funds."

"Would he talk to me?"

"If you can get ahold of him."

After we hung up, I texted Ty that I had a hearing tomorrow morning and suggested another time. Then I emailed my freelance paralegal, who works remotely from another state, and asked her to research all the Magic Works board members over time.

When I got back to the townhome, Lauren was logging out of her iPad. No one else had appeared.

"You're sure you've never seen that man before?" I said.

She shook her head. "No. And the name he signed in with is so generic. T. Allen. No email address."

We looked at her future open house schedule to make sure she could have someone with her for each one. I apologized to Dylan for how the day had gone. He assured me he didn't mind. But he couldn't go with me to the magic store now. He was rehearsing with a blues band he'd just joined.

I decided to try the store another time anyway. It had been a very long week. Lauren and I headed home to have some wine on my deck. As Lauren opened the bottle my email dinged. Julia had forwarded her email exchange with Randall's land-lord, Oscar. In it, she noted the office suite lease between him and the managers of the Monadnock Building didn't say anything about Randall or his office. She asked for any written lease between Oscar and Randall for the office.

Oscar responded in four words.

That's the only lease.

With Lauren looking over my shoulder, I reread Oscar's lease on my iPad. He agreed to rent the full office suite for seven years total. The rental period started about eight months before Randall moved in. The lease didn't list Randall as a party, mention his name or his office, or include his signature.

"And he seriously thinks that means Randall had to stay for years and years?" Lauren said. "You can't bind a tenant to a lease for a single year, let alone seven, unless the lease is in writing. And the tenant signs it."

"That's true for business leases, too?"

Because I grew up in an apartment building my Gram owned and managed, I knew about leases for apartments. In Illinois, if you want a residential lease for a year or more it has to be in writing.

"Yep," Lauren said. "It's just like apartments. Even if Randall promised to stay six or seven years—"

"Which I doubt."

"But if he did, if it's not in writing the only lease that formed was based on how often he paid rent. If he paid once a year, then he had a year-to-year lease."

"And since he paid monthly, it was month-to-month."

"Absolutely." Lauren poured two glasses of wine. "Either Randall or Oscar could end the lease with a month's notice."

"I wonder why Oscar didn't just have him sign a lease," I said.

Lauren, who is very fair skinned, shifted so the umbrella on my patio table shielded her from the sun. "A lot of business landlords like month-to-month leases. It's easier to kick someone out who doesn't pay or causes trouble. Or Oscar might have wanted to be able to jack up the rent on a month's notice if the market changed."

"Or maybe he just didn't know the law," I said. "He does mostly traffic cases."

"He should still know a little property law."

"You'd think," I said. "Not that I remember a ton of it from law school."

Property had been my least favorite class. Not surprisingly, it was the only one Lauren liked.

Whatever Oscar's reasons for failing to ask Randall to sign a long-term lease, I still wasn't sure Randall moving out created a motive for murder. But people have killed for lesser reasons. I needed to talk with Oscar again.

CHAPTER 17
CATCH ME IF YOU CAN

Ty and I never set a time to talk. I told myself it was just as well
as I stepped into the Daley Center courtroom for my hearing.
Not having a call before it meant I slept a little later and felt
more alert for the argument. The judge ignored the plaintiff's
filing from Friday and warned him not to do something like
that again. But she ruled in his favor on one issue and in mine
on another.

It was the exact compromise I proposed the month before. If I
were less busy, I wouldn't have minded so much for myself. But
it irritated me on my client's behalf. That was ten hours of extra
research, writing and arguing this small plumbing company
had to pay me for.

The Monadnock Building, where Randall's office was, is
between the Daley Center and my office. I stopped in the coffee
shop on the ground floor for an Earl Grey tea. They made it
with loose tea leaves, which meant waiting five minutes for it to
steep. As I stood near the counter, I did some research on my
phone and then scrolled Facebook. Still no response from the
Afterlife Facebook Group on my request to join.

Upstairs, Oscar's office was dark, but the insurance agent down the hall was in. She said she knew Randall but not very well. Nothing she told me about him was new. She had no idea what type of lease Randall might have had with Oscar.

A round faced woman with a wrist brace on her right arm sat at the end of the hall. Her desk was sandwiched between two walls with a table behind her and a window overhead. She was on the phone but waved Hello as I approached. Her smile and the warmth in her voice made me think she might be someone people confided in. And her spot near Randall's office meant she probably knew him well.

After she hung up, I introduced myself and said I was helping Randall's wife take care of his affairs. The woman's name was Flora. I asked if she was the office manager. She laughed and said No but she ought to think about adopting that title. She worked for two personal injury attorneys who shared the largest office in the suite.

Flora lowered her voice and scooted her chair closer to me. "I heard you asking about a lease between Randall and Oscar. Don't let Oscar fool you. He knew Randall was moving out. Didn't like it, but he knew. Randall told him about three weeks before he died."

"How do you know?"

"I heard them arguing. Oscar popped into Randall's doorway and tried to get him to stay the rest of the year. Randall said No."

"Oscar claims Randall agreed to stay over six years."

"Doesn't surprise me at all." Flora spread her hands wide. "When the three of us looked at this space, Oscar said he'd throw in this alcove and desk for me free. No one had used it in forever. His last tenants didn't have a secretary."

"And?"

"A month after we moved in—after we changed our address with the court—he decided we had to pay another three hundred dollars a month for this desk."

"Was it in the lease?"

"There's no lease. Not in writing. We keep thinking we might move to the suburbs where office space is cheaper. Or go virtual. So we kept it flexible."

"Which meant Oscar could ask for more and if you didn't like it, you had to move."

"Exactly. The crazy thing is if he told us up front that's what he wanted, we still would've taken the space. Sandbagging us just made the guys not like him."

"Do you think Oscar was planning to up the rent on Randall?"

"Oh, probably." Flora tilted her head. "But why so interested?"

She didn't sound hostile, just curious. If I told her about the murder investigation, though, she might clam up. It's one thing to share a little office gossip. It's another if you think what you say might make someone a murder suspect.

"Curious nature." I rolled my eyes. "It gets me in trouble every now and then."

That was all true. More than once it almost got me killed.

"Oh, me too, me too." Flora nodded. "Well, it's no secret. Oscar isn't quiet. Three or four days after they talked that first time, Oscar's hovering in Randall's doorway again. He said something like he would've charged him more per month if he knew he was only staying a couple years."

"Do you think he gave Randall really low rent?"

"Knowing Oscar? Probably not. But Randall said something I couldn't hear. Next thing I know, Oscar storms down the hall and slams his door. Things were icy between them for a week or so after that."

Flora's phone rang. I thanked her and decided to work in Randall's office for a while. It was quieter than my office suite, and maybe Oscar would eventually come in.

I called my friend Detective Sergeant Beckwell. After some grousing, he confirmed without out-and-out telling me about the investigation that Randall's father, Ivan, had been at the memory care unit visiting his wife the night Randall was killed. It wasn't impossible that Ivan could have slipped out for as long as thirty minutes. Stretching that to forty-five, with perfect traffic, Ivan could have ducked out, driven to Randall's place, and returned. But that didn't leave time for the two to get into an argument that led to a physical fight. I felt reasonably sure Ivan was off the hook.

The police hadn't gotten anywhere with the AngryHusband email sent two weeks before Randall's death that said he didn't deserve to live. Beckwell agreed the sender was a suspect. But the email didn't link to any physical address, name, or landline.

"And I can't run that partial license plate," Beckwell said. "Sorry. Department's really cracking down. But if anything else happens that's concerning, let me know. If there's any way to justify looking into it, I will."

The mention of the license plate of the man who appeared at Lauren's open house reminded me that I'd promised Lauren I'd try to talk to Joe's ex-girlfriend. I massaged my temples with my fingers. I was starting to feel pressure in my forehead. This month I'd taken six or seven Ibuprofen more days than not. I didn't want to down more if I could help it. And the only other medication that worked for me made me too sleepy to work.

I owed my dad a call, too. He works for himself, so he could likely talk mid-afternoon. And I knew from my sister Kendra's not-at-all-subtle prompting that he was disappointed we hadn't talked more lately.

But after checking the time, instead of calling him or looking for Heather I opened Facebook. I messaged six people on the Afterlife page who referred to the private Facebook Group in their comments. I'd gotten no answer from the Group Administrator. I asked each member for tips on gaining entry, sharing the same information I did in my request to join.

Next I searched online for information about Mario Orvino, the disbarred former Magic Works board member. And I searched for Illinois non-profits and fraud.

I found a thread on a site similar to Reddit. The discussion was dated six months before the golf fundraiser. It started with a post headed "What Movie Describes Your Board?" Someone with the screen name NewGuy2744, a recent college graduate, said he went to a board development seminar. The leader used the question to help attendees identify issues their non-profits needed to address.

Someone named MarioLawyer answered and the two exchanged messages.

Hah. The Sting? Catch Me If You Can? Family Business?

- MarioLawyer

Dude, what kind of board are you on?
- NewGuy2744

We help sick kids. And board members help themselves.

- MarioLawyer

You should tell someone.
- NewGuy2744

Or join them. Hah. JK.

- MarioLawyer

MarioLawyer's list of movies suggested a lot more going wrong than a single fundraiser. And posting on a public forum showed how careless he was about his non-profit's reputation and his own, which fit with someone who later got disbarred. MarioLawyer wrote "JK" for Just Kidding. But if he was Mario Orvino, he'd been serious. I copied the message string and logged out.

Clearly I needed to look a lot harder at the whole Magic Works board.

CHAPTER 18
JOE WEIGHS IN

I HAD a court status call the day after I visited Randall's office. All the plaintiff's attorney and I needed to do was update the judge on the progress of the case, but I arrived early. Running into the lawyer for the other side before court sometimes leads to settlement talks, which my client wanted. And I like the view from the twenty-seventh floor of the Daley Center. I texted Ty as I perched on one of the wide, flat benches with a view of Lake Michigan. But I got an automatic *Can I Call You Later?* message.

The other lawyer was nowhere in sight, so I researched Randall's office landlord, Oscar Miller. He lived in Homewood, Illinois, a south suburb that's fairly affordable and isn't far from the Indiana state line. Oscar had been running his solo law practice for ten years. It looked like he mainly handled traffic tickets and DUIs where no one was injured or killed.

My friend Danielle, a criminal defense attorney I used to share an office with, gets referrals from lawyers like that. She's at court most days. But if she's free she responds to texts. I sent her one asking if she knew Oscar Miller. She must have been waiting, as I was, for her turn in a courtroom because she answered right away.

Met him once or twice. Mostly traffic. Was at Kominsky and Associates for a long time.

That firm wasn't mentioned in Oscar's attorney bio. Most lawyers list previous employers. It shows you have more experience. It made me curious about his relationship with the Kominsky firm.

After popping into the courtroom to see how many cases were left before mine, I returned to the hall and looked over the Kominsky and Associates website. All three attorneys there had the last name Kominsky and all handled traffic tickets, Secretary of State hearings to reinstate driver's licenses, and DUI claims. The firm's senior partner used to be a Secretary of State hearing officer. He and the firm's other partner handled workers' compensation cases, too.

The youngest Kominsky's ARDC listing told me he started practicing the same year Oscar started his firm. I guessed the Kominskys didn't have enough business to add the lawyer who was probably their son and keep Oscar.

After peering through the glass courtroom doors to be sure the last set of attorneys was still talking, I called Danielle. I got voicemail, but she called back a few seconds later.

She sounded aggravated. "I'm waiting for my client. I told him nine-thirty, but is he here? No. But it's only a gun charge that could put him away for six to twenty years. Why should he worry? Ugh. Sorry. I'm done. What's going on?"

"Is it odd that after practicing decades Oscar handles only traffic and low level DUIs?"

"Not sure if I'd say odd. Boring maybe. But it's a lot less stressful. No one's going to prison, not for more than a year anyway. And for traffic, you get the whole fee up front. No hounding the client to pay the bill. And lots of times you only go to court once and it's done."

"Those sound like the kinds of cases you do to learn the ropes before taking on more serious ones."

"Sometimes. And some defense attorneys go back to them at the end of their careers. When you don't need to earn as much but want to stay in the game."

"This guy Oscar doesn't fit either scenario."

"Some people want a less challenging practice. Traffic tickets and misdemeanor DUIs don't tax the brain. But you've got to hustle to get enough of them to make a living."

I thanked Danielle and hung up. My case would probably be called soon. I spoke a quick email into my phone, sent it, and ducked into the courtroom.

Hello Oscar,

You and I spoke the other day at your office about Randall Petrov. His wife, Julia, asked me to look into your rent claim. I'm not clear why or how your lease with the building management could apply to Randall. I'd like to hear from you, though, before I advise her.

There's another matter I hope to talk with you about, too, relating to Randall's death.

Could I buy you a drink or coffee some evening after work and we can talk? This week is pretty open for me.

I'd very much appreciate it.

Quille C. Davis

After court, which was uneventful, I spent all day reading deposition transcripts in another case. By the time I finished, pain pulsed up the sides of my neck into my skull. I got the cold pack I keep in the office refrigerator. Then I lay on the couch I'd recently inherited for my office from another tenant who moved out. After about twenty minutes of deep breathing with the cold pack under my neck and shoulders, I was able to sit without pain.

Careful to keep my head and neck aligned, I returned to my desk. The Family Business comment about a board that sounded a lot like Magic Works had surfaced in my mind while I lay on the couch. I read through board member information my paralegal sent me earlier in the day.

I already knew Mario Orvino was Colleen's cousin once removed. It turned out the current Chairman of the Board was her brother. I hadn't caught on before because they had different last names. Colleen took her husband's name when she married, then she kept it after the divorce. Her brother joined the board about five years after Colleen became the Executive Director. Then three years before Randall's death, right after Mario resigned over the golf fundraiser issues, the brother was elected Chairman. Two more board members resigned after the election. One of those was the previous Chairman.

The other time two board members resigned together was early in Magic Works' history. That was right after Randall hired Colleen.

I texted Joe to see if he had time to talk. I'd been meaning to pick his brain since the night of the benefit. He'd been on the boards of both for-profit and non-profit companies. It helped him meet people and find new clients. And do something he felt was meaningful. He called right away.

"You're sure I'm not interrupting anything?" I said.

"Lauren's here. But it's not a problem. We're watching *The Bodyguard*. Again. I can miss it."

That reminded me that I had yet to stalk Joe's ex-girlfriend for Lauren. But if Joe, who hated movies with any type of romance in them, was willing to sit through *The Bodyguard* twice I doubted she needed to worry about his commitment level.

"He's never watched it all the way through," Lauren called out in the background.

I told Joe about the board members who resigned when Colleen was hired.

"Might be a bad sign," he said. "Sometimes a person joins a board and can't stand sitting through meetings or doesn't like the other board members. Or life happens and they realize they can't fit board service in. When two members leave together, though, there's more of a chance it's due to a dispute."

"But it could be both decided it wasn't for them?" I fished my lavender-scented neck wrap from my bottom desk drawer and took it to the kitchen.

"It could be," Joe said. "Randall bringing in his best friend means any disagreements were more likely to be resolved in his favor. The two members might have left because Randall's vision, not theirs, won out. Not because anyone did anything wrong."

I popped the neck wrap into the microwave. "What if it happened again? Three years ago, two more directors resigned after a new Board Chairman was elected."

"I'm assuming some people came and went in between that, too?"

"Yes. Magic Works started two decades ago. Most board members stayed between one and ten years. Colleen's brother has been on nearly fifteen years. Three years ago he became the Chairman."

"Hm."

"What?"

"Even ten years is long. Boards need turnover. Fresh ideas. New people to fundraise."

"It doesn't sound like this board does much." I settled the warm neck wrap so it covered my shoulders too, and sat at the table. My shoulder muscles loosened a bit more. "The brother, who is the Chairman, almost never comes to meetings. He wasn't there the night he was elected. That's a problem, right?"

"That's like having no Board Chairman at all. It might be why people resigned after he was elected."

"That's what I'm thinking. One of the recent resignees was the Board Chairman who got voted out. It can't feel great to have people prefer an absentee over you."

I told him about Mario being Colleen's cousin and asked what he thought about relatives on boards.

"It happens a lot in small non-profits. One or two founders make things happen because they're passionate about the mission. It's no surprise the easiest people for them to recruit are friends and family. And those people tend to recruit other friends and their family, too, not strangers."

"So it's not a problem?"

I heard the suite door open. Keeping the neck wrap in place, I peered out the doorway. It was the nighttime cleaning crew. I waved and returned to the kitchen.

"I didn't say that," Joe said. "Say Colleen figures out something's off about that golf fundraiser. But her cousin Mario offers her a cut, so she doesn't say anything. If the Treasurer's not too sharp and doesn't catch it, the next line of defense is the rest of the board. But if the Chairman trusts Colleen because she's his sister, his faith can discourage anyone else from asking questions."

"Or he might discourage them because he knows all about it."

"That too."

"I hope nothing like that's going on. Julia just joined the board. She wants to carry on the mission in memory of Randall. She'll be devastated—more than she is already if that's possible—if it turns out Randall's friend was cheating."

"Assuming there isn't any cheating, Julia ought to push the board to be more active. A board that approves whatever an Executive Director does is a big red flag."

"Like a board that's a rubber stamp?" I said, thinking of how Mario described the Magic Works board.

"Exactly. The Executive Director doesn't have a boss other than the board. If the board members let her decide everything because they're family or don't understand their role, an ED can rob a non-profit blind."

"Huh."

"What?"

I told him about the movies Mario compared his board to on

the online forum. I hadn't mentioned it before because I didn't want to influence Joe's take on anything.

"That comment was around the same time the two members resigned?" Joe asked.

"Yes. I'm thinking these are people I need to talk to."

It was after eight-thirty when we hung up. Between the ice and the heat, my muscles felt relaxed. The short walk home helped, too. At my condo, I started to watch a new series on streaming. After a few minutes, though, I grabbed my iPad and found the phone number for Kominsky and Associates. I planned to call tomorrow morning.

I wanted to find out what Oscar Miller's former employer had to say about him.

CHAPTER 19
MONEY MATTERS

I TRIED Kominsky and Associates first thing the next morning and left a voicemail for the senior partner. The rest of the day I focused on my legal work with a break around mid-day. Though it meant I'd need to work all evening to finish the day's work, I walked to the lakefront and back for the exercise. Before returning to the office, I stopped at Totto's Market, a small corner market in my neighborhood, for a premade box of cheese, fruit, nuts, and olives. I ate sitting near the fountain in the plaza half a block from my office. A group of pigeon admirers gathered near my feet hoping for crumbs. They and I enjoyed the sun and warm weather.

After four more hours of work I ate dinner—a ham and brie sandwich from Café des Livres downstairs—at my desk. I only noticed how late it had gotten when the evening cleaning woman, Eva, came in to empty my waste basket and recycling bin. With all my late nights, we'd gotten to know each other. She told me about her daughter, who was leaving for college in the fall. And she told me I ought to go home for the day. But a call came in on my office line.

It was Rebecca Noxonian, the woman who served as Vice President of Magic Works until the board elected the current Chairman. She lived in Arizona now. After shutting my door so Eva would feel free to hum as she worked, something she liked to do, I filled Rebecca in as quickly as I could.

"You think someone on the board killed Randall?" Rebecca said.

"It's possible."

"But they're all wonderful people." A sigh came through the phone. "I suppose you'll tell me some murderers are charming."

"Some are. Some aren't. But you definitely can't tell based on their personalities. Right now, though, I'm more interested in fundraising issues."

I explained about the golf fundraiser. Rebecca didn't know Mario Orvino very well. She remembered Randall asking about the funds from the golf outing. But she didn't think Mario purposely stole money or held a grudge against Randall.

"What do you think of Colleen?" I said.

"She'd never hurt Randall if that's what you're asking. They were best friends. Peas in a pod."

"How about when it came to money?"

"Oh. Let me think how to say this." There was a long pause. "I never thought she was scamming. But she was a bit slipshod with money. Though that was understandable."

"Slipshod how?" I turned on the tiny fan I kept on my desk and pointed it at my face. The building air conditioning shut off at seven. It was after eight now, and my office felt warm and stuffy.

"Sometimes families of the children we helped hosted fundraisers. They split the money with us. Half to whatever foundation they set up in their child's name or for medical bills and half to us. But Colleen never pressed them for a clear accounting. She accepted whatever they said about how much our share was."

"There were no procedures to track that?"

The accountant in me was appalled. I love numbers and tracking things. Long before I took a college business class I recorded exactly how much I earned as an actor and what my professional and personal expenses amounted to in spreadsheets.

"There were," Rebecca said. "But it's hard, believe me, to push a family whose child is ill or who, God forbid, just died, to dot all the i's. Colleen hated to add to their burden."

"She had a lot of empathy for people."

"That and she just wasn't a businessperson."

Except supposedly Colleen was. She said she ran the business of the illusionists she worked for. I made a note to try to track them down.

"Didn't the Treasurer follow up with the families?"

"When I was on the board he looked at the big picture only. Put together financial statements for the outside accountant, but didn't do day-to-day tasks."

"So Colleen handled the bookkeeping?"

"Well, Magic Works had a bookkeeper who did some other office work too. She reported to Colleen."

"Any chance Colleen was skimming from those family fundraisers? Or someone else on the board was?"

"I doubt it. These were good people."

I wiped sweat from my forehead. "Why did you resign? Did it relate to the new Chairman?"

"You heard about No-Show Beau?"

"Beau? I thought his name was Theo."

"It was. Is. But his middle name is Beauregard. I called him No-Show Beau out of frustration. He came to so few meetings that a newer board member had to ask me who he was when she saw his name on the ballot for Chairman."

"Did he get elected just because he was Colleen's brother?"

"That was part of it. But he brought in a lot of donations," Rebecca said.

"The other members didn't do that?"

From my research I knew most non-profit boards have a Give or Get requirement. If you join, you pledge to donate or raise a certain amount per year.

"I did. The others, not so much. They felt they were there to offer expertise or experience, not money."

I put the phone on speaker and pulled my hair, which hung heavy on my neck and back, into a ponytail high on my head. "You sound skeptical."

"Honestly? They were nice people, but didn't do a lot. They suggested a tweak to the website here and there or spitballed ideas for new programs. But the best idea came from our bookkeeper. A website page where people could donate clothes that might help families."

"I didn't see that," I said.

"It never raised a ton. Maybe it was discontinued. But at least she was trying to think of new things. Sharp young woman."

The sound of a vacuum cleaner came through my closed door. I took the phone off speaker.

"What about the Chairman who got voted out?" I said. "People must have been unhappy with him to choose an absentee instead."

"Colleen didn't like him. He's the one who suggested freezing her salary."

Rebecca explained that Randall promised to match Colleen's salary with the illusionists. But that salary was about double the average starting pay for someone with no experience running a non-profit. Randall won the day. That was the first time board members resigned in protest. When Rebecca and the man who later became Chairman joined the board, Colleen's high salary shocked them. They got the others to vote to freeze her salary.

"Years and years later we gave her a raise. But it was nowhere near the amount she wanted. We said No again the next time, but got outvoted. And the Chairman got unelected."

"Let me guess," I said. "No-Show Beau was a big supporter of a raise for Colleen. Which I suppose as her brother, he should be."

"Oh, yes. He made it to every meeting where Colleen's pay was up for a vote. Skipped the rest."

"Did you and the old Chairman resign to protest his election?"

"Not exactly protest. But it was the straw that broke the camel's back. Once Robert got voted out as the Chair his heart sort of went out of being a board member."

I wanted to talk to Robert, but Rebecca told me he'd died of a heart attack last year. She did give me the name of the book-keeper. After the call ended, I sent my notes to my paralegal and asked for some more research.

The office suite door slammed. Eva had finished cleaning and left. I wished I could, too, but I still had hours of documents to review. Logically, I knew I wasn't the only one working late tonight. The building had twenty floors and plenty of lawyers worked on them. But with all the other offices in my suite dark and the air conditioning off, I felt like I was all alone in the world.

Two hours later I was about to head home when an email came in from my paralegal. She often worked evenings and must have been doing so tonight, too.

> Okay, meant to take only a quick look tonight but couldn't stop once I started down the rabbit hole. A month after Rebecca Noxonian and the old Chairman resigned, two new board members joined. One had a finance background. He was mid-fifties, got an early retirement deal from his company, and had time on his hands. He volunteered to serve as Treasurer and do the day-to-day bookkeeping for free. Save Magic Works some money. The bookkeeper was let go. The old Treasurer shifted to being just a board member. Six months later he left the board. He died two months after that. Cancer.

> Here's the kicker. The new Treasurer? He was the college roommate of Colleen's brother, Theo/No-Show Beau. Social media links and the contact info attached.

I spent about double the time you suggested, but I hope you'll think it was worth it.

I did think it was worth it. But I was deeply troubled. If we were in a court of law, none of the facts so far proved beyond a reasonable doubt that Colleen, her brother, or his old roommate were scamming Magic Works. But they suggested it. And solid evidence might be out there.

The problem was that everyone described Colleen and Randall as best friends. Peas in a pod. If Colleen scammed Magic Works, there was more than a small chance Randall knew it or was in on it. Or that he found out and got killed for it.

How did I tell Julia the love of her life might have been stealing from his own charity, been killed by his best friend, or both?

CHAPTER 20
MEN AND MEETINGS

Around nine-thirty that night I at last curled up in the corner of my couch at home. A mug of lavender and vanilla herbal tea sat on the cedar chest beside me. My sliding glass doors stood open, letting in the warm night air. Normally after a day like this one I'd sit on my deck and inhale the fresh earth smell from my neighbors' potted plants, ignoring the tinges of car exhaust and diesel that linger in the neighborhood. But it felt like too much work to step onto the wooden deck.

My phone sat at my side. Today's task list still included texting Joe's ex-girlfriend. I clicked on Instagram instead. A video of a green, blue, and yellow parakeet using his beak to roll a small plastic aspirin bottle across a rug played. Next I watched one of the same bird racing up and down a bright green ladder.

If I tracked down Heather, I risked Joe's anger for who knows how long. And if I dug deeper into Magic Works and found something terribly wrong, Julia was going to be more miserable than she already was, especially if it didn't solve Randall's murder.

And yet, for better or for worse, I'm not wired to drop the ball. Especially if somebody's getting hurt. If Colleen or other board members were running scams, I couldn't let it go.

"Of course you can't," Ty said.

I'd gotten into bed after another half an hour of bird videos. Ty's FaceTime call awakened me as I drifted off to sleep around eleven.

I shifted so my elbow propped on my knee, making it easier to hold the phone in front of my face. "But this isn't what Julia hired me to do."

"Isn't it? The resignations happened years ago. But the golf fundraiser guy lost his license right before Randall was killed. If there's a running scam or series of them and he was involved, and Randall uncovered it, why couldn't it relate?"

"Mario's got an alibi. Detective Beckwell himself confirmed it."

"You've seen alibis fall apart before."

"True." I felt happy Ty remembered so much about my current investigation despite how rare our calls had become. And he remembered details from earlier ones.

"I trust you, Quille. If something's nagging at you, it matters. And if you find out something Julia doesn't want to know, it'll be hard. But from what you told me, she'd never want to turn a blind eye to anyone stealing from a non-profit she supports."

"She's more than supporting it. She's on the board. But you're right. I need to look into this. Then, if there's real evidence, tell her about it."

We talked for a few minutes about what we'd been doing, which for both of us was mainly work. Ty needed to start getting ready for a meeting soon. I asked how it was going with rescheduling his visit. He wanted to get away for at least a week and a half. With a fifteen-hour flight each way, coming for less time didn't make sense.

"I thought I had it sorted out. But deadlines on a key project all got moved. Forward for a change. Good for the client, not good for you and me."

"So not the usual Delay Delay Delay?"

"No, the one time I wish it were. It'd be easier to get away."

Ty's company had promised he could fly home at least once a quarter. But it was no easier to make that stick than it was for me to be sure I wouldn't need to work any particular weekend. A judge could always enter an order that required me to be in court, or a lawyer on the other side of the case could file a motion that meant I needed to spend the next few days researching and writing a response brief. Or a new case could come in that I couldn't afford not to take.

"I get it. I might get the brownie case resolved next week." I rubbed my forehead. "I wish—if I hadn't taken on this investigation—"

"You'd fly here? It would've been fantastic to see you. But I would've felt terrible. You'd spend all your time working on your laptop while I was in meetings or at site visits."

"We'd spend more time together than zero." I wasn't sure why I was pushing the point. My schedule didn't look any better for a long trip than Ty's did.

"True. But don't feel like you ought to have turned down this investigation on my account. Okay? We'll sort it out."

I slept pretty well that night. But in the morning I felt discouraged. Ty's work was a lot like mine in a key way. Once we took on a project, the project took on a life of its own. And all our plans went out the window.

Oscar Miller never answered my email asking to meet. When I had a free hour the next day, I headed to the Monadnock Building. If I couldn't catch Oscar in his office, I could at least go through the books and papers in Randall's office. I'd focused on his digital files with little success. Maybe I'd find something on paper to help track down his murderer or explain the Magic Works board.

I finally had some good luck, though. Oscar's door was open. Reading at his mahogany desk, he didn't look up when I popped my head into the office.

"I know you're busy," I said. "But I need your help. Not just about the rent issue. Julia asked me to look into Randall's murder."

At last I got Oscar's attention. His arms flopped onto his desk and the paper fluttered to the floor. "Murder?" Oscar bent to retrieve the page. "I thought it was a robbery gone wrong."

"Where did you hear that?"

"The police. They interviewed me. They wanted to know if Randall had been in the office that day. I had no idea. I don't work Sundays."

"Robbery is their theory. But Julia thinks it was someone he knew, and I'm investigating. If I could buy you dinner, pick your brain—"

"I don't see how I could help."

"You saw Randall day after day. You might be able to tell me things about him that could help piece it all together."

Oscar frowned. "But I don't know who killed him."

"Probably only the killer knows that. The way I work is I interview people who knew a victim, try to understand the victim's life as much as I can. Sometimes that points to who killed the person."

Oscar's forehead creased. "There's no one I know who'd want to kill Randall." He looked genuinely puzzled, though I wasn't sure anyone could fail to grasp what I was saying.

"That's okay. If I could just ask you some questions about Randall, I'd appreciate it. Julia would too. She might be more apt to agree to keep the office a bit longer."

I didn't know that last part for sure. But she'd been clear that I should spend what was necessary for the investigation. That would just have to include some extra rent.

Oscar glanced at the calendar app open on his desktop monitor and named two dates.

I looked at my phone app. "Is there anything else open? I've got a bar association networking event for the first one and—"

"Does it help?"

"What? Networking? I've gotten a few referrals."

"Where's it at? Can you meet before it?"

The event was in Lincoln Park. But Oscar was in court in the south suburbs that day, so that wasn't going to work. And the second date he had open was the arbitration for my brownie case.

"Arbitrations don't go into the evening, do they?" he said.

"No. The afternoon hearings end by four."

"Great. Five-thirty at Shaw's Crab House works for me. I'll meet you in the bar. You make the reservation."

"But I—"

"Take it or leave it. That's my only free night."

"I'll meet you there," I said.

Dinner at five-thirty, though, meant almost no time to decompress, relax, and shift gears after the arbitration.

I'd just have to deal with it.

In Randall's office I found paper copies of some Magic Works financial statements. It prompted me to pull the rest from Randall's digital folders. A discrepancy nagged at me. It might be nothing.

But it might be everything.

CHAPTER 21
MOTIVES

DESPITE TWELVE AND thirteen hour workdays, I barely kept up with my caseload the rest of the week. The task "research Heather" slid down my Reminders app every day. I told myself that was only because it had no set deadline, unlike everything else.

I spoke with two current board members and three more past ones, plus four Magic Works magician volunteers. None shed any light on Randall's death. Or the fundraising issues. I phrased questions on possible money scams in roundabout ways, not wanting to suggest a problem if there was none.

Despite being twenty-eight years old, the bookkeeper who'd been let go, Laquita Williams, had almost no online presence. I hadn't known anyone in their twenties could survive offline. One of my subscription databases showed she lived in an apartment in Oak Park, a suburb that borders Chicago. She worked at a non-profit in a professional building about five blocks from the apartment.

I hadn't found a home phone number or cell phone. It was late Friday night. I debated calling Laquita at work Monday. But it was far too easy to hang up, especially on a stranger. By finding two of her coworkers on social media I learned that Laquita left work at five each day. On Mondays and Thursdays, the three of them attended a spin class together after work. There didn't seem to be any routine Tuesday evening plans.

On Tuesday I rode the Green Line to Oak Park. Not wanting to waste time, on the way I signed onto Facebook on my phone. Three Afterlife, Alchemy and More Facebook Group members answered my request for tips on being admitted into the private group. Two said the administrator admitted them right away. They didn't know why I was having trouble. But a third shared more.

> I'm sorry to hear about your sister's death. But some people join the group to poke fun at us or worse. Your message didn't sound like you were that kind of person, so I looked at your profile. It doesn't say where you work or live. You don't have many friends. You need to show the administrator you're not a troublemaker. I had to do that because my work doesn't want any of us on social media for PR reasons, so my profile isn't under my real name.

> Try applying again. Explain yourself and include links. A website with a work bio if you've got one, online photos of you, ways to contact you. That kind of thing. If you can link to your sister's obituary, that's good too. That's what I did and a week later I was admitted.

> Good luck.

I clicked the Facebook pages of the group members I'd messaged. One person had a few hundred friends and posted a lot of photos of himself and his wife. He lived in the Czech Republic. The English translations of some of his posts suggested he might be AngryHusband, the anonymous emailer who threatened Randall. And warned him not to post a video I so far hadn't found despite scouring every cloud-based account Randall had.

Two members had thousands of Facebook friends. Photos of themselves filled their pages. They listed the schools they attended, their jobs, and where they lived. They were a nightmare when it came to exposing their personal lives to strangers.

The home page of the woman who sent me the advice, though, looked a lot like my Cathy Dearborn profile. She shared little. Her photos mostly showed antique cars and railroad tracks. None included her or other people. She was probably right. I needed to share more about my real life to get into the group.

After getting off the train, I made my way to the building where Laquita worked, stopping at the Starbucks next door to it. Then I stationed myself on a bench in the lobby near a chiropractor's office. The caffeine in my London Fog from Starbucks helped keep me awake. The latte part added a few calories. I'd missed quite a few meals lately as I got ready for my arbitration and waded through giant troves of email in another case. It involved four law partners suing each other over who got what when their law firm imploded. It was like a business divorce and just as messy as a marital one.

I knew I was flirting with disaster. Restless sleep and not enough food equals migraines for me. I promised myself a relaxed evening after I talked with Laquita. Or after she refused to have anything to do with me.

Laquita emerged from the north elevator bank just after five. She chatted happily with another young woman about her age, gesturing with her hands, the beads at the ends of her narrow braids bouncing.

I stood. "Laquita?"

She paused. Her eyebrows, one of them pierced with a small gold hoop, raised. "Yes?"

"My name's Quille Davis. I'm a friend of Randall Petrov's wife." I held out my hand to shake. "And a lawyer. I'd like to talk with you about Randall if you have a few minutes."

Laquita's grip was firm and her hand warm. Whatever her views of Magic Works, I hoped she felt positively enough about Randall to consider talking to me. And if not, that would tell me something, too.

"Oh, that was awful what happened to him." She turned to her coworker. "This man from where I used to work got killed."

The other young woman gasped. Laquita gave her a one-sentence version of what the news reported. After the two said good-bye, Laquita turned to me. "Why do you want to talk about Randall?"

"Julia—his wife—thinks there might be more to it than a robbery gone wrong. She thinks someone he knew killed him."

"Really?" Laquita pursed her lips. "Well, she's a smart lady. But it's years since I saw Randall or anyone from Magic Works."

"That's exactly why you can help. I'm looking for background from someone who's not there anymore. Could I buy you a latte or a margarita?"

I'd seen photos of her drinking both out with her friends.

"Looks like you already got a latte."

"I can drink another."

People flowed around us as we spoke. Laquita studied me,

hands on her hips. "First I need to know you are who you say and Julia really hired you."

I showed her my ID and pulled up Julia's courtroom information on the Circuit Court of Cook County website. "She's been in chambers late these days. You might be able to reach her there."

I texted her Julia's cell phone number, too, and texted Julia that Laquita was calling. Laquita crossed the lobby so she stood out of my hearing range. Her caution was smart. And unusual. Most people I talk to, after pushing back a little, open up because they like being listened to or are longing to tell their story. Laquita's wariness and avoidance of most social media made me wonder if she'd had a bad experience in her past.

Laquita joined me again as I finished answering my brownie client's emailed question about our arbitration.

"Okay, let's go. But I need to leave by six-fifteen."

The Mexican restaurant down the street had a large brick-floored patio. Laquita got a margarita and we shared chips and guacamole made table side. As the server chopped avocados, I asked if Colleen's salary struck Laquita as high.

"That was my first full-time job. I didn't know one way or the other. But the Treasurer—the one before this one—told me Colleen's pay was high. But he said Randall never took a salary at all so it balanced out."

"Was there some reason you asked about her salary range?"

"I didn't ask. He just told me. He was what my mother calls a motor mouth."

I asked how often she saw Randall.

"Pretty often. Everyone at MW worked from home before that was a thing. But Colleen and I met twice a week at a Starbucks in between where we lived. Randall usually joined us. He filled her in on the volunteers and recent events."

Laquita told me Randall rarely disagreed with Colleen. They made a lot of decisions together about Magic Works.

I squeezed a lime slice into my ginger ale. "Without the other board members?"

"Usually. But I'm pretty sure Colleen always informed the board. They could veto anything they disagreed with."

"None of the board members besides Randall came to your Starbucks meetings?"

"That new Treasurer did during my last three weeks. I showed him the books and passwords and such. But besides that, no."

Laquita told me Colleen's sister took over the administrative assistant tasks Laquita handled. The sister worked on an independent contractor basis for eight or nine hours a week. Another way to save Magic Works money. And another family member of Colleen's working there.

"Was it hard training your replacements?"

Laquita shrugged. "I wasn't thrilled. But they gave me two weeks' severance pay. And I lined up a new job right off. Colleen gave me a great recommendation."

"I hear you set up a donor page before you left. Why ask for clothes as donations?"

"Because we—that's MW, I still say 'we' a lot—could easily donate any items left over. I learned from my mother's experience. She worked for a veterans' outfit that asked people to donate clothes or small items. People used to bring in everything from toasters to printers, and lots of times they were broken. It costs too much to fix things like that, and sometimes you've got to pay a junk dealer to take it away."

"Is this the page?" I showed her my phone. I had finally found it after a lot of hunting. It wasn't on the Magic Works website menu.

Laquita nodded and said the families Magic Works helped were given links to it and to another webpage. That one showed photos of each piece of clothing.

"That one's searchable. So if a parent needs a winter coat for their toddler, they can find it. It's a little like those Buy Nothing Facebook pages."

"That other page didn't come up in any of my searches."

"You have to have someone send you a link. That was my idea, too. That way people outside MW won't just jump in and grab things for free."

"And the clothes none of the families asked for were donated somewhere else?"

"Not all of them. The plan was to sell designer or really nice vintage pieces on Etsy or eBay or some such site. Then put the money into the fund for families."

My hunting online had uncovered no Magic Works eBay page. The Etsy store sold T-shirts, buttons, and other Magic Works swag, but no used or vintage clothes.

"Where do people send items they donate? Since Magic Works doesn't have a physical office?"

"The official address is one of those business suites where you can rent a mailbox and use the conference rooms for a fee. They accept packages, too."

That address was in Blue Island, a southern suburb of Chicago.

I asked Laquita how she'd planned to record money from the clothing sales. She said it was supposed to go under Sales, along with the swag Magic Works sold. Swag, though, brought in very little. Fifty cents or so on a button and a dollar on a fifteen dollar T-shirt.

Laquita glanced at the time on her phone and stood. "I hope this helped. And I hope Magic Works goes on without Randall. That's what he would have wanted."

I nodded. "Julia thinks so, too. Thank you."

"You don't really think his death has anything to do with MW do you?"

"It's too hard to say."

That was true, literally. I didn't have the heart to tell Laquita that she might have pinpointed a very big potential motive for Colleen, her brother, or both to kill Randall.

CHAPTER 22
A CRIMINAL MATTER

On the train home, I scoured the income statements I'd downloaded from Randall's laptop. As I remembered, there was no listing for Sales other than Swag. And the dollars in the Swag column were low. Too low to reflect the sale of donated designer clothes.

I rechecked what I'd found when researching Colleen personally. She sold designer and upscale clothing, as well as antique dishes and glasses, on several sites. Her sales history began around the time Laquita was let go. That didn't prove Colleen was selling clothes she got through the Magic Works donor page. She might scour secondhand stores and garage sales to buy items for resale.

I had an idea on how to find out which was true.

Lauren's not quite as much of an early riser as me. But she was awake when I texted her the next morning after my weight lifting session. I work out in the basement exercise room of our condo building. She told me to stop by on the way to my office.

Half an hour later, showered and changed, I knocked at her door. "Know anyone with a distinctive item of clothing to donate?"

Lauren still wore a tank top and sweat pants. "Um, is your memory seriously failing you? You've been in my closet."

Her walk in closet looks like an upscale designer resale shop that sells garments worn no more than once.

"It can't be you." I followed her to her kitchen island, which is just like mine only at an angle to her living room area. I explained what I suspected. "If Colleen's behind it, she might recognize your name."

"Hm. How distinctive?" She waved to the cabinet where she keeps tea bags just for me. She's a diehard coffee drinker.

I shook my head. "I only have a few minutes. Distinctive enough that a similar item probably won't be donated around the same time. I want to recognize it if it appears on one of Colleen's sites."

I spent that afternoon calling and emailing people related to Magic Works who shed light on how the donations were meant to work. Just as I ended a call with a volunteer, Lauren forwarded a photo of a pristine three-year-old royal blue Chanel pantsuit with silver piping. One of her real estate agent friends had bought it on Thred Up. She offered it to Magic Works through the donor page. An hour later Lauren forwarded a return message. It asked the donor to send the suit to an address that matched Colleen's home. That wasn't proof of scamming. Colleen might have gotten tired of the hour and forty minute drive each way from her home to the official Magic Works address and back.

A Magic Works volunteer had sent me the link to the webpage where families could view photos of available clothing items. I kept an eye on it and on the Magic Works eBay site as I reviewed emails of law partners in my business divorce case. But there was nothing. I reached both of the illusionists Colleen worked for. I learned a lot. But I started to think I might be wrong about the designer clothing scheme.

The next day, though, Lauren texted me a link to a brand new listing of what looked like the same Chanel suit on The RealReal. She called a few seconds later. "I can't tell if Colleen is the seller. The screen name's too generic. SF_24879."

"Let me see if that's in Randall's notes." I opened and scrolled the PDFs of recent board agendas. Randall had scanned them after meetings. They included handwritten notes in the margins with all kinds of abbreviations I didn't understand. No SF_24879, though.

"When did Magic Works let that bookkeeper go?" Lauren said.

I told her as I closed the Agenda folder.

"Well, Seller SF_24879 started their store two weeks after the bookkeeper left. They've sold over three thousand items since then. Everything ships from Woodstock, Illinois."

"From Colleen's address?" I said.

"It doesn't give the exact address. But it says you can pick up if you're local and don't want to pay shipping."

Colleen was very foolish, or arrogant, if she used her own address for pick-ups. But my former officemate Danielle, who was a cop and then a prosecutor before becoming a criminal defense attorney, always tells me most criminals aren't rocket scientists. And the board members didn't look closely at anything Colleen did.

I called my friend Carole, the owner of Café des Livres. She agreed to buy the suit. Lauren felt sure she could resell it online, so Carole would only be out the money for a short time and might make a profit.

Three hours later Carole messaged me. The pick up spot was Colleen's home address.

Sometimes I longed for a judge's schedule. It was only four in the afternoon. Yet the judges' chambers and the hallways between them and the courtrooms were silent. I met with Julia to tell her I suspected Colleen might be stealing funds from Magic Works. I started with the illusionists, who confirmed she was their stage assistant for years. But Colleen never ran their business or handled any business tasks. And Randall never spoke to them about her, probably because he trusted her.

"No, no, no." Julia shook her head with each No. Her elbows rested on her large polished desk. A bookcase of law books with worn bindings towered behind her. "None of that shows Colleen was scamming. All she did was pad her resume."

"A lot," I said.

Julia spun her chair to look out the floor-to-ceiling window. The view included a wide expanse of Lake Michigan, bright blue on this cloudless summer day.

"Randall would have hired her anyway," Julia said.

"Agreed. But in some ways that makes it more troubling. Why lie if she didn't need to? Is it a habit?"

Julia swiveled to face me. "Maybe she did need to. The board might not have agreed to hire her."

"Randall was the founder. He had a lot of influence."

"But he could be outvoted."

"Then there's her salary. She tripled what she claimed to be making with the illusionists, then got Randall to match it."

"People puff their salaries during negotiations."

But Julia's shoulders drooped. She looked so defeated I felt more determined, if that was possible, to find the killer, whether it was Colleen or someone else. Julia needed some sort of good result from my investigation.

"They do," I said. "But exaggerating that much, especially with a friend begging you to help him start his non-profit, strikes me as more than puffing."

Julia sighed. "She ought to have just told Randall how much she wanted to make the move worth it. But surely you don't think Randall found out about those lies and she killed him? That's absurd."

"There's more."

I revealed what happened with the Chanel suit. Then I told her about the donated clothing. Colleen had at least five sites where she sold upscale clothes. Over half the hospitals where Magic Works placed collection bins were in pricey suburbs. Suburbs where the clothing donated was likely to be high quality and very gently worn. Similar items sold for hundreds of dollars online. But my IT consultant, who dug through Internet archives, couldn't find any designer items ever listed on the Magic Works family page. None of the income statements showed any money coming in from sales of clothing.

Julia folded her arms over her chest. "This is just—I almost wish you hadn't told me. This type of scandal, if you're right, could tank Magic Works. Randall's whole legacy."

But she called an Assistant State's Attorney she knew well. He worked with the Chicago police Financial Crimes division. That division had resources I didn't. I shared all I learned about Magic Works. It would take time to build a case against Colleen and check out the rest of the board members, including her brother and his roommate. But it was a criminal matter now, and up to them.

CHAPTER 23
LONG DAYS

My day started at seven the next morning. I worked on the business divorce case for a few hours, then the owner of the bakery that made the "chocolatiest" brownies arrived. I spent three hours getting her ready to testify at the arbitration. After that, I caught up on my other cases. Around three, a gnawing in my stomach reminded me I needed to eat.

I settled at a table in a corner of the outdoor patio at Café des Livres with my laptop, an iced Chai tea, and a salmon and cream cheese sandwich. My phone rang before I took a single bite. It was Burton Kominsky Junior, who told me I could call him Burt. He was returning my three calls to the firm asking about Oscar Miller.

His voice sounded young, serious, and a little self-important. "My father forwarded your voicemails to me. I handle personnel matters. I need to understand exactly why you need this information. A rent dispute and a murder? Strange combination."

"It is in a way," I said. "My law practice is business litigation. I handle murder investigations on a very limited basis. This one started when Judge Julia Lopez asked me to look into her husband's murder."

I'd decided being up front with these lawyers about my work for Julia gave me the best chance to get them to share information.

"I'm surprised the judge didn't call us directly. She went to law school with my parents."

My research told me that while Julia attended the same law school as the Kominskys, she graduated five years earlier. That meant they wouldn't have had classes together, though they might have crossed paths later.

"Her husband, Randall, rented an office from Oscar Miller. Julia tells me Randall planned to move out at the end of this month. Oscar claims Randall agreed to stay for another four years plus."

"Well, we know nothing about that. We'd like to help the judge, but no one here has heard from Oscar in years."

It was a little too hot out for me. I shifted my chair into the shade from the building behind me. "Can you tell me what he's like to work with?"

"Well, you've probably guessed he's not Mr. Congeniality. That was part of the problem."

"In what way? He didn't get along with clients? Or couldn't bring in new ones."

An electronic beep sounded in the background and I heard a few keys clicking.

"He brought in clients. Some speeding tickets. DUIs where no one got hurt. But he groused about why he had to find new clients at all if he had enough work for the month."

"Always a challenge," I said. "I'm working long hours this whole month. But I'm still planning on the monthly bar association cocktail party in Lincoln Park."

Very large law firms tend to have corporations as clients. Many send steady streams of business to their firms. Things can always change, so the firms still need lawyers who can snag new clients. But no one lawyer needs to do it all.

For small firms and solos like me, though, it's an endless roller coaster. If you're very busy, as I was now, you work all the time. And still worry that six months down the road you'll be playing solitaire on your office computer, unsure how to pay the bills. My brownie case and another for a local plumbing company took up nearly half my time these days. But both were going to resolve one way or another soon. That's why as hectic as things were at the moment, I needed to get in front of people so they remembered I was around when it came time to refer cases.

"Yeah, I go to that sometimes. And two or three other networking events a month," Burt said. "Oscar didn't think he should have to do that. He said he was here for his brains and skill, not to bring in business." A phone rang in the background. "Hold on."

I took advantage of the time to eat a few bites of my sandwich. When he returned, Burt told me he couldn't talk more now, but he could meet some evening for drinks or coffee.

"You can't tell Oscar you spoke to me or anyone here, though," Burt said after we picked a place and time. "Things were rocky when he left."

"How rocky?"

"Restraining order rocky."

Three days later Julia asked me to meet her after work to talk about the murder investigation. But not in her chambers. She said she'd spent far too much time there since Randall's death.

We sat instead on a wide expanse of lawn along the Chicago River in large bright pink Adirondack chairs, the only two left open this summer evening. To my left at street level an L train rumbled across the river. Across the river, a wide, shiny glass apartment complex soared. The area is known as Wolf Point. It's where all three branches of the Chicago River meet. The city's first taverns and its first hotel, drug store, church, and theater company were built there.

The spot was a favorite of Julia's and Randall's. I hadn't known it was there. I never walked that far west on the Riverwalk.

"It's all so stupid of Colleen," Julia said.

"She was used to no one questioning her. She got careless. Or was careless from the start."

I reminded myself to relax my shoulders. Two or three hours of work still waited for me at my office, both on my brownie case and on investigating Joe's girlfriend. Lauren's quick help with the Chanel suit left me feeling guilty that I hadn't done the favor she asked for.

"I can't believe Randall never checked into what she was doing," Julia said.

"Maybe he did when he flagged the Mario Orvino golf fundraiser issues."

"No. He would have told me." She folded her hands together and rubbed one thumb over the other. Her diamond-crusted wedding band glinted in the sunlight. "Magic Works will never survive. Financial Crimes already traced that RealReal account back to Colleen. At best, the board members, including Randall, were negligent in not knowing."

The breeze shifted and I smelled fresh cut grass along with river water. "Magic Works might make it through. Or you could start a new non-profit with the same goals. I'm sure the volunteers will want to continue."

She shook her head. "They'll have to do it without me. Magic was Randall's passion. He was mine. Without him, there's no magic."

She asked about the rest of the murder investigation. I filled her in, adding that Colleen's scams didn't mean she killed Randall.

"I'm certain she didn't," Julia said. "The prosecutor verified Colleen's and all the board members' alibis."

"That helps. I can concentrate on other leads now."

"No," she said.

"You want me to doublecheck on Colleen and the board?"

Julia stared at the river, avoiding meeting my eyes. Three green kayaks whizzed past. "I don't want you to investigate anymore. I wanted to believe there was a reason for Randall's death. That it wasn't just bad luck that he was on the 606 and ran into a mugger. But I was avoiding the truth. Thinking I knew better than the police. And all I did was stir up trouble. It's done. We're done."

I opened my mouth to argue. But I had no idea what to say. Or why I wanted to say it. Julia wanted peace. My work brought her anything but.

She told me to send my final bill as soon as possible. We climbed the concrete stairs up to Wacker Drive in silence. We ordered separate Ubers home.

CHAPTER 24
THE UNEXPECTED

I LONGED to call Ty from the Uber. But it was three-thirty in the morning in Dubai. I worked from home the rest of the evening. I tried Ty at eleven-thirty. It's later than I usually go to bed, but I didn't feel like trying to sleep anyway.

He answered right away, but he had a meeting in fifteen minutes.

I should have called sooner. But morning meetings are rare for Ty, so I'd been more concerned about waking him up.

I plumped my pillows to lean against them and drew my knees up to my chest. "The whole investigation's off. And not because I found answers. The only good thing out of it is I can visit you. As soon as my arbitration is done. Danielle's got a light couple weeks, she can cover my court calls." I pulled my comforter over my knees. "Ty? You still there?"

"Yeah. Yes."

"The firm's still willing to pay for the flight aren't they? They said once a quarter."

"That's not a problem."

"So what do I do to book?"

"Ah, Quille. I'd love to see you. But coming all that way, disrupting your practice when—"

"It's okay if you're busy while I'm there. I just need a break. Even if it's mostly working in a different conference room in a different country."

"This is more than a ten-minute conversation. Can we try for tomorrow?"

My stomach felt like it dropped straight down through my body. It was as much his tone as his words. "We can. But give me the high points now. Or I'll lie awake all night wondering."

A sigh came through the line. "It's more like low points. I had a talk with your mother—"

I gripped the phone so tight my fingers ached. "You had a—you called my mother?"

"She called me. Concerned about this long-term long distance thing being unfair to you."

"My mother knows zero about me. Or my life."

"She knows what a kind, loyal person you are. And how you put other people's needs ahead of your own."

"I can't believe you're listening to my mother."

"She didn't say anything I wasn't already thinking. Honestly, Quille, is there anyone in your family—or any one of your friends—who thinks this relationship is good for you?"

I got out of bed barefoot and paced between my bedroom area and my couch. "Do not tell me you're breaking up with me for my own good."

"I'm not. I said this all wrong. It's not for you. Not only for you. I feel all wrong about this. First I put you on the spot last spring to tell me if I should take this job. Then without giving you time to think it through I took it. After that I arm-twisted you into staying with me when I have no idea if I'll come back to the U.S. when the two years are done, let alone Chicago."

I perched on the sofa arm, pressing the phone to my ear. "A year and a half now. And there are all kinds of developments here. Conversions from office to condo—."

"Conversions. Not brand new buildings like so many places overseas."

"And you're sure that's the only thing that will make you happy?"

We'd talked before about his career plans, but he never seemed so set on only developing new construction.

"I'm not sure. But you are. Your practice is taking off. You love investigating crimes. You told me how hard it would be start all over somewhere new, even in the States."

"Almost impossible," I said.

If I wanted to work for a firm or a company I could get a job in another state and get licensed there. But I wanted to keep working for myself. It was one of the main reasons I went into law. Starting a new practice requires knowing a lot of people and being part of a community that trusts you and respects your work. I wouldn't have that in another state. And I wouldn't have people who knew about my crime-solving and trusted me to help them. In another country I wouldn't be allowed to practice law at all. Unless, maybe, I worked for some sort of multinational corporation.

The exact opposite of what I wanted for my life.

"I know," Ty said. "That's so clear whenever we talk about it. And still I did some research myself. The barriers to practicing law in other parts of the world...none of it seems like it could possibly be worth it."

"But long distance..."

"Forever? Look at how it is even now. I knew when I agreed to move it would be hard to make it work. But I just couldn't let go."

"Except you could. You are. You're doing it right now." I stopped in front of my sliding glass doors. My own ghostly reflection peered at me. I shut my eyes, feeling tears beneath my eyelids. I could let them out, but why? It wouldn't change anything.

"Quille, I'm so sorry. If there were a way I could be in two places at once, I'd do it. Or if you could. But we can't. When I'm done, when the two years are up, if I do end up—"

"Don't." My free hand closed into a fist. "Don't do that. If you don't want to try anymore, stop trying. Don't tell me maybe someday. That's keeping me hanging in there without taking the trouble to visit."

"Quille—"

"I need to go."

CHAPTER 25
WOMEN WHO HELP

My mother, a night owl, answered on the first ring.

"What were you thinking calling Ty?"

"Oh, hello, Quille. I'm fine. How are you?"

"Not fine." I crossed the floor to my kitchen, took out a mug for tea, then put it away and took out a wine glass.

"Ty talked to you."

"Ty broke up with me."

"Oh. Really, it's for the best."

"Is it? You liked him. Why would you do this? Why would you interfere?"

"I do like him. But long distance was never going to work. Not when he couldn't make a commitment."

"And you needed to call and tell him that." I grabbed a bottle of Pinot Noir from my cabinet and fished out a bottle opener.

"No one else was going to tell him. You weren't."

"You have no idea what I was going to do." The bottle opener slipped as I twisted it. Fragments of cork scattered all over my counter. I flung the opener into the sink where it clanged against the stainless steel basin. "It wasn't your business."

"If you and Ty had both been set on making this work, nothing I said could change that."

"That wasn't your call."

"You deserve better than a man who might, maybe, possibly return to you after two years overseas. You think I don't know you, Q.C.—Quille. But I do. You never let things go. You try and try and try. All I did was remind Ty of that and ask him if it was fair when he wasn't doing the same."

After putting the phone on speaker, I grabbed the wine opener and tried to screw it into what was left of the cork. "If I didn't try and try and try you still wouldn't have answers about Q.C. The real Q.C."

I hadn't called my deceased sister that in decades. Not since a therapist in college convinced me to call her the original Q.C. rather than implying she was real and I was fake. But that still made me a copy.

"I'm not saying it's bad that you stick with things."

"Except you decided it is when it comes to Ty."

"I was trying to help. I'm sorry."

My hands, still struggling with the wine opener, froze. My mother never apologized. She said the words "I'm sorry" as sarcasm or to gain sympathy for herself. But she never sounded like she meant it.

Except now. Maybe she had been trying to help.

That still didn't excuse what she did.

"It's just—I don't need you, I don't need anyone, sorting out my relationships for me." I put the bottle opener on the counter and drifted back to my ghostly reflection in the glass door. "Or sending me new potential boyfriends for that matter."

"Dylan told you what I said? He wasn't supposed to."

"He's a tell-it-like-it-is person."

"All right, so what does it matter? He was smitten with you, Quille, and he was already going to UChicago. He would have looked you up whether I said anything or not. Eventually."

"Then why tell him to?"

"You're from his hometown. He needs that."

"I spent six months of my life there. As a baby."

"But you're from here. And he spent all that time here caring for his mom. His dad never so much as thanked him for it and has never been kind to him."

That sounded like a parent I knew. But my head ached too much to argue. My mother's tunnel vision has more to do with her mental health than with me. I wish she would try harder. But after a lot of therapy I know, though I don't always feel in my heart, that she might be trying as hard as she can.

Barely pausing for breath, my mother told me Dylan's brother did little more than fly in at Christmas every year to see their mother during her long illness. "And poor Dylan wasn't excited about anything after his mother's death. Including grad school. Then he met you, helped you with the investigation—."

"Wait, wait, wait. How do you know any of this? You told me you barely saw the Sabatinis after Q.C.'s death."

My parents and Dylan's parents had been close when Q.C. was alive. I had questions about how close. But both my parents insisted there was nothing beyond Reverend Sabatini offering some marriage counseling.

"I didn't," my mother said. "I learned all this the month before Dylan left. He stopped by a few times for tea. Though he's really more of a coffee drinker, which I'll never understand."

"Dylan 'stopped by'?"

I've never known anyone to go to my mother for tea and a listening ear. I've never known her to listen. Yet she learned a lot about Dylan in a few visits. Likely more than she knew about me. I felt sure, for example, that she had no idea what type of law I practiced.

"Oh, yes. He likes espresso, double shots."

"No, I mean—never mind." I shifted to lean against the interior brick wall between the doors and my small dining area.

"You need to stop getting so worked up about things, Quille. It'll all be fine. You just—"

"Mom. Stop. I'll talk to you later."

She kept talking. I clicked the phone off and let my body slide down the wall, the brick scraping my back through my cotton T-shirt, until I sat on the hardwood floor. Knees to my chest, I rubbed my thumb over my right ring finger near the knuckle. For over a year after my boyfriend Marco's death, I wore an amber and diamond ring he bought for me. Just before I met Ty, I switched the ring from my left hand to my right. A while later I stopped wearing it every day. Not on purpose. One day I forgot to put it on. It had been at least six months since I'd worn it.

I shuffled to my closet and opened my jewelry drawer. The amber-colored gem gleamed in the faint light from the kitchen island. At least Marco hadn't meant to leave me.

Lauren appeared at my door fifteen minutes after I texted her. She wore sweats and flip-flops and brought a plate of home-made chocolate chip muffins.

I sat on my couch, holding a throw pillow against my chest. "I had the weirdest conversation with my mother."

"And here I thought I needed to pick you up off the floor over Ty." She swept the cork fragments off the counter and finagled the half-cork out of the bottle I'd tried to open.

"That, too."

As I told her everything about Ty, she plated the muffins and poured the wine.

"And I haven't researched Heather for you yet," I said.

"No rush." She settled on the couch across from me and bit into a muffin.

"You were right, too. What you said when we were in Edwardsville." I took a long drink. The wine was dark red, with faint jammy and peppery notes. "I kept telling myself what a great city Chicago is for architecture. But it's mostly developed. Ty wants more excitement. More challenge."

"The same reasons you investigate crimes."

"I guess." I thought of myself as looking into crimes because it was the right thing to do and it helped people. But there were lots of right things to do. I picked a dangerous one. "And I wouldn't stop doing it to be with Ty. Which maybe says we aren't that in love."

"Or it says you both need someone whose life fits the other's better. But I'm sorry. Really sorry."

"Me, too."

"Your mom—who knew if she started noticing you exist she'd jump into managing your love life." Lauren raised the wine bottle. "Should I top it off?"

"Why not? You're here to talk me down if I head for a ledge."

Because of my mom's history with depression, and my own tendency to feel blue with too much alcohol, I usually avoid more than one drink if I'm feeling low.

"I will be your not very sober companion," Lauren said.

My plan was to sleep late, or at least late for me. With the investigation over and no visit to Ty to fit in, at least I didn't need to work such long hours. But at five the next morning I lay in bed wide awake, head pounding despite that I stopped at two glasses of wine the night before and drank plenty of water. After half an hour of trying to sleep, I crawled out of bed. Exhausted and wired, I downed four Ibuprofen and got in the shower. The viselike grip on my head eased as I stood under the hot spray.

I vowed to take better care of myself. I didn't see any way to fix things with Ty. But I could try to feel less bad, starting with eating more regularly and taking a break now and then.

Café des Livres opens early for the stock traders who live or park in the neighborhood. I caught the lull just after they scurried off to the trading floor a few blocks away. It was a sunny day but, my head still throbbing, I chose an armchair inside by the unlit fireplace. I was halfway through a bowl of yogurt and granola when my friend Carole, the owner, set a fragrant mug of dark hot cocoa on the side table next to me.

"*Mon petite chou*," she said, "*je suis desolé* for saying so but you look *horrible*. What happened?"

I reached for the cocoa, inhaling the rich and slightly bitter scent. "That bad?"

Carole's long, colorful skirt swished around her as she dropped into the chair next to mine. "Your eyes, the circles under them speak volumes. And six is early even for you. *Dis-moi tout.*"

Because it was Carole, a woman always there for me in ways my mother never had been, I poured it all out. The ups and downs and the end with Ty. My disappointment at how hard everything was with my mother despite that I finally resolved Q.C.'s murder. The long hours on my cases and the investigation. My fear that I only made things worse for Julia mixed with frustration that I couldn't finish what I started. And Ty again.

I worked so hard at everything, including my relationships, and in the end it didn't matter.

Carole squeezed my hand. "Ah, *mon petite*, you are not wrong that good relationships take effort. But the converse is not true. Effort does not guarantee a relationship will work."

I nodded and wiped my eyes with a paper napkin with a silver *fleur de lis* emblem on it. "That'd make things too easy, wouldn't it?"

Carole brushed my hair from my eyes. "For some, yes. I want to tell you to take some time off. But I suspect that might make you feel worse, no?"

"I am going to cut back a little." I drank a little more of the cocoa. It was thick and warm and felt comforting. "But my mother was right about one thing. I do try. And try and try. And now—I feel wrong giving up."

"On Ty? Surely you don't plan to fly there anyway."

"No, no. Though I'd love to fly off somewhere just for the change of pace. I mean giving up on Randall. I've got a meeting tonight I set up before Julia pulled the plug, and I need to cancel it. But I don't want to."

It felt like ages ago that I arranged to meet Burt Junior, son of Oscar Miller's old bosses, though we spoke only four days before.

"Must you cancel? Julia still wants you to handle this office rent dispute you mentioned, *n'est-ce pas?*"

"She didn't say to stop." I sat up straighter. "It's a stretch. But the meeting could help with that. If I know more about Randall's landlord I might be able to negotiate a compromise."

"There. So you meet and if you learn something that helps with the murder, too, where's the harm in that?"

"I bet Julia still wants me to sort out Randall's office and files, too."

"Ah, and if so, who knows what you might come across that relates to the murder?"

I drank the last of the cocoa. "Who knows."

CHAPTER 26
WAITING TO POUNCE

ALL THE OFFICES in my suite were dark, which was good. My head still ached a bit. Quiet and dim lighting felt better. I left my blinds closed. Out of habit, I glanced at the clock, calculated the current time in Dubai, and opened my message app. Then I sighed, sat, and checked email. To my relief, there was nothing new. But an old message about Facebook notifications got me thinking about the private Afterlife group.

My whole life I've avoided, as much as I can, sharing my private life publicly, including when I was a child and later a teenage stage actress. There was no real social media back then. But I never talked to people from the local newspapers or tried to get on community cable channels as some of my friends did. After my sister's kidnapping and death, my family feared anyone knowing anything about us. On some level, if only unconsciously, that probably influenced my decision not to pursue acting.

My law firm has online profiles. If someone took time to dig, they could find my office and home addresses online. But it would take some effort.

At least with the investigation closed, I didn't need to share more with Nova Moon or the Afterlife Group Administrator, whose real name never appeared. They were known only as The Admin Alchemist. Yet my fingers hovered over the keyboard. I wanted to know if the last sting Randall carried out involved the Afterlife people and Nova Moon. I wanted to think about something other than Ty.

I told myself I'd only reveal what was already online about me. And it would only take a few minutes to write to Nova. I wouldn't bill Julia for the time. If I got into the private Facebook Group and found something that touched on Randall's death, maybe I could use it to persuade Julia to let me keep investigating. If she still refused, I could go inactive in the group easily enough.

I started typing.

> Hello, I applied before to the group but I haven't heard from you. My FB profile is under Cathy Dearborn. But my real name is Quille C. Davis. I'm a private person and don't like to share online except for professional reasons. Below is a link to my law firm and the Illinois Attorney Registration and Disciplinary Commission site. You can check for yourself to see that I'm a licensed attorney.

> Before I was born my sister, the original Quille C. Davis, was killed. Her death has hung over my entire life and affected my whole family. If joining the group helps me know for sure that she's at peace I can share that with my family. It might change many things for the better.

> I hope you'll let me join.

I reread the message, making sure each sentence was true. I find that works better in any investigation. People, even ones who have bad motives, respond to honesty and real emotion. It makes you look vulnerable. In most people, that triggers a desire to help or at least connect. To a predator, it signals prey. Whichever type of person Nova Moon was, my message ought to work. I hit Send before I could change my mind.

The rest of the morning, I checked my phone regularly, drank a lot of water, and worked on my most urgent tasks. I paused only when my shoulders started to ache. My dad texted to say he was sorry to hear about the break up and to call if I wanted to talk. No texts or calls came in from Ty. He probably thought a lot about breaking up with me before he did it, so he might have nothing else to say. But it felt awful that he didn't at least ask how I was. I sighed and took my half-full mug of tea to the office kitchen to reheat. A text from Ty wouldn't fix anything. My Gram, I was sure, would tell me no contact was better.

In the early afternoon, I picked up a sandwich, downed four more Ibuprofen, and lay for thirty-minutes on an ice pack on my office couch. My head finally stopped hurting. My brain, though, felt overloaded. And no wonder. My timekeeping program showed I'd worked ten to thirteen hours every day, including Saturdays and Sundays, for the last three weeks.

Sticking with my take-care-of-myself plan for now, I logged off my computer. Then, sunglasses on, I walked a mile north on Dearborn Street to the Chicago River. I sat on a bench there and let my mind drift as people jogged past. Tour boats, speed-boats, and a small yacht with an open hot tub motored by on the water. The breeze across my face kept me feeling cool despite the sun beating down on my head. It felt good to zone out. I forgot Ty, the investigation, and all my clients.

The trill of my phone timer startled me far too soon. It was time to meet Burt Junior, son of Oscar Miller's former employers.

Some summers, when the City Council votes for it, Chicago cordons off two entire blocks of Clark Street in the River North neighborhood. During that time, restaurants spill into the road. Tables are everywhere, as are twinkling white and colored lights and giant planters that divide the seating areas.

Vehicles can't drive through. It makes outdoor dining slightly less noisy and the air a little clearer.

Burt Junior already sat outside at Ema, a Mediterranean small plates restaurant at the south edge of the two blocks. He looked like his law firm photo. Slim with symmetrical hazel eyes, wire-rimmed glasses, and very white teeth.

We ordered drinks and a pita platter. After some small talk where we discovered we'd attended a few of the same bar association conferences, though we hadn't met at any of them, I asked if his practice was the same as Oscar's.

He waved his fork. "No, no. The website's behind. I handle workers' compensation, too."

"Oscar didn't?"

"Nope. He claimed focusing only on traffic and misdemeanor DUIs made him way better at them than anyone else."

"You sound skeptical." I wrapped my hand around my glass of ice water to cool off. The air wasn't steamy. But it was warm enough that my neck sweated under the weight of my long hair. I should have taken time to wind it into a bun high on my head while I sat along the Riverwalk.

"It's easy to be an 'expert' in those kinds of cases." Burt smeared some feta spread on a triangular piece of pita. "After a year you can do them in your sleep. Or a couple months if you're me and you work at the firm a long time before becoming a lawyer."

"Could Oscar?" I remembered how stressed Oscar seemed about an upcoming trial the first time I met him. "Do them in his sleep?"

"Not so much. I sound like an arrogant jerk saying that about an attorney practicing almost twice as long as me, but it's true."

There definitely seemed to be a rivalry thing going between Burt and Oscar. I wasn't sure why. Oscar got kicked out the moment Burt graduated. He posed no threat to the younger man, who had the advantage of two parents running the firm. But that might be the issue. Burt needed to believe he earned his place through his own merit.

"Did Oscar think he got let go to make room for you?"

Burt's lips pressed together, hiding those bleached teeth for a second. "That's not what happened. My parents wanted to keep him, too."

"So he chose to leave."

"No. But he didn't try that hard to stay. He refused to learn work comp. And if you insist on sticking with just traffic cases, you need to turn over a lot of them. And focus on more than one case at a time."

"Every lawyer has to do that."

"Not Oscar. If he was prepping for a Secretary of State hearing, he refused to return phone calls. Once my dad told a new client to call him about a speeding ticket. Oscar didn't call back for a week. By then, the client had already hired someone else."

If Oscar couldn't multi-task, that explained the lack of response when I tried to talk with him. I like doing one thing at a time better than jumping around, too. But judges and clients don't line up in a neat, orderly fashion and demand that you do new things only after you finish what's on your plate. It's why I can never take time off without checking email and voicemail every hour and bringing my laptop everywhere.

"Oscar must have done something right. He worked at the firm for ten years," I said.

"My parents kept thinking he'd get up to speed. By the time they realized it was hopeless, I was almost done with college and planning on law school."

"So they kept him on another four or five years despite being that unhappy with him?"

I wondered whether Oscar read the writing on the wall early on. If he figured out Burt Junior would take his place no matter what, he might have adopted a quiet quitting strategy. Done just enough to keep his job but no more. I could never do that for years, or likely at all. But some people did.

Burt turned sideways in his chair, looking away from me. "They hate to fire people."

"They did it once you graduated."

"He deserved it."

"You said things went badly with that. What happened?"

Burt resettled his wire-rimmed glasses on the bridge of his nose. "He saw it coming. Started pilfering office supplies a few months before I took the bar. No one said anything. But then he started calling clients. He told them he was starting his own practice and they should come with him because no one else at the firm knew about DUIs or traffic. My mom overheard him mid-phone call and lost it. She went in his office and hung up the phone. And she told him to get out that second."

"She told you this?"

"I heard it. I worked in a cubicle right outside his door. When Mom started yelling I ran in there. He flung the receiver at her. It was a clunky old desk phone, so it was heavy. It hit her face. I had to take her to the ER."

"How badly was she hurt?"

"Her nose swelled up, but it turned out it wasn't broken. She had a black eye. I shoved Oscar against a wall. I'm not proud of that. But I didn't know what else he might do. He swore at both of us, grabbed his briefcase, and ran out."

"Pretty bad temper," I said. "And abusive." That didn't make him a murderer. But it didn't exactly rule him out.

"To be fair, that's the only blow up I saw in ten years. And I can't see him planning a murder." Burt rocked his chair back and crossed his arms over his chest. "At least not one the police don't figure out in ten minutes. My mom called him dumb as a box of rocks."

I finished my piece of pita with lemon hummus. "He can't be completely clueless. He got his law practice up and running."

Burt shrugged. "It's not that hard to do."

"Says the attorney who's never done it." I kept my tone light. I wasn't there to argue with him.

"I saw my parents do it. You hire a couple people, buy some laptops, rent some office space. Big deal."

I took a long swallow from my ginger ale and refrained from lecturing him about what it's like to start a law practice versus walking into one ready-made for you by your parents. While I had no sympathy for Oscar's actions, I didn't need much imagination to guess that Burt Junior sitting in a cubicle outside his office, waiting to pounce the second he left, got on his last nerve.

"Forget about what he could or couldn't plan," I said. "What's your take on Oscar as a person? Can you imagine him killing someone?"

"After seeing him attack my mom? No question."

Oscar looked more and more like a potential murderer. The question was what to do with that information.

CHAPTER 27
PAUSES AND POWERS

THE NEXT MORNING I called Detective Sergeant Beckwell to tell him what I learned about Oscar. If Julia found out, she might be mad that I was still gathering information about suspects. Also known as investigating. But I couldn't live with myself if I knew something that could help find Randall's killer and I failed to share it.

Beckwell starts work early. He answered on the first ring and asked how I was. I claimed I was doing great, though I felt worn out after another sleepless night. I didn't want to talk with him about my break up. We were more friendly-ish acquaintances than friends.

Before I could share my news, Beckwell confirmed what the prosecutor already told Julia. The alibis of Colleen Cahill and the other Magic Works people held up.

"That's good." I opened my Petrov file on my laptop. "It'd be awful if Julia thought Randall's best friend killed him. Bad enough that Colleen probably cheated him."

"Off the record, 'probably' isn't a strong enough word."

"I take it we're talking about more than an eBay scheme or a golf fundraiser?" I said.

"No question. This Colleen did a lot of flying under the radar."

"It is a scammer's perfect world," I said. "You run everything. The Chairman is your brother, the Treasurer is his old roommate, the administrative assistant is your sister, and no one pays attention."

"That's about right. Remind me again why you and I work so hard for a living."

The dim office was starting to feel depressing. I opened the blinds. Sunlight flooded the room. "Ethics? A strong desire to stay out of prison?"

"Some days it doesn't feel like enough," Beckwell said. "Anything you want to tell me about your investigation?"

"It's on pause. At Julia's direction."

"Really. And you're pausing."

"Sure." I dropped into my chair again. "Though I do know a little more about a potential suspect. Oscar Miller. He lashed out at someone physically when he was fired from his previous job."

"How long ago?"

"Ten years. It's quite a while back, but it was a serious incident." I filled him in on what I learned from Burt Junior.

"I'll let the team know. But Quille? A little advice. If you've got paid work to do, go do it. If you don't, take some time off. Your life is busy enough without working for nothing."

"Good advice."

"Any chance you'll take it?"

"Some."

"Good luck."

After putting in a few hours on my law firm cases, with Beckwell's advice in mind, I headed for Randall's office. It was time to do one of the things Julia was still willing to pay me for.

Oscar's darkened office saved me from trying to pry more information from him. Instead I sorted through Randall's physical files, throwing out duplicate documents and organizing and boxing the rest to ship to Julia. It wasn't easy. Sheafs of paper held together with binder clips filled unlabeled accordion folders. Several contained medical records for Randall's mother, Ava Petrov. Bright pink, yellow, and green sticky notes flagged hundreds of pages. Notes in Randall's handwriting questioned prescriptions and therapy choices. More than once he caught dosage errors.

Behind physical therapy records I found a clipped bundle of papers about Nellie Havel. She was the psychic whose letters appeared in the Alchemy folder on Randall's hard drive. And she might or might not be the same person as Nova Moon, the psychic in the Afterlife Facebook Group.

I didn't know if Randall lacked organizational skills or used a mental filing system that made sense only to him as another way to keep his mind sharp. But either gave me an ideal reason, which some might call an excuse, to read everything.

A 2004 New York Times article covered a United States Postal Service Office of Inspector General report about Nellie Havel.

The Inspector General is an arm of law enforcement that's become far less active in recent years. Most scams now are conducted over email, text, or social media, not through paper mail.

According to the article, Havel, or whoever used her name, mailed tens of thousands of letters over a fifteen year time span. She sent them to people whose names appeared as next of kin in obituaries. Quotes from the letters matched the ones I read on Randall's computer. As I'd guessed, whenever people wrote back, Nellie responded. She asked people to send objects that belonged to their deceased loved ones, especially watches or jewelry. She then wrote back to share "personal" messages she claimed came from the loved one's spirit without returning the items. She used about twenty templates depending on the age of the person who died and where they lived.

The file included a copy of the Inspector General report itself. Randall received the report through a Freedom of Information Act request about five months before his death. It included more sample letters. Some promised greater health and happiness if the recipient sent higher donations. In others, Nova warned that the deceased person foresaw a cloud around their loved one. A cloud that could be removed, of course, by sending far more money.

Nellie Havel's letters came from four different addresses. The Inspector General traced them to small storefronts in the United States that rented mailboxes to businesses. The rent was paid by a foreign company with so many layers of corporate ownership that the Inspector General never found any human owner. The lawyer who paid the rent for the mailboxes said he never met Nellie Havel. He dealt with her by phone and fax. The mailbox centers forwarded mail to an address in Hungary.

Not getting enough cooperation from local authorities, an investigator finally traveled to a small town near Budapest and found the address. But by then the building was vacant.

Three years after the investigation began complaints about Havel stopped. The scheme either ended or morphed into something different enough that the Inspector General never connected it.

I subtracted the time looking at the Havel materials from my timekeeping app. Julia had told me not to investigate, so I wasn't about to bill her for it. Down the line, though, I hoped the facts about Havel might convince her to let me go forward again.

The next few folders included records from the complex where Ava lived at the time of her death. She and Ivan, Randall's father, moved to a townhome there about a dozen years before Randall died. The retirement community section included restaurants, a golf course, and outdoor and indoor pools. When Ava's health declined eight years later, she moved to a one-bedroom apartment in the assisted living part of the complex. Ivan remained in the townhome but could stay with his wife any time.

Then, six months before Randall's death, Ava moved to the complex's skilled nursing facility. Specifically, to the memory care unit. A thick, clipped set of documents about Petrov's Pizza was wedged in the middle of memory care unit bills. At first I thought the Petrov's Pizza papers were unrelated. Then I saw a power of attorney for property. Ava's signature appeared on it, dated only a week before she moved into the memory care unit.

A yellow post it note in Randall's writing said, "How? Why?"

A power of attorney, or POA, for property allows someone else to manage your finances. Here, that someone was Randall's brother, Max Petrov. Randall's note suggested he didn't know about the POA before Ava signed it. And the date suggested Ava likely had no idea what she was signing.

I glanced at the time. Julia was in the middle of her morning motion call right now. I left a message with her clerk asking her to call as soon as she got off the bench.

CHAPTER 28
SACRED SPACES

Two hours later, Julia still hadn't called. But I got a notice that I was admitted into the Afterlife, Alchemy and More private group. I signed on. After the group rules, I found a post from the administrator suspending group video sessions where Afterlife mediums, who were called emotional alchemists, tried to contact the dead.

Dear Friends,

As you know, meeting in person increases the chances your emotional alchemist will reach the spirit you seek. This is especially true in a group, as many spirits appear whether called or not. All the same, for many years Nova allowed group video sessions because it was the only way some of you could take part. Certain events, however, showed the process could be corrupted, so the group video readings were paused.

After much meditation, Nova has received guidance on how best to use video. Going forward, you may join a group video session if you meet with an alchemist in person no more than six months before the group session.

Nova knows travel can be a hardship. She offers several options for in person meetings. You may visit an alchemist in person at the Center in Prague. In addition, alchemists travel frequently throughout the world. (DM the administrator for the schedule.) If one is in a city near you, with at least two days' notice they will be happy to meet you privately. Finally, if you gather a group of at least eight seekers in one area, we will arrange for an alchemist to travel to an airport near you to meet everyone in person.

DM the administrator with questions or call the Center.

The post was dated a month before Randall's death. In his threatening email, AngryHusband referred to a video he warned Randall not to release. That email and this group post fit with the theory that Randall's last sting targeted Nova Moon and the Afterlife Group. And Randall recorded it.

Randall's digital video files, unlike everything else in his office, were organized in labeled folders. But none showed Afterlife, Nova Moon or Alchemy as part of the title. I spot checked each to be sure the content matched the labeling and it did. I ran more searches of his shared drives. But again I found only the videos already on YouTube and shorter clips from them for other social media platforms. He might have stored the sting video on an external drive to be sure no hacker could get at it. But I hadn't found any storage device anywhere.

I was tempted to work through lunch. Instead, sticking with my vow to take better care of myself, I walked to the Farmers Market in the plaza behind the downtown post office. I got fresh tamales at one of the stands for lunch and an Italian ice for dessert. I ate on one of the benches, then spent half an hour reading a book rather than email. I only checked my phone twice to see if Ty might have texted.

Back in my own office, I logged into the Afterlife private group again. Most group members had lost someone close to them. About twenty percent of comments and posts came from the emotional alchemists, who claimed they could contact the dead. The tone of some of Nova's comments reminded me of the letters from Nellie Havel. But I guessed many psychics might write that same way, so the similar wording might mean nothing.

Nova offered words of comfort and, sometimes, free services. Those included single card tarot readings and fifteen-minute emotional alchemy sessions, all done through online posts. Her paid services included one-hour emotional alchemy sessions or tarot readings for groups or individuals. Her goal, she said, was to help people handle their grief or get in touch with loved ones on the other side.

I found a group post from the administrator dated about two months before Randall's death that confirmed Randall ran a sting.

> Due to a breach of the sacred space last night, online video sessions are suspended. Resultantly, some of you who desperately are needing help to reach loved ones may wait for a session.

> There have been questions asking how the man who breached the sacred space "fooled" Nova. He did not. Nova correctly read this man and listened to the spirits around him. He held his "false" identity strongly in his mind and heart. This man did not know it himself, but his "false" identity spoke to deep needs within his spirit that overrode his "real" identity. Nova told this "false" identity what it needed to hear, aided by a soul who was the spiritual father of that identity. The soul was speaking through Nova to comfort this empty, skeptical man.

Sadly, we must inform you that we believe this man, Randall Petrov of Chicago, Illinois, USA, may have recorded video of the session in the sacred space using hidden technology. That was his practice when he was "exposing" people seeking help from other mediums and psychics. He then published the videos on the Internet. Past videos were edited to hide names of seekers and to blur their faces. But we cannot guarantee he will continue that practice if he publishes his video of the alchemy session. Nova informed him that we will take legal action if he shares the video on the Internet or with anyone at all.

If you have questions, please message the administrator. Nova desires that all your concerns be met.

"Do not let yourself be tainted with a barren skepticism." — Louis Pasteur

If they checked the Facebook Group regularly, everyone who attended the session Randall joined knew his name, that he lived in Chicago, and that he made a practice of recording stings of psychics and mediums. Any one of them might have contacted Randall and arranged to meet him the night of his death.

I sketched out a timeline.

- <u>1990s</u>: Nellie Havel (may be Nova Moon) sends letters claiming spirit of deceased speaks to her, requests items and donations
- <u>5 Years Before Randall's Death</u>: Nova Moon helps police search for missing boy in Krakow
- <u>5 Months Before</u>: Randall gets copy of Inspector General report about psychic Nellie Havel (may be Nova Moon)

- <u>2 Months Before</u>: Randall records group video session where he exposes Nova Moon's methods
- <u>2 Months Before (day after sting)</u>: Video alchemy/psychic sessions canceled, Randall identified as person who infiltrated group session and recorded it
- <u>1 Month Before</u>: Video alchemy/psychic sessions resumed if people meet in person first
- <u>2 Weeks Before Randall's Death</u>: AngryHusband sends email saying "You do not deserve to live. If you publish the video, if you expose everyone...you will regret it."

Julia finally called an hour after I finished the timeline. I told her about the power of attorney Ava signed just a week before entering the memory care unit.

I heard a sharp intake of breath. "I can't believe Randall never told me about that."

"You said he rarely talked to you about the family business—"

"Because he stayed out of it. But this POA—is it an original?"

"Photocopy." I had run my fingers over the handwritten signature and date and the paper was smooth, with none of the indentation that occurs from the pressure of a pen on a page.

"If he found it while going through his mom's things and raised it with Max, they might have gotten into a fight."

"Exactly," I said. "I know you want me to leave the murder alone. And I'm sure you don't want to believe Max could have killed his brother. But we know they fought physically when they were young. And we've only Max's ex-wife's word to corroborate Max being with her that night."

"It could have been accidental," Julia said. "They take a walk to hash things out. Talking turns into an argument turns into a physical fight. They're too close to the railing and Randall goes over."

"It could be," I said.

The slashes on Randall's palms, though, meant whoever killed him pulled a knife. To me, that made an intent to kill more likely. But in a rage people do things they otherwise might not. One of many reasons my retired police instructor advised that, nearly all the time, owning or carrying a gun poses more danger to the owner and those close to them than to strangers.

"But then why not call 911?" Julia said. "Try to save Randall?"

"I read the autopsy report," I said. "I won't go into detail. But there was no saving Randall once he hit the pavement. Calling 911 wouldn't help him. But it probably would tank Max's life."

"And devastate his father."

I drummed my fingers on my desk. "I'm not saying that's what happened. But I'll keep investigating if you'll let me. It seems clear no one at Magic Works was involved in Randall's death. And if they were, that's up to the police to uncover. But there are other possibilities. Not only Max. I really want to keep trying."

Julia sighed. "I've barely slept since I told you to stop. Not that I've been sleeping well anyhow. I know finding the murderer won't bring Randall back—"

"It could stop someone else from getting killed. Whoever did it used violence, whether they intended murder or not. They might take that route again."

She sighed again, a long exhale as if letting all the air out of her lungs. "There's a reason I hired you in the first place. I knew you wouldn't let it go."

"You were right."

"All right. What else have you learned?"

No one in my family has ever been in a nursing home. At least as far as I know. My Gram, not yet eighty, is in great health. Her husband died when I was a toddler. I don't know much about my other grandparents because they and my mother cut ties not long after the first Q.C.'s death.

I volunteered in a nursing home, though, during my theater days. I was in a play set in one and wanted to get a better sense of what it was like. I remember wide hallways with scuffed tiles, the faint odor of antiseptic and ammonia, and a mix of voices. Visitors murmuring, some clients moaning or yelling, wheelchairs squeaking along corridors.

The skilled nursing facility where Ava Petrov finished her days was far nicer than the one I volunteered at. The lobby looked like that of a fancy hotel, with chandeliers, leather couches and chairs, and large windows facing a wooded lot. A giant glass enclosure ran along a wall between the lobby and the residences. Inside, green, blue, and yellow parakeets fluttered. They squeezed themselves through hanging hoops, swung on bright pink swings, and flew back and forth in the large glass cage.

"They make the clients smile," the woman who walked me toward a seating area said. Her name was Caroline Cruz, and she knew Julia and Randall from their many visits to his mom. At Julia's request, she'd agreed to talk with me. She was the same woman who checked the video surveillance and verified that Ivan, Randall's father, was at the facility during the hours when the police believed Randall was killed.

"Julia told me Randall did magic shows for the clients."

Caroline's face lit up. "He did. He even revealed some of his secrets. A few clients drove me crazy for a bit by practicing their card tricks on me."

Her warm smile told me she didn't mind at all.

"It sounds fun."

"It was. We always asked him to come in around the holidays. It can be a sad time for people. Even if their families come, the clients still know, at least the ones who are aware, that they're missing out on the big celebrations."

"Do some families not visit?"

"We have a few clients with no family or friends left. Others have family members who hardly ever show. I'm sure there are reasons. But it's awful. That's why Randall was such a gift. He talked with everyone. And visited the rooms of people who couldn't come to our social center for the show."

"He sounds like a wonderful person. I wish I'd known him."

She gestured for me to sit on a loveseat with fluffy green throw pillows. "I never met anyone who cared so much about other people."

Her words echoed what hospital personnel and Magic Works volunteers told me. It was a big contrast to Max's and Ivan's insistence that Randall rubbed people the wrong way. But we all show up differently in different parts of our lives.

CHAPTER 29
DECODING

"You know I'm looking into Randall's murder." I sat and took out my notepad. "Anything you can tell me about Randall or the Petrovs could really help."

"I can't tell you about Mrs. Petrov's medical condition or her care." Caroline perched on the other side of the new-looking blond wood coffee table. "Because of HIPAA."

"I'm more interested in people who visited."

"Well, Randall and Julia did."

She confirmed that Ivan Petrov was visiting his wife the night Randall was killed. He came in around four in the afternoon and didn't leave until eleven. The video feeds showed the front desk, the back and side exits, and the common areas. There were no cameras in the clients' rooms.

"Any chance Ivan left Ava's room without being seen, then returned?"

The police ruled out Ivan because the nursing home was a thirty to forty-five minute drive from the 606 where Randall's body was found. But I wanted to be sure.

"Only if he climbed out a fifth-story window, jumped, survived, and scaled the wall to climb back in."

"So if he's Spiderman."

"Right."

I nodded. "I'd love to take a tour, if I could. My Gram is reaching that age."

Gram would kill me for saying that. She's as sharp as ever, does more volunteer work than most people do at paid jobs, and can easily walk a few miles a day. But if Caroline ever did a background check on me, my Gram's official age qualified her.

Caroline smiled. "Julia mentioned you might want to. No talking to clients, though."

"Agreed."

Caroline seemed knowledgeable and vigilant. But I wanted to see for myself whether someone could get in and out without being caught on camera. As we walked, I noted where each camera was. And I asked how the program worked. Caroline told me people bought in by purchasing a townhome and paying a monthly fee. That guaranteed them a spot in assisted living and later the skilled nursing facility, which included the memory care unit, if they needed it. Once in skilled nursing, if they ran out of money for fees they were guaranteed one of the facility's Medicaid-designated beds.

We turned a corner. I noted a camera at the end of the hall above the doorway. So far nothing made me think Ivan could have left and returned without being filmed.

"How do people decide when to shift to skilled nursing?"

"It's whenever it's medically necessary. Most people wait as long as possible," Caroline said. "We do our best to keep it upbeat and homelike here, but no one wants to be in even the nicest nursing home. People like their independence."

"Is it unusual for one spouse to move from one complex to the other without their partner?" I said.

"Not at all. People don't age the same way or have the same needs. A husband—usually it's the husband—might move more quickly into the assisted living or skilled nursing. As long as one spouse is well enough to stay in the townhome, they stay. We only release it for others when both have had to move out."

"I'm assuming none of it is cheap."

"No. I'm afraid it's out of reach for all but the very well off."

Caroline used a key fob to access the memory care unit. The flooring shifted from mauve carpet to white tile. The artwork on the walls was abstract but calming, all blurs of pastel colors with some glitter here and there.

As we headed down a brightly lit hall that smelled of cleaning solution I told her I'd heard that Randall and his brother Max argued a lot.

"Doesn't surprise me." Caroline pushed through a set of double doors. "They rarely visited at the same time. It was like they were on shifts."

I followed her into a large dining hall with a few long tables and many smaller square tables near wide windows. "Randall was upset about a paper Max had his mother sign. Do you know anything about that?"

Caroline paused a few feet from a long buffet table filled with three-tiered platters, bowls, and plates but no food. She opened her mouth, then pressed her lips together.

"You don't need to tell me anything Mrs. Petrov said or did," I said.

She glanced around the room. It was deserted. "I wasn't there. A temp who floated between departments told me. She went into Mrs. Petrov's apartment when Mrs. Petrov hit the call button. Max was there at the kitchen table. He had his hand curled around Mrs. Petrov's hand. She was holding a pen."

"Was that why Mrs. Petrov hit the button?"

"Mrs. Petrov didn't remember hitting it. Max said she bumped it by accident when they both sat down."

"And that made the temp suspicious?"

"Not really. But a week later she was working in the memory care unit and saw Mrs. Petrov had been transferred there. That's when she got concerned, and she told Randall. He was visiting that day."

"She told Randall without talking to you first?"

"She said it just came out when she saw Mrs. Petrov. Randall got really angry, so the temp filled me in. She worried he was going to complain about her not reporting the incident earlier. But he never did."

"I'd love to talk with the temp."

"She's long gone. She covered vacations for two different people in a row. But the next time we needed a temp, someone else came."

"Do you know her name? Or the agency's name? It would really help me help Julia."

I promised to never let on how I got the information. Caroline said she'd see what she could find out. By the time I parked

Lauren's car, which I'd borrowed for the drive to the facility, there was a message on my office voicemail.

When I heard the agency's name, I smiled. At last, a bit of luck. A manager there wrote and directed one-woman plays. The agency work was her day job. I'd met her back in my theater days. If the temp was still around, the manager might be willing to pass on a message to her.

In keeping with my vow to take better care of myself, that night I picked up dinner at Totto's, the neighborhood corner market. I took my rotisserie chicken salad sandwich, honey crisp apple, and cut carrots and celery sticks onto my deck and enjoyed a warm breeze as I ate. Only after I finished did I open my iPad to dig deeper into the Afterlife private group.

Members got discounts on readings, retreats, and workshops at Afterlife's Center in Prague. Alchemists provided services elsewhere, too, at yoga studios, psychic fairs, and spiritual centers all around the world. The roving psychic spaces reminded me a bit of pop up stores. Prices ranged from a hundred to tens of thousands of dollars. Video sessions were cheaper but not very common now that participants—known as seekers—needed to meet in person in advance with an alchemist.

Some Afterlife alchemists appeared in videos on YouTube or other sites demonstrating their skills. But I found no videos or photos about Nova Moon.

I wondered again if she was a real person or an avatar. Yet people in the online group raved about her. They must have met someone who called herself Nova Moon. I created my own post. In it, I claimed I was thinking of asking Nova for a reading about the loss of my sister. I asked anyone with advice to reply or send me a private message. Around nine I forced myself to log off and read for a while.

Later, as I lay in bed, I tried to keep my mind off Ty by listing fun things I could do in the city without him. I kept remembering places we'd gone to together instead. Finally, I turned on an audiobook edition of *The Lion, The Witch, And The Wardrobe,* one of my favorite childhood books. I set the timer for thirty minutes. I drifted off around when Edmund tried Turkish Delight in the land of Narnia.

The next two days were frustrating. And sad. Group members answered my post with encouraging words about getting a reading. But no one wrote anything about Nova or the Afterlife Center that helped my investigation. I heard nothing from Ty. I didn't doubt that he'd answer if I texted or called. But as much as I longed to hear his voice, each time I started to text I reminded myself nothing good would come of it.

I thought about calling my dad. He worked mid-afternoons at a music store he co-owned. If I caught him there we could talk at length without my mother interrupting in the background. But I rarely spoke about my love life with my dad. And it might too easily lead to topics I didn't want to discuss ever.

That's when my tendency to overwork came in handy. I dove into my cases, doing more than I really needed to. When I finished my workday around seven, it was the middle of the night in Dubai. I had to wait until the next morning. But my mornings were too busy to think very much about Ty. Just as I liked it.

My contact at the temp agency, at least, was happy to hear from me after all these years. But she didn't know who the temp for the nursing home was. A lot of records were corrupted after a hacking incident. My contact promised to ask around to see if anyone remembered. But she didn't sound optimistic.

I emailed Max and asked to meet or talk on the phone with him again soon. I wanted to talk about the power of attorney, but I didn't say so. Better to catch him by surprise when I asked about it in person.

In between reviewing more paper files at Randall's office, I researched cryptography online. I hoped to make sense of the initials in Randall's calendar. None of the simple code breaking tips I learned fit the entries. I began to think Julia must be right. They referred to times and initials. I confided in Flora, the secretary with the end-of-hallway alcove, about my investigation. But she had no idea what Randall's system meant. She did tell me that Oscar, stingy as he was, took each tenant out to lunch during the holiday season.

I didn't find Oscar's initials in any November and December entries in Randall's calendar. And no dates other than the day of Randall's death included the initials PRG.

Finished with Randall's desk and file drawers, I turned to his bookshelves. The books looked pristine, so I started with the boxed decks of cards on the top shelves. Randall owned dozens of beautifully illustrated decks, including tarot cards, soul cards, dream cards, and angel cards. Most decks showed some wear. A bent card corner or two, faded colors, a drop of ink or a coffee stain. The most worn cards were lined up on the top shelf, the newer cards on the shelf below.

The box at the far end of the newer cards had a European cityscape design under a starry sky. An online search showed it was sold at select stores, including several in the Chicago area. One of those was The Mystical Mile in Andersonville, which must be the magic store Dylan told me about what felt like forever ago.

The store's name seemed like a play on the Magnificent Mile, a stretch of Michigan Avenue once known for luxury stores and brands. But it was on Clark Street, far north and a bit west of that part of the city. I spent a lot of time in the area one summer when Joe, Danielle, and I used to sing together at a club nearby, opening for more well-known acts.

The club hosted an open mike, too. A quick search showed it was every Wednesday night, traditionally a slow evening for bars.

I rolled my office chair forward and back as I looked at the website photos of the club. The one fun thing I thought of when trying to fall asleep the other night was singing. And the last time I sang was with Dylan at an open mike in Edwardsville. That was fun. More than fun. It took me out of myself when everything about the investigation into my sister's murder and my family felt overwhelming. Dylan's laid back style and his skill—he made part of his living as a studio musician—set me at ease in a way I rarely felt on stage or off. Our voices blended beautifully.

I couldn't think of a single reason not to call him.

CHAPTER 30
MYSTICAL MOMENTS

THE MYSTICAL MILE smelled like old paper and sea salt. Books overflowed the shelves and teetered in stacks on tables. Electric candles flickered on glass display counters that held jewelry, crystals, and stones. Flute music played in the background.

A young bearded man, whose name tag said Oberan, stood behind a checkout counter. He wore an emerald green T-shirt with a V neck that plunged to his belly button. Tattoos of astrology symbols decorated his arms. An orange and green felt hat with tassels sat on his head. I felt out of place and ultra-conservative in my dark jeans, fitted T-shirt, and chunky garnet necklace.

Because of my theater background I think about what clothes, makeup, and hair convey. Oberan's jester-like hat made me wonder if he was making fun of the customers. But I didn't know this world. He might be quite serious. I wondered if Randall Petrov, known for debunking psychics and mediums, ever visited the shop and how its patrons felt if he did.

Two customers browsed near the back of the store in a section that featured vials of colorful liquids and jars of powders and dried herbs.

I introduced myself to Oberan and asked if we could talk for a few minutes. "I'm not with the police, but I'm investigating a murder."

His dark blue eyes widened. "I'm sure we don't know anything about it."

"It didn't happen anywhere near here. But you might be able to help with some background information."

"I suppose we could try. Depending what you need to know." He called over his shoulder. "Bram? Lady here needs to talk to us."

A second man, whom I guessed was Bram, emerged from a black-curtained doorway a few feet away. He wore skinny jeans and a long tunic that swirled around him. A mandala in dark red ink decorated the back of his left hand.

After I reassured both that I didn't suspect them or their customers or think any of their spells were involved, I asked if they'd heard of Randall Petrov. They hadn't.

"He was a magician who debunked psychics and mediums. I'm not sure how you feel about that."

Oberan scratched the side of his face just above his beard. "False prophets. Never good. If they can be debunked, they should be."

"How do you know false prophets aren't buying your products?" I waved toward a shelf with crystal balls and spell books.

"We don't. Lots of people enjoy owning magical things," Oberan said. "Some people are gifted in using them for good. Others lack any real gifts but pretend to have them."

Bram crossed his arms over his chest. "We don't like it, but we can't test everyone who buys at our store for real ability."

"If someone were pretending and Randall exposed them, how much damage would that do to the person?"

"Exposed them how?" Oberan said. "If he just explained cold reading techniques, or how to make a table move, no big deal. Tons of videos all over social media show how to fake a psychic reading."

A chime sounded behind me. Dylan entered the store carrying his guitar case. I introduced him to the owners before returning to the topic. He drifted over to study the shelves of tarot card decks near the front window.

"I'm thinking of something more specific to an individual," I said. "Let's say a video shows exactly how the psychic got information they claim came from the spirit world."

"Oh, oh, oh." Bram tapped a finger on the glass case near me. "Randall Petrov. Now I know who you mean. He did a video sting maybe seven, eight years ago, exposed a psychic in New York. The guy went out of business for a year or so. I read about it."

"Just a year?"

Oberan tugged a tassel on his hat. "He laid low for a while. But he built a practice again. Found new clients. Might have gotten some old clients to return. People forget. And people want to believe."

"Do you think it's reaching to imagine Randall might have been killed by someone afraid he'd expose them publicly as a fraud?"

Dylan turned away from the shelves and stepped over to the counter. "That's high stakes if they're making a very good living as a psychic."

Oberan frowned and shot Dylan a look. "And it's high stakes being wrongly accused. You might see this as make believe. But it's a calling for those of us who practice."

"Agree." Bram glanced at the two shoppers as they drifted toward the spell books. "Magic—spells—can be dangerous. If Randall challenged someone with real power, he took a big risk."

Dylan pointed to scrolls of paper with handwritten notes next to them explaining each type of spell. "You're saying these spells can really harm people?"

"We encourage good motives and good practice always," Bram said. "But yes, these can harm. They're not to be played with."

I don't believe saying certain words in a certain order changes the world for good or ill. If that worked, my mother's prayers would heal the mental illnesses she's struggled with all her life. And, for that matter, my sister would never have been murdered. But lots of people believe words have mystical power.

I opened a photo of Randall on my phone. "Ever meet him?"

Oberan barely glanced before shaking his head. Bram peered at the phone, then said he hadn't.

"Have either of you heard of a medium named Nova Moon?"

Dylan's eyebrows raised, but he stayed silent.

"Sounds familiar." Bram stepped out from behind the counter. "Does she write books?"

"Not that I know of," I said. "She runs a center. Afterlife and Alchemy."

"Alchemy, alchemy." Bram ran his fingers over new-looking books on the nearest bookcase. "There was a book signing."

Oberan tapped the store's iPad near the checkout area. "By Nova Moon?"

"No," Bram said. "But an author mentioned her. Denis someone. The book had stars in the title. He talked about emotional alchemy."

"When was this?" I said.

"Oh, right." Oberan clicked a few keys. "*Touching the Stars: Mysticism and Magic.* Last weekend in July. Friday night."

That was two nights before Randall's murder.

"Any chance Randall attended?" I said.

Bram and Oberan answered together. "No."

"How can you be sure?" Dylan asked.

"It was a terrible night." Oberan shuddered. "Pouring rain, flash floods, lightning everywhere. Three or four people at most came. All women."

Neither owner remembered what the author said about Nova Moon or the Afterlife Center. But he used the term emotional alchemy for helping people process their grief and contact the spirit world.

The author's name was Denis Jednyak. Oberan disappeared through the black curtains to find me a copy. Bram excused himself to help the other two shoppers.

In a low voice I told Dylan about Randall disrupting Nova Moon's group video reading.

"Then two days before he's killed an emotional alchemist's in town," Dylan said. "Big coincidence."

Oberan returned with the book. Its black, gray, and tan color scheme and architectural design themes looked familiar. The author's photo showed a man in his late twenties or early thirties with pale blond hair, very light skin, and a strained smile. His bio stated he worked at the Afterlife and Alchemy Center.

"So he traveled here from Prague for the signing," I said.

"Long trip to sign some books," Dylan said. "And I thought the music business was brutal."

Oberan's chin drew in toward his neck. "Our store's known throughout the world."

Dylan shot me an apologetic glance.

"He obviously thought it was worth the trip." I took out my credit card. The book, a hardback, cost more than I wanted to spend. But I felt it was the least I could do after the time the owners spent with me. And I might learn more about the Center.

"Jednyak visited other stores, too. Here and in Milwaukee."

Oberan didn't know all the author's tour stops but said they might still be listed somewhere online.

"Oh, and he had his own specially designed deck." Oberan pulled a black, gray, and tan box from the shelf of tarot cards. The front showed stars across a night sky over old-world European buildings. "Would you like these, too?"

I declined. I already knew where I could find them. This was the newest of the tarot decks in Randall's office.

Dylan twisted the tuning peg for the low E string on his guitar, his lips pressed together as he listened to the note rising. It's always harder to hear outside. We sat on a wrought iron bench a few feet apart in a cobblestone square at the center of Andersonville.

He finally got the string where he wanted it and let his hand rest on the guitar neck. "So I mostly sucked at being your wing man. Got any suspects to tackle? Because that I can do."

Dylan, a former high school wrestling coach, aided me in dealing with a dangerous suspect a few months before.

"I'll let you know," I said. "By the way—your poker face? You don't have one."

"Sorry. Selling people spells to bring love into your life or speak to the dead reminds me too much of my dad talking money out of people who could barely cover their rent. But they wanted to get into heaven. Or were afraid of hell. And they opened their wallets."

"I got the impression your father's congregation was pretty well off."

Dylan shook his head. "Some people are. Not all. And a lot of times people with the least money give the most. My dad says they need the hope more."

I opened the Notes app on my phone to the set list Dylan and I worked out over email. "That's why I wish I could find this video Randall might have made when he exposed Nova.

Someone who attended that session might be angry enough to kill if he stole their last hope."

"You think this author from Prague could be the killer?" Dylan's fingers traveled over the guitar, expertly but quietly playing the break for *Give Me One Reason* by Tracy Chapman.

"I think he at least knows something. But his initials are DJJ, not—" I stopped to think.

Dylan stopped playing. "What?"

"What if the initials aren't for names but airports? Prague's airport code—" I broke off and searched on my phone. "PRG. Those are the letters in the bottom corner of Randall's calendar on the day of his death."

"Does that fit other notes in the calendar?"

"I have to check."

"Now? We can skip the open stage if you want."

I shook my head. Part of me longed to return to work right now. But the night before when Dylan and I sang together over Zoom to practice had felt wonderful, despite the occasional timing glitch the WiFi caused. I didn't want to skip tonight.

I sipped water from my thermos. "Let's run through the set."

The first song was *How Can I Keep From Singing?* We sang the old hymn a cappella, though Dylan played a note to start us off. Joe, Danielle, and I rarely include that one in our sets. Joe's not a big fan of songs with religious themes, though we don't modify it to make it more preachy the way religious choirs do. I see the original lyrics as being about the power of love and truth.

We kept our eyes on one another's faces, watching for slight movements that signaled the end of a note or a faster or slower tempo. By the second chorus our voices melded. As I had on stage in Edwardsville, I felt a sort of hush inside. We held the last note an extra two beats, then hit the "g" on the word "singing" at the same instant.

People around us applauded, pulling me out of the moment. I hadn't noticed them gathering.

My phone rang, plunging me into real life. It was Max Petrov, once more calling me out of the blue. And once more, he was angry.

CHAPTER 31
FINDING RANDALL

MAX'S SPUTTERING and swearing replayed in my head as Dylan and I sang on the small raised platform that served as a stage in the back of the club. From what I could gather on the phone, Julia told Max we had questions about his mom signing documents right before moving to the memory care unit. Max's and my schedules clashed for the rest of the week. He finally agreed to meet me in the morning. Unfortunately, he felt the need to yell at me a lot first about why I had no business asking about his mother.

At the end of the night, Dylan shared his Uber ride, an SUV that smelled of lemon air freshener, with me. Hyde Park, where he lived, is a neighborhood nearly ten miles south of mine. He propped his guitar case in between the two back bucket seats, one arm resting on it so it didn't tip or bang into anything.

"Thanks for the saves," I said, "when I lost track of the harmony."

Dylan had switched without hesitation to harmony when I accidentally sang melody during two of our four songs.

He gave me a half-smile that, another time, might make my heart flip. "That's the fun of open stages—less practice, more chances to improvise. And the audience never noticed. Especially the guys at the bar."

"I didn't remember the place having that many TVs. All on the same sport, though I couldn't tell which."

"I'll go out on a limb and say it involved a ball and drunk people cheering. The people who listened loved us, though. You know you sounded fantastic, right? I was shocked when you told me you've barely been singing lately."

Headlights whizzed past us on DuSable Lake Shore Drive, bright spots against the black expanse of Lake Michigan. To the west, lit up buildings soared toward the sky. "What? Oh, right, I had a great time."

"Everything okay?"

"Just a little distracted."

"Based on your song choices, can I risk another wild guess? You're not seeing your long-distance beau anymore?"

"More like he's not seeing me," I said, but I couldn't help smiling a little at the old-fashioned word choice.

"He's a very foolish man."

"I don't know about that. He's an ambitious one."

"I'll concede he might be both." Dylan reached around the guitar case and squeezed my hand for an instant. "I know you wanted it to work out."

"I did."

We rode the rest of the way in silence, but it felt comfortable. I kept watching the lake and was rewarded by the colorfully-lit

Ferris wheel at Navy Pier against the night sky. When the SUV pulled to the curb, Dylan touched my shoulder. "Text if you need anything. Crime-related or otherwise."

"Thanks."

I went inside, feeling better than I had since the call with Ty. I didn't need to ping pong from one relationship to another. Dylan seemed to get that. But the evening had been fun, and I enjoyed his company. Sorting out what that meant, if anything, would need to wait, though. It was past midnight, and I had a meeting with Max Petrov at six-thirty the next morning.

Most people talk more freely with one person rather than two peppering them with questions. But Julia joined us for the morning meeting. She wanted to assess for herself whether Max was telling the truth. As a judge, she'd developed a good feel for witnesses in court, so I decided it couldn't hurt to get her take on it. And given Max's short fuse and his clashes with her, his anger might prompt him to spill things he normally wouldn't.

At least Max agreed to meet at Café des Livres. He had a meeting with a potential investor whose office was near the Chicago Board of Trade, three blocks from the café.

My friend Carole, the owner, squeezed my shoulder as she passed by and set down my mug of Earl Grey tea. Julia had black coffee and Max got an espresso.

Max glared across the table at Julia and me. "So tell me. What's your problem now, ladies?"

The tea tasted stronger than usual. I added half a teaspoon of sugar. "Randall's notes show he had questions about documents you had your mother sign."

"I answered Randall's questions. As I'm sure you know."

"We don't," Julia said. "That's why we're here."

"Oh, come on. We fought about it in the assisted living community room the day my mother moved. Don't act like no one told you."

"No one told me." I glanced at Julia, who shook her head. "Fought physically?"

"What, like college kids? No. We argued."

I tilted my head. "So you shouted like adults?"

Max almost cracked a smile. "Yes. Like adults."

Julia slid her untouched coffee to one side. "What did Randall say?"

"He didn't say anything. Like Quille said. He shouted. Accused me of trying to trick my mom. Said it in front of all the other old people. And my father. He was there that day, too. It was a regular family reunion."

"Were you trying to trick her?" Julia said.

Max huffed out a breath and folded his arms over his chest. "Of course not."

"I was told you put your hand over hers, moving her hand as she signed," I said.

"What?" Julia's eyes shot daggers at Max.

"She had bad arthritis. She asked me to guide her hand."

"Guide her hand? That's forcing her to sign," Julia said.

"She wanted to sign. It made it easier on everyone."

"It's fraud. It's criminal." Julia banged her fist on the table.

Max opened his mouth, but I raised one hand in a stop gesture and rested my other hand on Julia's shoulder. "Let's take a breath." I focused on Max first. "If she was a week from moving to the memory care unit, how could you be sure what she wanted?"

"Look," he said, "dementia's not all or nothing. There are good days and bad. Toward the end, good moments and bad. She was lucid sometimes. But every time we needed her to sign something—say a major decision about the new location—we had to wait to catch her at a good time. The attorney finally suggested she sign a power of attorney to make it easier."

"Easier as in you could do what you wanted? With her vote plus yours, you controlled the company," Julia said. "And it's still fraud. She couldn't have had capacity to sign."

"I did not—" A young woman two tables beyond ours glanced at Max as his voice rose. He took a breath, rested his arms on the table, and spoke again, this time quietly. "I didn't do it to steal her vote. My father and I figured out what Mom wanted based on her earlier views. And we asked her when she had good moments. I didn't do anything underhanded."

"You might not have thought so," Julia said, "but that attorney should have known better. I deal with cases like that in my courtroom all the time."

"Thus, the great Julia speaks."

I doubted any judge would find Ava Petrov had the legal capacity to sign a power of attorney. But not everyone who does things the way Max did has bad motives. Sometimes they're trying to do what a loved one who can no longer function wants without having that person declared incompetent, which is an upsetting thing to do. Others were trying to cut other relatives or heirs out of businesses or wills, though.

"If it was just for convenience, why was Randall shouting at you?" I said.

"Who knows? Ego? Control issues? He had no voting rights, so he didn't lose anything."

"What if he agreed with your mother more often than your father?" I asked.

"You're not getting it. Randall didn't care about the business. He never took a position. When he cooled down, he apologized. He said he found the power of attorney when he looked through things Mom asked him to store before her move and he lost it."

I glanced at Julia.

She sighed. "He was very upset about his mom's downhill slide. But Max is right, he wasn't that concerned about the family business."

"And he never told you Max had his mother sign something?"

"He never mentioned it. He tried to keep me out of the family business. Said there was no reason I needed to hear it."

I glanced at Max. "Your father will confirm what you told us?"

"Not the apology part. He stalked out before that."

"And you let him think you and Randall were on the outs?" I said. While my relationship with my mother isn't great and my sister Kendra and I aren't terribly close, I couldn't imagine letting one believe something negative about the other when I could make things clear.

Max shrugged. "If it didn't affect the business, my father didn't care. He'll confirm that. And why does it matter? You know where I was the night Randall was killed."

"Only according to your ex-wife," I said. "She might not want to see the father of her children in jail."

"You think that, you don't know my ex-wife. I hope you're looking at someone besides me."

"I am."

Max asked who. I glanced at Julia before telling him the Magic Works people were ruled out for the murder but I was researching a psychic named Nova Moon. I skipped over the fraud issues with Colleen. I doubted Julia wanted to hear Max expound on how he'd known the Magic Works director was shady.

Max grimaced. "Nova Moon? What is she, a fortune teller?"

"After a fashion. Did Randall ever mention her? Or Nellie Havel or Denis Jednyak?"

He shook his head. "None of those names ring a bell."

"How about Afterlife, Alchemy and More?"

"Afterlife I remember. I thought he was talking about what to do with Mom after she died and lost it. Told him she'd walk on his grave." His face turned pale. "I forgot about that. And now she's dead and so is he."

I reached across the table and squeezed his hand. "I'm sorry. Do you remember what he told you about Afterlife?"

"Just it was some sort of mystical thing he was looking into. Oh, and how he felt like a pilgrim exploring new worlds with this group."

"A pilgrim? Why?" Something about the word felt important, but I couldn't put my finger on why.

"I didn't ask. He seemed to think it was funny. I never got why he spent so much time on that instead of doing some real work."

At first, I didn't think the talk with Max was much help. But when I logged into my computer in my office it came to me. I double-checked that Randall's middle name was William. Then I opened the Facebook Group and searched for Billy Pilgrim. The screen name stuck out back when I was reviewing group posts because of the literary reference. I never read the novel *Slaughterhouse-Five,* but I recognized the protagonist's name from hearing people talk about it in college.

I glanced over Billy Pilgrim's posts. I'd found Randall.

CHAPTER 32
BROWNIE ON TRIAL

Knowing Randall's screen name didn't give me access to private messages he sent within the group because I didn't know his Facebook password. But I searched for all his posts and comments.

The Billy Pilgrim profile appeared nearly two years before Randall's death. It included many details. Both Billy's father and his dog died shortly before he joined Facebook. His About section stated he was lonely as a result. That's why he was venturing onto social media for the first time. Billy was a Vietnam War veteran, lived in Buffalo, New York, and liked to watch and play football. He posted often on his own page and accumulated over a hundred "friends," which was fascinating since he didn't exist. The profile photo showed a middle-aged man with a crew cut who looked a bit like Randall. He stood next to an older man. The man wasn't Ivan Petrov, but he looked enough like Randall to pass for his father. The dog was a Great Pyrenees Billy adopted as a puppy.

In Billy's early comments in the Afterlife group, which started about three months before his death, he wrote about the loss of this beloved dog. It was so moving I made a note to ask Julia if the dog was real. He claimed he worked for a decade as a Las Vegas dealer, something Randall must know about from his years there. He said the dog helped him through his grief when his father died of lung cancer. That history appeared on his Facebook page, too, spread out over two years.

Group members commented to sympathize with his losses. On the fourth post, Nova Moon chimed in. Another member then suggested Billy book a session with Nova, sparking more comments.

She'll help you get in touch with your dog and with your father. You'll find out if they're at peace. And that will ease your sorrow.

I did it and it turned my life around. Cured my depression.

You'll never find anyone as intuitive and kind as Nova.

As I read, I copied posts and comments into a spreadsheet with dates. After a few weeks, Billy posted that he might want to meet with Nova but wondered how it all worked. Nova answered twenty minutes later.

> Send me something your animal companion loved if you can, like his favorite toy. If you don't have anything, print a photo of your dear friend and mail it. I'll direct message you the Center's address. For your father, send something meaningful to him. A watch. A cufflink. If you have no items, send a photo. We will then talk through DMs about whether a group or individual session is best.

A month later Nova posted about Randall infiltrating the session. No doubt she knew Billy and Randall were the same. And anyone who attended the group session could put it together. But Nova didn't share that within the larger community. Billy Pilgrim simply never posted or commented again, no doubt banned from the private group.

I updated my timeline for Randall and the Afterlife Center and reordered it from the latest events to the earliest.

- <u>2 Days Before Randall's Death</u>: Denis Jednyak reading at magic store in Chicago
- <u>2 Weeks Before</u>: AngryHusband sends email saying "You do not deserve to live. If you publish the video, if you expose everyone…you will regret it"
- <u>1 Month Before</u>: Video alchemy/psychic sessions resumed if people meet in person first
- <u>2 Months Before</u>: Video alchemy/psychic sessions canceled, Randall identified as person who infiltrated group session and recorded it
- <u>2 Months Before (day before video sessions canceled)</u>: Randall records group video session where he exposes Nova Moon's methods
- <u>3 Months Before</u>: "Billy Pilgrim" starts posting in private Afterlife group
- <u>5 Months Before</u>: Randall gets copy of Inspector General report about psychic Nellie Havel (may be Nova Moon)
- <u>2 Years Before</u>: Randall creates Billy Pilgrim social media profile
- <u>5 Years Before</u>: Nova Moon helps police search for missing boy in Krakow
- <u>1990s</u>: Nellie Havel (may be Nova Moon) sends letters claiming spirit of deceased speaks to her, requests items and donations

Unfortunately, I couldn't dig deeper into any of the events on the list now. The chime over the office suite door sounded. It was my client the bakery owner. She was here to get ready for the arbitration this afternoon. And this evening I had my dinner with Randall's landlord, Oscar Miller. It had been a long morning already. It was going to be a longer day.

After two hours practicing to testify and withstand cross-examination, my client wanted out of the conference room. After a quick lunch outside at Café des Livres, the client returned to my conference room to make some phone calls. We had twenty minutes before we needed to leave. I was tempted to spend the time in the Facebook Group. But I didn't want to get too immersed in anything other than the brownie case.

I decided to text Joe's ex-girlfriend Heather. I owed it to Lauren to follow up. And I had Heather's number from the few times we were on a group text when she and Joe were dating.

Heather, it's Joe's friend Quille Davis. Could I buy you a glass of Chardonnay sometime soon? There's something I'd like to talk with you about.

I could have pretended to run into Heather. Social media told me enough about her, including her love of Chardonnay, without needing to check the paid people-finder database I subscribe to. But I didn't want to do anything that sounded shady if Joe later found out. Being as up front as possible was the only way I felt okay about doing reconnaissance for Lauren.

A few minutes later, my client and I left the office. The temperature was low seventies with a nice breeze. The arbitration was in a building on Wacker Drive—the opposite end of the Loop from my neighborhood. But we were both full of nervous energy. City people used to traveling on foot, we agreed to walk. The buzz of traffic and people around us helped us set aside everything else and focus.

Arbitration is less formal than trial. The lawyers and witnesses sit at a long conference table throughout. Three arbitrators sit behind a formal-looking wooden counter that looks a bit like a judge's bench, but it's not raised above floor level.

My opponent was a clean shaven young lawyer named David who inherited the case six months ago. During his opening statement, he slapped his hand on the table and told the arbitrators my client was a swindler, not a baker. She engaged in a widespread scheme to bilk the people of Chicago out of their hard-earned money. After he finished, I quietly said this was a simple case about one $4.25 brownie. The supposed scheme was a series of ads calling the bakery's brownies "the chocolatiest in Chicago." Ads the plaintiff admitted in his deposition he wasn't sure he saw or heard before he bought his brownie, which he ate all of.

The plaintiff testified first. He claimed that while he didn't remember seeing any particular ad, he might have heard one on a podcast he listened to. He did remember seeing an advertisement on a park bench a week after buying the brownie. He got angry because the brownie he ate hadn't been the chocolatiest one he ever tasted in Chicago. Starbucks, for example, was chocolatier.

"Which is sad," he added. "A chain shouldn't be better than a neighborhood bakery."

He sat across from me at the table. On cross-examination I asked if he felt strongly that independent businesses sold better products than chains. I knew the answer to that question was

Yes. And I knew his answers to all the other questions before I asked based on his testimony under oath at his deposition.

He nodded. "For sure."

"That's why you go to independent bakeries whenever you can, right?"

He agreed that was true, and volunteered that he stayed away from Starbucks because he thought they had too much economic power.

"And baked goods are at most a once-a-month treat for you because you try to eat a low sugar diet, correct?"

He leaned forward in his chair. "Absolutely. That's why I was so disappointed it wasn't a better brownie than Starbucks. Because I hardly ever have brownies."

He agreed that he last ate a Starbucks brownie four years ago at an airport in Houston.

"And you never ate the brownies at the other bakery you go to near your home because you like its cherry pie better?"

"Right."

"The brownie from my client's bakery was a big brownie— about four inches square?"

"Uh, yeah, I guess. About like this." He made a square with his hands.

"And you ate all of it."

"Well, I didn't want to waste it."

The room was hot. I pushed the sleeves of my blazer above my elbows. "And you didn't try to return it or tell the person at the counter it was bad."

"No."

"Because you thought it was pretty good when you ate it."

"Right. But I realized later it wasn't the chocolatiest."

"And you realized that when you saw an ad about a week after you ate the brownie?"

"Right."

"Which cost $4.25?"

"Right."

"And you don't know if that's more or less than Starbucks charged when you bought it?"

"Uh, right, I'm not sure."

"Because Starbucks is powerful and evil and you almost never go there?"

"Exactly."

In my closing argument I pointed out that "chocolatiest" wasn't a fact that could be true or false, it was an opinion. It existed in the eye of the beholder, or the tastebuds of the taster. In this case, I argued, the taster didn't know himself. He hadn't eaten brownies at any other bakery in Chicago. Plus, the "chocolatiest brownie" was puffing, a common advertising tactic the public recognizes, not a factual claim. All of which meant there was no fraud. And even if there had been, and there hadn't, the plaintiff got what he paid for. A four-inch square chocolate brownie he liked enough to finish for $4.25. He never presented proof that supposedly chocolatier brownies cost more or were worth more. So he hadn't proved he overpaid. The law he sued under required showing money damages. Being disappointed or angry, if he really had been, didn't count.

The plaintiff's attorney got to speak last because he had the burden of proving his case. I only needed to show he failed to do that. He struggled a bit on damages but finally said it must be worth something to be or not be the chocolatiest brownie or my client wouldn't advertise about it.

The arbitrators usually take fifteen or twenty minutes to decide a case. My client needed to leave, as she had a private catering event to run that night. I settled alone in a vinyl chair in the waiting area and reviewed my list of questions for Oscar Miller. I kept rereading each one, though. While it's not as intense as a trial, an arbitration requires the same concentration and performance skills. A mix of leftover adrenaline rush and looming fatigue made my brain fuzzy.

I clicked over to the private Facebook Group. Unlike the brownie plaintiff, whose supposed anger and disappointment I didn't buy for a second, someone who joined the session Randall disrupted might have felt Nova harmed them deeply. Or they might have felt Randall caused the harm and tracked him down.

The author Denis Jednyak was in Chicago the weekend Randall was killed. Maybe someone else from Afterlife was, too. The profiles I could access showed one member who attended lived in Green Bay, Wisconsin. That's about a four-hour drive from Chicago. Another lived in Prague.

Many group members who didn't seem to have attended the group session all the same ranted about Randall. They felt angry he tricked people, and Nova, by pretending to be someone he wasn't.

I sent a private message to each commenter, saying I was new to the group and concerned about what I read. I didn't want to risk appearing on a video like the one Nova said Randall recorded. And I didn't want to be taken advantage of if Randall was right about Nova. In case someone else forwarded the message, I sent a copy to Nova and to the Group Administrator. If I got banned from the group, so be it. I'd learned a lot.

David approached and shook my hand. "Good job."

My eyebrows raised. "Widespread scheme?"

He shrugged and grinned. "I got a little dramatic. Should we try to work something out after the verdict?"

Either party can reject the arbitrators' decision if they pay a fee. Then the case heads to trial. If both accept the decision, everyone gets to stop paying their lawyers. Other times the arbitrators' ruling prompts one side or the other to change their view of their chances of winning and the case settles.

"We're not the ones who shut down settlement talks. And by the way, I think you'll find Starbucks brownies cost more than my client's did all last year."

"I believe you."

The head arbitrator walked to the counter, gave a piece of paper to the clerk, and left. David and I waited a moment, then got our copies. It was a verdict for my client.

"Congratulations." He held up two fingers in the old peace sign gesture. "Give me a couple minutes."

I texted the client about this chance to settle, but I didn't have a lot of hope. We'd been down this road before.

The plaintiff hurried out, not looking in my direction. A few minutes later, David emerged from the hallway.

"Officially, you and I are spending the next twenty minutes negotiating."

"Okay. And then what happens?"

"I tell you that if your client is still offering the thousand, we accept."

My client had already decided that if she had to, she'd pay the one thousand dollars. She'd already paid me ten times that amount, even with the small business discount I gave her. It wasn't fair for her to pay when she did nothing wrong. But she wanted the bleeding to stop.

"We last offered the one thousand two months ago—before it cost her more legal fees to prepare for today. I can't advise her to pay that now. We won. But if you tell me your client will take it, I'll recommend that she offer five hundred."

"I figured." He heaved a sigh. "He'll kill me if I suggest five. But if it will settle the case, we'll drop the demand to seventy-fifty."

"Your client's willing to go to trial over a few hundred dollars?"

"Is yours?"

"I don't think the jury's going to be more outraged than the arbitrators."

"But there'll be twelve of them. You never know."

"Six fifty's the most I'll recommend." I said.

"I will if you will."

I nodded. Our fingers flew over our respective phones, though I was only deleting email. The client already told me what she'd be willing to do to settle. David's client probably had already told him, too.

"Deal," he said.

"I'll send a settlement agreement first thing tomorrow."

I didn't want his client to change his mind. And I liked being the one to put in the language I wanted.

"Perfect," he said. "Though I'm sort of sorry. I could have told everyone I put a chocolate brownie on trial. Want to grab a drink now that we're done?"

"Sadly, I'm not done working yet."

"Sorry."

My client was so pleased when I called her from the first floor lobby that she wanted to take me to dinner as soon as we could both fit it in. The case had been great publicity, too. She had more customers than ever because the lawsuit was so ridiculous it got featured on two local news shows.

I felt like I ought to play the lottery. I'd had cases settle after arbitration before, but never while standing in the waiting area.

I still had an hour before my meeting with Oscar. Not enough time to make it worth walking back to my office, which was the opposite direction, but too soon to head to River North where Shaw's Crab House is located. I stayed where I was and opened Facebook on my phone. Four answers to my messages awaited me. One sent a sentence filled with colorful words to tell me to mind my own business. But others gave me information I needed.

CHAPTER 33
UNCERTAINTY

Nova is a gift from heaven. Worth every penny. You will find peace and closure. But be careful—that evil man Randall Petrov pretended to belong to the group. He's gone and will never hurt anyone again but there might be more like him. You never know. Not all evil men come to justice.

He's a vulture who wanted to make money off people's grief. That's why he recorded our session. I hope his video was never found or maybe the police destroyed it. It's terrible for Nova because a lot of people like me will never trust a video reading again and that's how she touches so many lives.

That evil man messaged us before he was cut off the session that he'd hide our faces and names except for Nova's but you can't trust someone like that.

Why are you asking questions? You sound like a scammer just like that guy that scammed us. I'm reporting you to the administrator.

I would not buy video reading from Nova. You'll pay for nothing. Randall was third in group call. Nova read for him. He agreed with reading. Then while she read for others he wrote chat to all of us. Long message before very last reading. He told his name and explained he created fake Facebook identity two years ago. He sent links and screenshots.

All things Nova said in reading for Randall came from fake profile Randall created. I saw that when I looked over fake profile. Then I looked at profile I have on Facebook. Almost everything she told me came from there. The rest like Randall said is because Nova asked good questions and used my answers, saying to me what I told her but with new words. It seemed like she read minds.

I never enter Facebook Group anymore. My husband does. He still believes Nova. I saw message from you because I left notifications on. I hoped friends from group might contact me but no one does.

Think very much please before you buy reading. Contact me if you have more questions.

Sincerely, Beata Porinsky

I'D ALREADY SENT the administrator a copy of my message, so I didn't worry about the person who planned to report me. I wondered if I hadn't found the video because Randall sent it out somewhere to have the faces and names blurred or covered. But it seemed to me he would have kept a copy.

Beata Porinsky's comment that her husband still believed in Nova while Beata didn't made me think of AngryHusband, author of the threatening email to Randall. I pulled my copy of it. AngryHusband talked about the loss of a child and how he never lost faith in the woman of God, but his wife did.

Beata's profile showed she was married and lived in Prague. Little else was visible. Other members' profiles included tons of information, but nothing that proved where they were the weekend of Randall's death. I exited and shut my eyes for a few minutes, letting the sounds of people leaving the building flow around me. Five minutes later I headed for the door.

The successful day ought to have left me riding high. Instead, the idea that I might have used all my luck for the day nagged at me.

The underground streets are the quickest way to get from one side of downtown to the other by car. But I avoid walking any of them. They're too dark and dirty. Shaw's Crab House, though, is on Hubbard Street just before it plunges beneath an overpass to meet Lower Wacker Drive. Plenty of vehicles and valet parkers frequent the area. So I walked there, enjoying the warm outside air after being stuck in conference rooms and lobbies all afternoon.

Shaw's serves the best seafood in the city, but it was an odd choice for summer. The bar and the vast dining room are windowless. Both have a clubby feel with dark leather booths and Art Deco light fixtures. It's pricey, too, and Oscar didn't skimp on his order. When I joined him at the bar, he'd already gotten a bottle of red wine and a plate of Norwegian crab legs to share that were listed on the menu as market price.

I quickly drained half a glass of wine, feeling my muscles unwind as I did. Then I switched to ice water. I guessed, correctly, that Oscar wasn't the type to notice what anyone else did. Not good for my hope that he observed anything important about Randall. But it meant he didn't focus on my staying sober while he downed nearly a bottle of wine. I hoped that would make him more talkative.

It did.

After two glasses of wine, he gave me his alibi with only a little prompting. It wasn't exactly airtight, but it fit what Beckwell told me. Oscar claimed to have been riding his bike near his house in Homewood. He stopped to talk to a neighbor who was washing his car. That person vouched for him with the police. The neighbor liked to sit out in his own yard and read until late at night. He had a view of Oscar's yard and said after biking Oscar sat on his deck until at least ten-thirty.

I turned the conversation to Oscar's claim that the estate needed to keep renting the office until Oscar's lease with the building ended.

"I did some research," I said. "Under the Illinois Frauds Act—also called the Statute of Frauds—a landlord can only enforce a multi-year lease if the tenant signs a written document agreeing to it. A lease between you and the building that Randall's not a party to and didn't sign doesn't mean anything."

"Randall and I had a lease."

I squeezed hard on the tool that looked like a giant nutcracker to break open a crab leg. The shell crunched, breaking into tiny pieces that clung to the meat inside. "You mean an oral lease?"

"He knew I needed him to stay the whole time."

It sounded like they'd never even had a conversation about how long Randall agreed to rent the office. "Have you talked to a real estate attorney about this?"

"Why would I? I'm an attorney."

Most of the time, it's almost as bad for a lawyer to represent themselves as it is for a doctor to take out their own appendix, other than it won't actually kill you.

"But you don't practice in that area of law."

Oscar reached across me for the bottle and refilled his wine glass. "It's not your area and you think you're an expert."

"I don't think I'm an expert. But I researched. And asked a real estate lawyer to be sure I was reading the law correctly. There's nowhere you can go with this."

The lawyer I talked to was shocked that any landlord claimed to not know this law. She guessed Oscar was playing dumb and hoping to talk Julia into offering a few thousand to avoid a lawsuit. I felt less sure Oscar was playing dumb.

Oscar waved to the bartender and pantomimed a scribbling motion to let him know he wanted the check.

"I still have a few things to ask," I said.

"Fine, fine. Ask over dinner."

I thought a hundred and fifty dollars worth of wine and crab legs was dinner, but apparently I was mistaken. After paying on my business visa, we returned to the host stand and were taken to a table near the back of the main room.

Oscar ordered a cup of clam chowder, lobster, a side of whipped potatoes, and grilled asparagus. I got tuna and salmon maki rolls. Shaw's is one of the few places I feel confident the sushi is safe to eat, so the rare times I'm there I order it. And it's priced reasonably compared to everything else. Julia was paying, but I try not to spend more of a client's money than I would my own.

As Oscar's soup was served, a text came in from Joe's ex-girl-friend Heather. With the intense day, I'd forgotten all about messaging her.

OK, call me curious. The Albert on Ontario Street, 6:30 tomorrow night?

I wasn't familiar with The Albert, but I texted that I'd see her there.

Then I asked Oscar how Randall happened to rent an office from him.

"We knew each other in college. Then we ran into each other in the coffee shop downstairs. He was looking at an office in another suite. But the conference room on that floor was too small for him."

The move in date Oscar gave me was eight months into his seven-year lease for the office suite, making it more puzzling that he thought the lease bound Randall.

"Did you spend time with Randall outside the office?"

"We had lunch once a year the week before Christmas."

That I knew already from talking with Flora.

"That was it?"

"That was it. We didn't have anything in common." Oscar scraped the bottom of the soup bowl with his spoon. "My friends are lawyers. His were Vegas show people. I practice law. He did card tricks."

Randall's magic shows involved a lot more than card tricks, though the videos I'd found of them online didn't include make-a-tiger-disappear-level illusions.

"You went to college together."

"We weren't friends. He tutored me in some humanities courses. My grades were tanking my law school chances, and a guidance counselor suggested I hire him. He was smart. Too bad he never did anything real with his life."

"Did you know he started Magic Works?"

"Never heard of it." Oscar brushed his hand across the table as if flicking away crumbs.

I found it hard to believe Randall hadn't talked about the non-profit he loved and the reason he needed an office. But Julia told me he disliked fundraising and wanted to focus on training volunteers, so maybe it felt too much like a sales pitch to go on and on about it. Or Randall talked about it and Oscar didn't listen.

"It's a non-profit he founded. That's why he needed the office."

"Oh, right. That volunteer thing he putzed around with."

I was certain Randall hadn't said that.

The rest of the evening went the same way. Oscar had paid so little attention to Randall that it shocked me. He claimed to have no idea how Randall spent his days, who came to the office to see him, or why or when he used the conference room. A tiny bit of information emerged, finally, as Oscar forked his last spear of asparagus.

"Did Randall talk about a new condo he and his wife bought?" I said.

"Yeah, they bought it right before he died. He was meeting someone there that weekend about some sort of project he had going."

The server stopped at our table and Oscar ordered key lime pie and coffee. I asked for an herbal tea.

"Randall met someone at the condo the weekend that he was killed?" I said.

Oscar nodded. "He was planning to." Oscar didn't know, though, who Randall planned to meet or why. Any of that information might help me find out who Randall met on the 606.

"Any idea what type of project?"

The server appeared with our hot drinks and the pie. Oscar tucked into it, ignoring my last question. I asked again.

Oscar waved his fork around. "Some hocus pocus thing."

"Relating to Magic Works?"

"Magic. Hocus pocus. Whatever."

"How did you know about it?"

"On his way out that Friday, Randall told what's-her-name, that busybody secretary, he was meeting someone over the weekend to work out some deal. They were standing right outside my door while I was trying to finish reading a police report. Really annoying."

The conversation snippet supported Julia's view that Randall was meeting someone that weekend.

"Did you tell the police about that conversation?"

"They didn't ask about conversations."

It didn't surprise me that this point hadn't come out. I doubted any of the homicide detectives who handled the investigation spent a couple hours pushing Oscar for details or bought him lobster tail and crab legs.

I made a note to ask Flora, the "busybody," for details. I didn't understand why she hadn't mentioned it before. But I bet she'd remember more than Oscar did. Or than Oscar claimed to. I still felt uncertain about him.

CHAPTER 34
TRAVEL TIMES

THE NEXT MORNING I wrote the settlement agreement for the brownie case and sent it to the plaintiff's lawyer. My email In Box was nearly empty at last, and I had nothing due in any of my cases. I was free to head to Randall's office.

Flora remembered talking with Randall when he left the Friday before his death.

"Now that you mention it, he did say something about weekend plans. But what sticks in my mind is he asked how my little Schnauzer was doing. I missed work the day before because he had to have surgery. Randall was the only person who thought to ask after him."

Julia would probably be glad to hear how kind Randall was. But if only he cared less about the dog, Flora right recall something useful about the conversation.

In Randall's office, I looked over his shelves and found a copy of a book by Denis Jednyak. But it wasn't the newest release. An autographed hard cover, it was published two years before. The autograph lacked a date or any inscription. The book fell open easily, and its glossy cover showed a few fingerprints. Randall might have bought it new or used.

Randall's page-a-day calendar confirmed that for every numerical entry that could be a time, three letter codes appeared as well. Last year's entries included ORD and MDW, the airport codes for O'Hare and Midway, the two major airports in Chicago. That, too, suggested the initials PRG on the date of Randall's death stood for the Prague airport code.

Randall didn't fly to Prague the weekend he was killed. But whoever he met, whether Denis Jednyak or someone else, might have been from Prague.

Oscar had lunch with Randall around Christmas. The page for the third Friday in December listed two numbers and two sets of initials written: 100 530 and GYY DPA. I texted Julia, who called me fifteen minutes later. She found nothing on her personal calendar for 1:00 a.m. or p.m. on that date. But she and Randall had dinner in West Chicago that evening with some old friends, a retired couple with two grown children who lived with them. None of them had the initials GYY or DPA. And the dinner was at 7:00 p.m., not 5:30.

West Chicago isn't, as it sounds, part of the city. Instead, it's a suburb about thirty miles west of Chicago. Julia told me that on a Friday night it took about an hour and a half to drive there from Lincoln Park, where she and Randall lived at the time. Five-thirty might be the time they needed to leave to arrive for dinner on time.

A quick search told me DuPage Airport is located in West Chicago. Its code is DPA, one of the two codes listed on that day. The other code, GYY, matched the Gary/Chicago International Airport. While that's in Indiana, it's about the same distance from Homewood, where Oscar lived, as is

Midway, Chicago's South Side airport. Other small airports are near that area, too. Because of that, I wasn't sure Randall always noted the airport nearest to where he was going or the home of whoever he planned to meet. The memory prompt might simply refer to the airport Randall happened to recall being near that person's home.

I decided to ask Oscar if the December lunch date matched his calendar. If so, I'd feel more certain about the airport code theory.

Oscar must have stepped out of the suite to use the restroom, as his light was on but the office stood empty. His computer was on, too, with a calendar icon in the corner. I could find the answer without sparring with Oscar. And without him trying to extract another expensive dinner.

The door to the suite was close enough that I should hear him return in time to duck out of his office. I hurried to the screen, pushed aside his gym bag, which blocked the mouse, and opened the calendar to last December.

The suite door banged open as I found the 1:00 p.m. lunch with Randall. I took a quick photo, shoved my phone in my pocket, and came face-to-face with Oscar as I stepped through the doorway.

"What are you doing?"

"I stopped in to tell you I'll be done moving things out in two weeks. I'll email you the date, which will be the estate's written notice that we won't need the office after the end of next month."

As I hoped, telling him about the email distracted him from why I was in the office.

"Fine. But the estate owes rent for the rest of the lease."

"There's no lease other than month-to-month."

"Guess we'll see what a jury says."

I nodded and returned to Randall's office. The calendar page with the PRG airport code lay open on the desk. Whoever met with Randall that night almost certainly lived in or near Prague. That person might or might not be the killer, but they hadn't come forward.

After a little more research, I scribbled a list of Prague connections on a legal pad.

- **Afterlife Center:** Old Town neighborhood of Prague
- **Author Denis Jednyak:** works at Afterlife Center
- **Nova Moon:** works at Afterlife - no home address found
- **Beata Porinsky:** Afterlife FB Group member who warned against getting reading from Nova, lives in Prague, maybe AngryHusband's wife?
- **AngryHusband:** threatened Randall in email two weeks before Randall's death, wife attended video conference Randall disrupted, maybe Beata Porinsky's husband?

I wished I could talk to Denis Jednyak. But I only found his home address, not a phone number or email address. I took the tarot card deck that matched Jednyak's new book from Randall's shelf. The box itself was autographed by Jednyak. That signature, too, was undated. But it included a note: *To one who opened my eyes.* The ink was a bit smeared, making me think it might have been signed in person and in a hurry. The deck inside was still wrapped in cellophane. I broke the seal with my fingernail.

The shiny, glossy box and the backs of the cards inside featured haunting and beautiful renderings of buildings in Prague. But nothing in the tiny pamphlet inside or on the cover included a way to contact Jednyak. Neither did his books.

My phone buzzed with an email from David, the plaintiff's lawyer in the brownie case. He made one change to the settlement agreement. It looked fine to me. I told him as soon as his client signed I could transfer my client's payment.

The case concluded, and my other matters on long timelines, this really was the perfect time for an overseas trip. Were Ty and I together, I'd be getting on a plane for Dubai by the end of the week. But much as I felt the need to get away, we weren't.

I looked at my list again and at the images on the cards. I preferred talking to people in person rather than by phone or over Zoom, even if I had contact information for each name on the list. From everything I'd heard, Prague was a stunning city to visit. And Randall planned to meet someone from Prague the night of his death.

It was time for an overseas trip after all.

CHAPTER 35
SIDE BUSINESS

THE WOMAN who answered the phone at the Afterlife Center spoke in what I assumed was Czech. But when I asked for Denis Jednyak, she switched smoothly to English and asked what time my appointment with him was.

"I don't have an appointment. I met him at a book signing and was hoping to talk more with him."

Before pitching Julia on going to Prague, I needed to at least try to get more information by phone or video. If she didn't want to cover the cost of a trip, though, I might go on my own dime. Getting out of town appealed to me. And I found a flight with two connections for close to the price of flying from Chicago to New York.

"I am very sorry. Denis speaks only in person by appointment. But there is today no time available."

"What about a video conference?"

"Denis gives readings only in person."

I guessed the Center still didn't feel certain about how to keep someone like Randall off video readings.

"Is there any way to talk to him by phone? Could you ask him to call me back?"

The receptionist, though, wasn't swayed. Not only could Denis not talk on the phone, he was booked for the next three weeks.

"What about Nova Moon?" I said. "Is she also in-person only?"

"Yes."

"Does she have any appointments open?"

"Yes, but her rates are higher than those for Denis."

Seeing Nova for an hour at the Afterlife Center cost about two hundred dollars. If Nova thought I would benefit by it, she'd then arrange a nine-hundred thirty-eight dollar reading that same afternoon. And I could apply to see if I qualified for the in depth two-day seminar. I had a feeling everyone with money qualified.

Nova had three openings within the next eight days. After tonight's networking event, I had only one upcoming meeting —Heather at The Albert.

I made an appointment with Nova. After I answered a few questions, the woman told me to bring something meaningful that belonged to my sister. Because I needed to pay up front by credit card, I gave my real name. But the Afterlife Group Administrator and Nova Moon knew that already, and no one had any reason to think I was connected to Randall.

Now I needed to sell Julia on the trip. I called her toward the end of the day, after more research and reaching out to an Afterlife Facebook Group member. I explained why I wanted to go and offered to pay half of the travel expenses.

"You don't need to pay half. But you're sure you can't talk to these people by phone?"

"I tried again and the evening receptionist told me the same things. But I'm meeting a member of the Facebook Group who lives there. She and her husband used to volunteer at the Center. She should be a good source of information and make the trip more worthwhile."

I still didn't know if the woman's husband was AngryHusband, so I didn't mention that part to Julia.

"Just promise you'll be careful. I don't want you putting yourself in danger. I wish you weren't going alone."

"I will be extremely careful. You're sure Randall never mentioned Denis Jednyak or his book or tarot deck to you?"

"No. But if he was planning a debunking involving Nova, and Jednyak works for her, he wouldn't have."

I texted Lauren to see if she wanted to join me in Prague. She travels a lot with her parents during wintertime when her real estate business is slow. Because they go everywhere first class, she amasses tons of airline and hotel points she uses for her own trips. It likely wouldn't cost her anything to travel.

She texted back immediately.

Of course I'm coming with. Always wanted to see Prague and I'm not letting you investigate there without me. Send the itinerary.

Two minutes after I sent the flights and hotel I planned to book she called me.

"Seriously? No way we're taking those three flights. It'll take forever."

"It'll fit my budget. But you don't have to fly with me. Just meet me there."

"No, no, no. Absolutely not. I'll plan it. You can pay me whatever this sad excuse for a trip was going to cost and I'll take care of the rest. I've got a gazillion points."

"But not to use for my investigation."

"Why not? My parents pay when I go with them. And you know Joe hates to fly. I'll never get him to Europe."

We bickered more but in the end I agreed. Traveling with Lauren was much safer, especially in a country where I didn't speak the language.

Had the brownie case not wound up I might have skipped the networking event that night and spent the evening in a bubble bath with a glass of wine. But I needed a steady stream of business to keep my law firm on its feet. Conversations tonight could lead to cases months down the road.

At the end of the day, after touching up my makeup and hair, I hopped on the L to Lincoln Park. The back room of the Italian restaurant where the bar association met was filled by the time I arrived. Trays of cheese cubes and crackers and hot appetizers sat on one end of the bar. A bartender served wine, soda, or water at the other. I chose a plastic cup of Pinot Noir and headed for a group of five near a fake fireplace.

Chicago is a large city but a small legal community. I was reminded of that when one of the male lawyers turned around. It was David from the brownie case. We said Hello but both of us spent the evening talking to other people who might send cases our way.

When the event ended promptly at seven, though, David followed me toward the door. He was thinking of starting his own solo law practice and asked for advice. We walked together to the Fullerton L station. We waited on the platform near the outer track to catch the Brown Line downtown. The Red Line runs through Fullerton as well on the inner tracks. But the Brown Line stations near my neighborhood typically have fewer incidents of crime. And there's a stop close to Union Station where David needed to go next.

"Congrats again on the case," David said. "I think it settled at just the right amount."

The sun beat down. I took off my blazer, though it was lightweight and only had three-quarter sleeves. The platform is open air, making it hot in summer and freezing in winter. It smells less of urine than underground subway stations. But in August there's always a faint scent of sweat and often beer as well. The Red Line goes to Wrigley Field. Judging by the number of partially drunk people wearing Cubs caps, I guessed there was a game tonight.

"I think about zero would've been right." I shifted sideways as someone raced past me to hop on the Red Line. They made it just as bells rang and a disembodied voice announced that the doors were closing.

David laughed. "Of course you do. But off the record, it wasn't my favorite case. The client is the partner's neighbor. Sends tons of his corporate work."

I was about to ask about David's wife, who had just opened a fashion boutique. But from the corner of my eye I noticed someone edge around a crowd near the top of the stairs. Despite the heat and humidity, the person wore a bright red sweatshirt with the hood up, black sweat pants, and a black disposable face mask. The mask looked clean and fit well rather than sagging from breath and damp air. A few people wear masks on public transportation in Chicago to avoid catching all manner of airborne illnesses. But hardly anyone wears them over their mouth and nose outside in the summer.

After getting free of the crowd, the figure—likely a man based on height, broad shoulders, and straight body lines—barreled toward me. Adrenaline shot through me. I was far too close to the Brown Line tracks. No train was in sight, but that didn't matter. If you fall and land on what's known as the third rail, you'll be electrocuted. It's one reason for all the CTA signs warning against jumping onto the tracks to retrieve dropped phones or wallets.

"Watch out." I leapt forward, shoving David backwards into a group of people. He yelped, they grumbled. But the momentum pushed everyone toward the center of the platform. I was still partly in the attacker's path. Out of time, I crouched low so, at worst, he'd trip over me.

The attacker swerved to avoid tumbling over me and onto the tracks himself. He slammed into stocky young man wearing a baseball cap, who started swearing as a Red Line train pulled in.

I stood and shoved through the crowd of exiting passengers after the attacker, grasping his arm. In an action movie I would have caught up and used some fancy martial arts—despite the crowds—to detain him. But I'm no action hero, and he wrenched away and ran for the stairs. Four drunk teenagers stumbled between us. It was all I could do to keep my balance. By the time I got around them, my attacker was gone. David found me in the station a few minutes later, my trampled blazer in his hand. I'd dropped it when I crouched low to duck the attacker.

David put his hand on my shoulder. "You all right? Did he get your wallet?"

"No." My shoulder bag was still clasped shut. I hadn't felt a tug on it. A quick check confirmed my wallet and phone were still zipped into an inner compartment. "I'm pretty sure he was after me."

"You? What for?"

"I never told you about my side business, did I?"

CHAPTER 36
WHY

The uniformed CTA employee shrugged and said it was probably a purse snatcher. "Good that you picked up on it, didn't lose anything. It's over."

"I'd like to file a report."

"They'll never find him."

"I know. But I'm hoping to get to see any video of the platform."

She rolled her eyes. "Good luck with that."

Fortunately, it took only twenty minutes for two police officers to arrive and take my information. David stayed with me.

I described the person and the clothing, adding that I saw a zig-zag white stripe on the back of the sweatshirt when they ran away. The officers weren't any more optimistic than the CTA employee about video footage.

"If no one's dead, it's not a priority. Took a week to get it after a door was shot out near the university last year," the shorter officer said.

I texted Detective Sergeant Beckwell on the Uber ride home hoping he could help get the video. He called me as I was unlocking the door to my condo.

"Who knew you'd be on that L platform?" he said.

I dropped my keys on the side table near the door and stepped out of my low-heeled shoes. "That specific platform? No one. I would've taken an Uber all the way home if David wasn't heading the same direction. Anyone at the event could have followed us, but there wasn't much time to change from business clothes to sweats."

"Any chance this guy David lured you there?"

"I can't think why he would."

"This event—public?"

"You have to belong to the bar association to attend. But it's monthly, always at the same place. And it's listed on the website. That's public. Anyone who knew I was attending and knew where my office is might guess I'd take the L. Or watch the entrance and follow me."

The area near the restaurant is busy enough in the early evening that I might not have noticed a lurker, much as I try to stay aware of my surroundings.

"Given all the feathers you ruffle, you shouldn't follow any routines. Make it hard for people to guess where you'll be."

"I still have to live a life." As I passed my walk in closet, I tossed the trampled blazer into the dry cleaning pile.

"I'm not saying you can't."

"I know." I slid onto a stool at my kitchen island. I still felt shaky and too hot, and the cool granite felt good under my elbows. "I don't go to this event every month. But often. And I'm sure I mentioned it to people when I was scheduling cases. Or setting up interviews for the murder investigation."

I couldn't remember who, though. Typically, I recall what people say to me, often word-for-word. I'm less apt to recall exactly what I say, because it's the information I gather, not that I share, that helps me when I look at a crime. Apparently I ought to pay more attention to myself.

"You're sure it was a planned attack on you personally?" Beckwell said.

"I'm not sure. I've never been a victim of a random crime in Chicago. It might just have been my turn."

I didn't really believe that, though.

The next morning, the day before I was leaving for Prague, Julia emailed me. Oscar had filed a Complaint, which is the written court document that starts a lawsuit, against Randall's estate. The sheriff served it on Julia early that morning in her chambers. Based on the date and time stamp, Oscar filed it with the court just before meeting me at Shaw's. Knowing I represented Julia, he ought to have told me and given me a copy, but he wasn't required to do that.

Though I read it carefully, it made little sense. Julia hadn't stopped paying rent yet. So even if Oscar were right that the estate owed him rent through the end of his lease with the building, there was no breach of contract. And nothing Oscar wrote improved, in my mind, his odds of success when the estate did stop paying. But that didn't mean Julia could ignore the lawsuit.

The defendant has to answer each fact the plaintiff alleges in a Complaint or move to dismiss the case, which means it gets thrown out of court before any evidence is gathered. Nine out of ten times judges, who are required to lean toward letting people have their day in court, deny those motions. I'd tried five times to get the brownie case dismissed. But this case should be the one in ten the judge tossed out. And that was before you considered that no judge was likely to bend over backwards to keep a baseless case against Julia, a sister judge, moving toward trial. Especially after she suffered such a terrible loss.

Normally I ask for extra time to answer a Complaint. All but the most difficult of attorneys agree. But Oscar was representing himself, and he probably fell in the most difficult category. Plus I had no interest in dragging this out.

I outlined my motion. I could write a first draft on the plane. The rest of the day I made sure nothing in my other cases fell through the cracks while I was overseas. I finished by late afternoon, with plenty of time to meet Heather for drinks at six-thirty, then get home and get to sleep early. Lauren and I needed to leave for the airport by seven the next morning.

The Albert, where Heather and I were meeting, is in the EMC2 hotel, both names a tribute to Albert Einstein. The hotel is in Streeterville, an upscale neighborhood near the lake. I could have taken a bus or L or walked the two miles for the exercise, which I needed. But I splurged on an Uber. After my experience the evening before I felt like being more protected.

<hr>

I arrived ten minutes early and sat at the bar, enjoying simply looking around. Suspended bookshelves, paintings, drawings, light fixtures, and sculptures filled The Albert. It was a good choice for a meeting. Crowded enough that Heather's and my conversation wouldn't easily be overheard. But not so loud that we'd need to yell to be heard.

She arrived exactly on time. Despite the heat and humidity her makeup looked smooth and polished and her blond hair hung straight and sleek to her shoulders. Mine, on the other hand, frizzed from the weather and hung heavy on my neck. I brushed flyaway strands out of my eyes. My skin still felt tacky from sweat. The Uber sedan's air conditioning hadn't been working.

I felt underdressed, too. A moment ago my dark red ballet flats, capri pants, upscale tank top with lace edging, and a lightweight cardigan felt just right for The Albert's smart casual dress code. But Heather wore a pencil skirt with a mid-thigh slit, a silver chain belt, a sleeveless, fitted, button-down top, and three-inch designer heels.

"Hello, Quille." She slid onto a barstool kitty corner to mine without any move to shake hands. The bartender set a Chardonnay in front of her.

"I guess they know you," I said.

"I come here for a lot of meetings. What can I do for you?"

I'm not a huge fan of small talk. But a few words about the weather or traffic or the almost always terrible sports teams are customary in Chicago, especially when you haven't seen someone in a long time. Heather skipping that added to my suspicion that she never much cared for me. But it did save time.

"I have a personal question to ask you," I said. "I'm happy to tell you why I'm asking if you want. Why did you and Joe break up?"

She rested her fingers lightly on the stem of her wine glass. "You don't know." It was a statement, not a question, and her tone conveyed skepticism.

"I know what he told me. Something about the ring."

I hesitated to share exactly what Joe said. That felt like more of a betrayal than asking Heather for her reasons.

She snickered. "The ring. So at least you know he proposed."

"And that you said No."

"He didn't say what it was about the ring?"

"You didn't like it."

"You could say that." She tapped a ruby red fingernail on the bar. "How long have you been seeing him?"

"What? No. He's seeing my friend Lauren."

"Lauren? The bubbly blonde?"

"Yes."

"Lauren."

"Yes."

"After you?"

"Joe and I never went out. We've always been friends."

Heather half-laughed again. "Honestly, for someone smart you're clueless, Quille. And your friend is, too. You want to know why Joe and I broke up? You."

FIRST CLASS SECRETS

I WOKE up over and over during the night. Three times I calculated how long it was until I had to leave for the airport, then tried with no luck to clear my head and fall into a deep sleep. Around three in the morning I gave up, propped my back against the interior brick wall behind me and my laptop on my knees, and revised my questions for each person I hoped to meet in Prague. I started to text Ty, too, to tell him I'd be in a time zone closer to his. But I deleted it.

A headline about Magic Works flashed across my screen just when I finally felt tired enough to sleep. Word of the investigation had leaked. Donors were furious. The fraud, according to the Chicago Daily Law Bulletin, included not only donated clothing but about half of the cash donations collected over the last decade. The paper quoted sources who asserted Colleen funneled funds to herself and her family members.

I turned off the light and tried deep breathing, hoping it would lull me to sleep. When Ty slept next to me, it used to help me relax, though I mostly like sleeping alone so I can stretch out my arms and legs. But he breathed in a smooth, quiet rhythm. Hearing it and feeling the rise and fall of his chest was like drifting to sleep on the ocean. I reached for my phone. If he answered, he'd remind me that it was good that I stopped Colleen from cheating more people. He'd reassure me that I always had doubts about whether I could find the truth in my investigations and so far I always had.

But then what? I rolled onto my side. Nothing about our relationship or locations had changed. I slept at last, but awoke thinking of Heather. Lauren, I felt sure, wasn't about to blame me or take Heather's claim, which was that Joe was in love with me, at face value. But Lauren wasn't likely to stay silent. And I didn't see any way to avoid Joe learning I talked to Heather about him. If Lauren believed Heather was right about Joe's feelings for me, it might be the end of Lauren and Joe. And of the three of us being friends. I gave up trying to sleep.

After a shower I started writing my motion to, I hoped, get Oscar's lawsuit thrown out of court. I needed something to go right in my work for Julia. So far my efforts led to the near-demise of Randall's legacy and a lawsuit against her as executor of his estate.

An hour later I waited near the potted plants in my condo building lobby, scrolling through our flight itinerary. It showed us flying from Chicago to New York to Paris to Prague. It was the first time I looked past the departure and final arrival times. Lauren appeared a moment later, clutching a thermos of coffee and rolling a large suitcase. Her Christian Louboutin tote with its trademark red bottom was slung over her shoulder.

I showed her my screen. "Is this right? I thought you didn't want to take three flights, and we're taking three flights."

She rubbed her eyes. "I didn't want three flights with a stop in Iceland. This will take four hours less. And once you take La Première on Air France you'll never want to fly any other way."

We pushed through the side exit next to the revolving doors so we could roll our bags through.

"La Première. Sounds like it costs an arm and a leg." I had already sent Lauren the funds from my business account to cover what I would have spent on my original travel plan.

"Points are covering a big part of everything, my mom's covering the rest. She told me to tell you to enjoy the flight as a thank you for getting me to go to Prague. Finally. She thinks it's the most beautiful city in the world."

Lauren's parents freely gift her major items like sofas and designer shoes and first class travel. It was kind of them to include me so I could travel with her rather than arriving bedraggled four hours later. But I felt a bit odd accepting what I suspected was a very expensive subsidy of my work.

A black SUV pulled to the curb in front of us. It was from a car service I use for business if I don't want to drive and can't risk being late. I'd insisted on paying for that.

Lauren hopped in and slid across the seat. I climbed in after her and the driver shut the door behind me. "I saw Heather last night. I need to tell you what she said."

"Wait 'til we get to the airport. It's way too early."

Lauren shut her eyes and rested her head against the seat. She's not a morning person, so I didn't insist. The ride to O'Hare airport took less than half an hour, as it should based on the distance alone. When there's heavy traffic it can take an hour and a half, sometimes more, which was why we left ourselves so much extra time. I figured Lauren and I would be early and could talk about Heather at the gate. But something was wrong with the computer systems. Bag checking took forever, as did the security line. It was crowded and noisy and there was no faster first class lane open. We reached the gate only ten minutes before boarding.

The first class compartment had larger seats than coach, and it was nice not being sandwiched against someone else. But it was fully booked, and Lauren and I sat in different rows.

I finished a rough draft of the motion to dismiss Oscar's case during the flight. It didn't take much work. The law was clear. And contrary to my Gram's stories of meals on all first class flights in her day, breakfast—hot black tea and a plastic-wrapped donut—didn't require me to pause for more than a few minutes.

Everything was different at JFK in New York. We checked in at a quiet enclosure on the edge of the airport. There was no line because, as Lauren explained while the agent tagged our bags, there were only four seats in La Première Class. Business class had a separate check in and lounge. I never saw that or the lines for coach. A young woman in a blue uniform and heels took us to the front of the security line, showed a pass, and ushered us through in five minutes. After that, she led us to a room the size of a large studio apartment, complete with sofas, coffee tables, and a floor-to-ceiling window with a view of the planes outside. Despite a bowl of fresh fruit, a tray of Madeleines under a glass dome, and an array of cookies and snacks, the room featured dining tables where we could order a full meal.

"But don't." Lauren settled in next to me on the longer sofa and took her cosmetics bag out of her tote. "You don't want to miss the seven course dinner on the plane."

"This is—" I glanced at the expensive liquor bottles glowing under recessed lighting in a display case. "You travel like this all the time?"

"Only when we go New York to Paris. It's not an option for most flights."

After a server poured us glasses of Acqua Panna, I took out my notes from the conversation with Heather. I didn't need them, but having my iPad in my hand helped me feel steadier.

"So…Heather broke it off with Joe, and turned down his marriage proposal, because she thought he was in love with me."

Lauren's a straight talker, so I figured I ought to cut to the chase.

"Seriously?" She closed her handheld mirror and stowed her lipstick in her case. "And she thought that because of the engagement ring?"

"Partly."

"Well, Joe knows zero about jewelry. And he's a bad gift buyer. I've exchanged every present he ever got me."

"You've exchanged every one I've gotten you, too."

"I'm particular. Sue me."

"It's not that she didn't like it. Remember that ring Marco got me? With the citrine gemstone in the center and the diamond chips all around?"

"How could I forget? You wore it way, way too long. It kept other guys away when you needed to start dating again."

That had always been Lauren's opinion. I disagreed, but that wasn't the point.

"Joe bought Heather one almost just like it. Except with a diamond in the middle and citrine around the edges."

Citrine is a golden-yellow type of quartz. It's not very expensive and isn't usually seen in engagement rings. But it's my birthstone. Though Marco and I never talked about it, that was probably why he got me a ring with citrine in the center. Plus he knew I'm not fond of flashy jewelry.

"Odd for an engagement ring, I give you that," Lauren said. "But she seriously lost her mind over nothing. Your ring was pretty. Clueless Joe was trying to buy something pretty."

"Heather didn't see it that way."

"This is what you were so obviously worried about telling me?"

"No. It's not just—"

The door opened again and a woman with a French accent asked if we wanted facials.

Lauren stood. "Oh, absolutely."

"You do? I've got more to tell you."

She waved her hand. "Wait for the flight. I need to think anyway. You should get one, too. They redo your makeup after and everything."

Growing up, I was thrilled if my mom combed her hair and put on something other than sweats. What little I knew about makeup and clothes I learned from my theater work. I rarely got my nails done and had never had a facial. Those things felt too unnecessary to spend on.

I told Lauren to go ahead.

By the time Lauren returned, an older couple sat on the sofa nearer the window. Lauren wanted to leave the rest of the

Heather talk for the flight. Fifteen minutes before the departure time a uniformed attendant walked us outside to a car. We were driven to the plane and taken up a separate gangway into our cabin.

It was both wider and longer than first class in any plane I'd ever boarded. Each of us got our own compartment with two seats. The main seat had a high back and foot rest. A shallower, curved seat across from it was for a companion to sit in during dinner. Both folded together later to become part of a bed. Heavy curtains could be pulled across it to create a private area.

The world really is different when you've got an overabundance of money. No wonder Lauren enjoyed flying so much.

The older couple had the compartments in the center. Lauren and I had the spots on opposite sides of the plane. A counter ran along each plane wall with a small reading lamp bolted onto it. After we took off, the flight attendant opened the table between my two seats. Lauren popped over to my side of the plane for dinner. We each got a glass of champagne, which I decided was my one alcoholic drink, as I hoped to avoid too much jet lag.

Lauren tasted her champagne then set her glass on the corner of her tray where the lip kept it steady. "All right. Tell me."

CHAPTER 38
THE JOURNEY

I STARTED with the first moment Heather focused on when talking to me. "Heather was not happy when Joe came home early from that trip she bought for him at Christmastime."

"But she knew he'd promised to spend the holiday season with you. What more did she want?"

"For him to stay for the whole trip."

The first Christmas after Marco's death was hard for me. He and I talked so much about what we'd do for the season. Joe, as my oldest friend, wanted to help me through it. I convinced him to go with Heather, though, and he did. But he surprised me by appearing at my place on New Year's Eve for my traditional games night with my niece and nephew and friends.

Heather took it as a sign, or so she said.

"Well, she was kind of awful," Lauren said. "She totally got him that trip to make him choose between you."

"She'd just become a corporate travel consultant. She probably thought putting together a fantastic trip was a perfect gift. And she claims she asked if I had plans for Christmas Day and I did. With Marco's family."

The flight attendant brought two small plates with the first course—a single large onion ravioli with Comte cheese and porcini sauce.

Lauren thanked her and turned back to me. "I still don't see why you didn't come on the ski trip with my parents and me."

"I was fine. I needed some time alone."

I was trying to give Heather the benefit of the doubt. My reaction to what she said was much like Lauren's, but neither of us could be objective. And Heather came from a pretty close family. I wasn't sure she understood how much friends mean to some of us. Though Lauren was close with her parents and she got it.

"Marco and I weren't seeing each other that long. She might not have thought about it being my first holiday season without him."

"Maybe. But there's got to be more to all of this than the trip," Lauren said.

The ravioli tasted savory and a little sweet at the same time. I finished it in two bites. "There is. It's a lot of guesswork on Heather's part. But she thinks Joe never told me how he felt because I had just started seeing Ty."

Heather's words gave me a sinking feeling in the pit of my stomach. Almost from the moment they met, Joe was snippy to Ty and snarky about him. He stopped making time to sing with me and our friend Danielle, when before that our a cappella trio sang at local bars and sometimes festivals throughout the spring and summer.

Lauren drank the last of her champagne. "That's ridiculous."

"You didn't think so at the time."

Lauren had floated the idea that Joe might be into me and be feeling jealous of Ty.

She frowned. "Okay, sure. But then you asked and he said he didn't feel that way."

We were interrupted by the next course—asparagus with parmesan cream and a few bites of lobster tail in a citrus vinaigrette.

After we both finished, I said, "Joe and I talked on the phone about it. He told me seeing things going well with Ty and me made him feel worse about his break up. And then he felt guilty because he wanted to be happy for me so he started avoiding everyone."

Lauren shrugged. "Classic Joe. Avoid avoid avoid."

"That's what I figured at the time."

"You're saying you think differently now?"

"No. I wondered for a while. But then you two got together, and I saw how happy he was, and I didn't worry about it anymore."

Lauren pushed her empty plate aside. "Exactly. You're only thinking about it now because Heather stirred things up."

"True. But to be fair, I asked her."

Lauren's lower lip puffed out in an exaggerated pout. "Do you have to be fair to her?"

I laughed. "Absolutely not. All my fairness ought to go in your direction. I just want to make sure you feel your questions are answered. Heather did say a couple more things."

"Is it anything I really need to know now?"

I agreed it wasn't, and we dropped the subject for the next two courses—a tiny roasted chicken thigh with a sauce that smelled of saffron and lemon, and a side fennel salad.

Lauren pointed her fork at the last bite of her chicken. "A little chewy, but miles above any other airplane food."

"Nice pun." I toyed with the last few bites of salad but didn't eat them. Fennel tastes too much like black licorice for me. It's one of my least favorite flavors.

The last course was a lemon meringue tartlet. Then the flight attendant brought a saucer-sized plate with four square chocolate bon bons as another started making up the beds.

Each bed stretched the entire side of the plane compartment. Air France gave us each a pillow-sized pouch with pajamas and a set of facial cleanser and moisturizer. Thinking the pajamas might help me sleep on the plane, which I normally can't do, I changed in the small private room near the cockpit set aside for us.

As I exited, I found Lauren waiting for her turn.

"Obviously, don't say anything to Joe about any of this," she said.

"Only if he asks, and I'd still talk to you first. But the odds of him randomly wondering if I talked to Heather lately are pretty small."

"Absolutely zero, I'd say."

"Agreed."

The plane's movement and being able to stretch out flat lulled me toward sleep, despite the seat belt fastened across my waist over the blanket. The next morning, Air France's La Première service extended to taking us to the very front of the border police line at the Charles DeGaulle airport, past rows and rows of exhausted-looking travelers, many of them with children gripping their hands. I was exhausted, too. I'd slept about four hours on the plane, but it didn't make up for the bad night before departure. And we had another flight to take.

We arrived at our hotel in Prague in the early afternoon. My eyelids were drooping. Happily, Europe is much more of a tea-drinking place than the United States, and I had no trouble getting an Earl Grey tea to go from the restaurant off the lobby. Lauren chose the Four Seasons, one of the priciest hotels in Prague. But between the exchange rate and lower cost of living, it cost about the same as a good Marriott hotel in Chicago. We had a King-sized bed, a desk, and a separate bath and shower, plus a bowl of fresh fruit waiting for us.

It was a perfect location, too, just off the Vltava River and less than a mile walk from the main square and the Afterlife Center. First, though, we needed to meet the Afterlife Facebook Group member who told me to think hard before buying a reading. She chose Terasa U Zlate studne, a rooftop restaurant in Prague that she said had a beautiful view of the entire city.

Uber operated in Prague, too. The driver stopped where a street dead ended at the base of a steep incline in what looked like a residential neighborhood. I saw no signs for any restaurants. The driver pointed to a cobblestone passageway between houses. Still unsure, we got out. The street was so narrow there was nowhere for the driver to turn the car around. He had to back down the hill to turn onto the main road again.

Lauren looked doubtfully at the cobblestone incline. "Seriously not wanting to go up that in spike heels if I just have to come down again and order another Uber."

I glanced at the three-story homes towering over us and hoped the cell phone reception was good enough to order a new Uber. If not, Lauren had a long way to walk in those shoes.

"See, sometimes flats are better," I said. "I'll find out if we're in the right place."

At the top, another narrow path with more cobblestones led to a building with a sign that said The Golden Well. Inside was a small entryway with an unmarked elevator. Fortunately, there was cell phone reception. A quick online search showed that the restaurant was in a hotel called The Golden Well.

I called to Lauren, who managed to get up the hill without catching a heel on the way. We took the elevator to a dimly lit deserted waiting area on the second floor with an iron spiral staircase. We exchanged glances and climbed.

We were seated near the three-quarter wall at the outer edge of the dining area. It was the perfect spot to take in the panoramic view of the city. The Prague castle with its grand palaces and towers was a focal point to the west. Red-tiled roofs stood out across the blue sky, interspersed with the spires of churches and cathedrals.

I could barely tear my gaze away to look at the menu. It offered items similar to those on the plane. While the prices probably weren't high for that type of food, especially, according to Lauren, compared to Paris or New York, nothing was cheap. Lauren was eyeing the caviar when, to my relief, a woman I recognized from her Facebook profile photo stepped onto the deck. Beata Porinsky. The woman I suspected was married to AngryHusband.

CHAPTER 39
THE SQUARE

BEATA MOSTLY LOOKED like her photo, but her dark, curly hair had much more gray in it. She wore bangle bracelets on both arms. The host waved toward our table.

"Quille Davis?" Beata's voice was low and melodic.

I introduced myself and Lauren. When the server appeared, Beata recommended one of the less pricey bottles of champagne. It turned out to be crisp and tasted faintly of pears. After we ordered our meals, without caviar, she told us a little about the view and the city, then took a deep breath.

"You have questions about Nova Moon. I am good person to answer. I volunteered at Center for a time. But I need to know why." She tilted her head to one side. "I do not believe you travel so far only to get reading."

"You're right," I said. "Randall Petrov, the man who disrupted your call, was killed."

Beata pressed her hand to her chest, resting it on the open skin above her neckline. "This is true?"

Lauren and I assured her it was. I showed her Randall's obituary on my phone, then explained about Julia asking me to look into the death.

"This is bad. Very sad. I was angry at Randall Petrov after he did that but never wished such a thing to happen."

"You were angry at him, not Nova?"

"At first, yes, at him. Then her. And finally me. For being blind for so many years. For four years Nova read for me and I paid. Since my brother died. She said she talked to his spirit."

That didn't sound like AngryHusband and his wife. I said I was sorry for her loss and asked Beata about her brother. She told us he was a schoolteacher, a bicyclist, and a very kind man. After Randall's sting, Beata discovered everything Nova told her came from the brother's spirit was on her brother's social media pages, which had never been deleted, and the pages of family members.

"Was there anyone on the call who lost a daughter?" I said.

Beata shut her eyes for a moment. "Nova read for married couple. They were on screen together. Daughter was kidnapped or disappeared. Somewhere in Canada. Vancouver? Nova sensed things about her."

"What things?" Lauren rested her elbows on the table and leaned forward.

"That loving woman took daughter because she wanted child. Daughter sometimes is sad but mostly happy. Nova knew name of daughter's dog and names of teachers at school. And knew girl liked to draw. Randall showed all of that was on socials, just like Nova gave his reading based on his false profile."

"Did the couple get angry at Nova?" I said.

"The husband was angry at Randall, not Nova. Before session ended, he yelled that Randall is terrible person. That Randall better hope they never meet in real life."

"Any chance you know the couple's names?"

"The names showed on screen in session but I do not remember. They were not in Facebook Group. They found Nova some other way."

"Oh." My shoulders sagged.

She told me that there were a dozen people on the video session Randall interrupted. Four or five, including the Canadian couple, didn't belong to the Facebook Group. But the video recording of it should show everyone's full names. Nova required them to use their real names in group session.

"Now I think was to make it easy to check socials again during call and pretend to read minds." Beata tapped the side of her forehead. Her bangle bracelets jangled.

"I haven't found the video recording yet," I said. "Are you sure Randall made one?"

"He told us in chat message he recorded. He planned to expose Nova to world. But he promised to cover all names and faces except hers."

Beata didn't know if Nova ever went to Chicago. She did, though, know the author Denis Jednyak.

"Oh, yes. He is Facebook Group Administrator. And he reads at Center and lives in Vinohrady neighborhood."

She still had Jednyak's address from when she volunteered at the Center and sometimes brought packages to him. She texted it to me.

I knew what I was doing first thing tomorrow.

———

Our hotel stood about half a mile from Old Town Square, the historic center of Prague. It was an easy walk even for two sleep-deprived women. We passed a plaque about the writer Franz Kafka, over twenty crosses memorializing martyrs, a gothic cathedral from the fourteenth century, the Baroque St. Nicholas Church, and wooden food and craft stands. But we couldn't find the landmark Beata told us about.

"She said we can't miss it. Yet I'm missing it." I paused on the edge of an area of picnic tables and peered at the stone buildings around us. The smells of sugary bakery, grilled sausage and sauerkraut, and deep-fried cheese filled the air.

It was early afternoon, thirty minutes before my appointment at the Afterlife and Alchemy Center. Lauren and I had tried Denis Jednyak's apartment in the morning. No one answered his buzzer. We couldn't even get past the heavy door to the lobby. The only person who went in during the forty minutes we loitered glared at us and pulled the door shut behind her, blocking our way.

"What exactly is an astronomical clock?" Lauren spun around, looking for the landmark Beata had told us about.

I took out my phone to search for a photo of it online. It was supposed to be on a building known as Old Town Hall and include symbols of the sun and moon, statues of saints, and the figure of Death as a skeleton. Every hour the clock sprang to life and the figures moved in a choreographed dance. If the clock failed, local legend said the city would be in jeopardy.

"Good thing it's not depending on my sleep-deprived brain to keep working," I said after reading the information to Lauren.

She clicked on her phone. "Forget the clock."

Lauren called up walking directions. A warm female voice directed us across the Square and down one of the cobblestone streets that jutted out from it. Another turn sent us into what looked like an alley. Delivery trucks about the size of small sedans at home parked along windowless brick walls. A few men came out of a narrow passageway between buildings but the area was mostly deserted. The turn-by-turn directions stopped. Lauren had lost service.

I glanced over my shoulder, sure I heard footsteps. No one was there.

"Might be people in one of those passageways." Lauren pointed toward one of the gaps between buildings.

"I'm paranoid after that attack on the L platform. Though I'm guessing whoever it was didn't hop a plane to Prague after me."

"No. But we absolutely need to be careful. And we're absolutely in the wrong place."

I glanced at the time. I had less than ten minutes until my appointment.

We retraced our steps to the street that led to the Square. An antique convertible followed by a horse-drawn carriage, both available for hire to tourists, headed toward us. We scooted to the edge of the road.

Lauren clicked buttons on her phone. "At last."

She started the directions over. But I pointed to a crowd of people with their backs to a row of cafés, aiming their phones at an ornate clock. It angled away from the Square. The other buildings had blocked it from our view earlier. It started to chime, telling me I was late.

I studied the cafés and stores, at last spotting a door with a symbol I recognized from the Facebook Group. A circle with eight curved spokes that looked like a sun and represented alchemy.

"There."

"Go." Lauren waved at the cafés. "I'll wait at one of them."

Inside the building I raced up two flights, my ballet flats slipping a little because the steps were made of smooth, worn marble. A glass door with the same symbol opened into a small waiting area that smelled of incense and vanilla. Heavy double doors twice the height of any at home blocked access to the rest of the Center.

A row of connected seats that looked like they came from an old auditorium sat across from a marble-topped desk. One door creaked open. A man with wire-rimmed glasses and a wide face emerged.

"Hello. I'm Quille Davis. I have an appointment with Nova Moon."

"Nova—oh. Yes." His English was clear with a trace of a Slavic accent. "We are—there is—slight change."

CHAPTER 40
CHANGE OF PLANS

THE MAN clasped and unclasped his hands as he spoke. "We are very sorry. But there is unexpected event. Nova cannot meet you. But do not worry. We have alchemist for you. At discounted rate because it is not Nova."

I gripped the strap on my shoulder bag. I had no idea how I'd get to talk to Nova if she didn't read for me. "Is there any chance I could talk to her just for a few minutes, to say Hello? I feel like I know her from the Facebook Group."

"No, I am sorry."

"Then could I see Denis Jednyak? That's who I tried to make an appointment with first."

The man blinked. "Denis Jednyak? No, I am sorry. We want to accommodate, but Denis is not here. He reads in evenings and has no openings."

"Could I speak with him for a few minutes before he begins? Or at the end of the evening?"

"Perhaps at end of evening. I will message him. But it will be late. He will not finish until perhaps twenty hundred hours."

That was eight hours from now. My body, still on Chicago time, already felt like it was night. But I couldn't leave without seeing Denis or Nova. "If you can arrange that, please do. I very much want to talk with him."

The man ushered me down a long hallway that was clean but smelled of old paper and dust. My alchemist, Andrea, waited in a small, warm, windowless room. She wore bright red lipstick that contrasted her plain white blouse. A metal desk fan whirred on her table next to a lamp with a mosaic glass shade.

I sat across from her. "I was supposed to see Nova Moon."

"Yes, yes, I am so sorry." Her voice wavered as she sifted through a deck of tarot cards. "Nova cannot—she is not well. I fill in today."

"Is it serious?"

"I—I cannot say. I do not know details." Andrea's whole face, from eyebrows to cheeks, to chin, drooped.

I guessed either Nova was very ill or she discovered I was investigating Randall's death and didn't want to answer my questions. Or let me talk to Denis.

I asked if she knew Denis Jednyak and explained that I hoped to talk with him.

"I work here only a year but yes. But we only meet once or twice. I work mornings. He is afternoon or evening. We are I think you might say ships that pass in night. I will do best I can for you." She set the cards aside. "You brought an object of sister's?"

"Yes." I fished out a tattered fuzzy pink bear with a white circle over its stomach that I'd found online. It wasn't a real Care Bear, a toy popular when the original Q.C. was about five years old. But it was close. From what I knew of the real Q.C., she was more apt to have a girl doll with shiny blond hair. But reality didn't matter here.

"You were close with sister?"

I was tempted to hand her the bear and say, "You're the psychic, you tell me." But I wasn't out to debunk anyone. Only to find out about Randall.

I passed the bear across the table. "I never met her."

"What do you wish to ask if I reach her?"

"What she was like as a child. And whether she's at peace."

Andrea rested her palm on the bear's head. "This was favorite toy of hers, or similar to favorite. Perhaps purchased later to remember her."

That was a great way to hedge her bets and avoid someone like me buying a random toy to try to fool her. I just nodded.

"I sense violent death." Andrea shut her eyes, cradling the bear. "I see no one. But I hear Q.C. says she is not troubled. Pain of death fades. Those she left may feel sadness, but she does not."

Andrea opened her eyes on the last sentence. My thoughts flashed to Marco. I hoped he felt peace if his spirit existed somewhere. I felt plenty of sadness for both of us.

"This was not only loss," Andrea said.

"What?"

"You lost another. In recent past."

I nodded and reminded myself of what Randall said in one of his videos. It's a good bet anyone past a certain age experienced the death of someone they care about. If not a person, a pet.

And my memory of Marco probably made me look sad, giving Andrea a clue.

"Parent? Husband?" she said.

"Friend." It was a chance to bring up Randall in a natural way. At the very least I might learn if everyone at the Center knew who he was. "Maybe you can contact him?"

She frowned and placed the bear face down on the table. "It is most easy to contact spirit through object. But I know you were wishing to see Nova or Denis, not me. I will try."

"I have something of his." I took out the Denis Jednyak tarot deck and handed it to her.

She froze. Tears filled her eyes. "These are...where did you get these?"

"Why do they upset you?"

Her face crumpled. She blinked away tears as she opened the box. "There is much sadness around them. I see now why you wanted to see Nova."

"You do?"

"She designed cards. You thought she might connect to your friend."

"No, I didn't know about that. I only knew that Denis wrote the book that the cards match."

"Yes, but Nova is artist."

Nova wasn't credited on the cards or the book. Maybe she did artwork for everything that related to the Center and didn't care about personal credit.

"I'm pretty sure my friend, the one who died, knew Denis and Nova," I said. "Did they ever mention him? Randall Petrov."

Andrea's expression didn't change. "No. He is Russian?"

"American. I think Denis and Randall met when Denis came to Chicago on a book tour. That's where I live. Nova might have been with him."

I knew Nova hadn't been at the bookstore. But Andrea might know if she went to Chicago at all.

Andrea shook her head. "Denis toured with book in States. Nova planned to join him but was not well even then and could not. Her heart—not strong."

Nova's photo in the Facebook Group suggested a woman in her fifties, but I had no idea how recent it was. She might be decades older.

"Nova missed the whole tour?" I said.

"Yes. She stayed in Prague. Sometimes she joined Denis using video."

Depending how far in advance Randall wrote the note on his calendar, perhaps he expected to meet both Nova and Denis the night of his death. I tried to learn more. But Andrea turned the conversation to my sister's and Randall's spirits. She wanted to make sure I got my money's worth. I went along, not wanting to raise suspicions she might share with someone before I talked to Denis or Nova.

Lauren waited under the Astronomical Clock, bags from Prada, Gucci, and the Swarovski store across from the Square over her arm. I shared what I'd learned. We decided to stake out the

Center and watch for Denis Jednyak starting around eight-forty-five that evening. I wanted to be there early in case he tried to avoid me.

To prepare, we explored all the streets behind and around the Center. There were two places Denis Jednyak might exit. Through the main door that faced the Astronomical Clock or through a narrow side street. Unfortunately, there was no spot where we could watch both exits. I didn't want to split up and leave either of us standing alone at night. But we couldn't both be in both places.

Lauren insisted I wait near the main entrance. "If he leaves that way, you already asked to talk to him, so it will seem natural that you're there. If he goes out the side and sees me, he doesn't know me. It won't set off any alarms and I can text you and follow him."

"That makes no sense. He won't recognize either of us."

"He probably looked you up online after you left your name. And he knows you're the woman who joined the Facebook Group recently. Beata said he's the administrator."

"True."

"And he wouldn't be much of a psychic—or emotional alchemist or whatever they call themselves—if he didn't research you when you joined."

I hated the idea of leaving her alone. But at least while most of the stores closed by eight p.m., several restaurants stayed open past ten. We found a spot with a view down the narrow street where Lauren could duck into a half-hidden café area if Denis spotted her. We checked her cell phone reception and mine. We agreed to text one another the instant we saw him and combine forces as soon as possible.

It didn't make me feel good. But it was the best we could do.

Plan in place, we left the Square and tried Denis's apartment again with no luck. At the hotel we studied all the photos and videos we could find online of Denis to improve our chances of recognizing him, especially at night. I emailed Julia the motion I had finished writing on the plane so she could look it over. Then Lauren and I changed into dark clothes and headed out for dinner.

Our hotel was a few blocks from the famous Charles Bridge, a medieval stone structure that arches over the Vltava River. Though Prague is a secular city, statues of saints line either side of the bridge. We crossed it to get to a riverbank restaurant called Kampa Park. We ate at a table against a stone balustrade overlooking the river. As we finished, the sun began to set, turning the river stunning shades of gold, mauve, and pink. I kept checking my phone, but no one from the Center called or texted to say Denis could meet me that evening.

In the Square again, I waited in the outdoor area of a bar near the clock. At ten after nine, my phone buzzed.

Someone heading my way

I had already paid the bill. I made my way out of the seating area. A few moments later, another text.

Denis just passed me

I ran for the side street.

CHAPTER 41
CATCHING ON

Denis emerged from the narrow lane into a wider street where it intersected the Square. I melted into darkness between gas lamps against the nearest building, hoping my black clothes and dark hair hid me from sight. Lauren stepped onto the street about a quarter block behind Denis. I recognized her silhouette. Tonight she wore low-heeled boots, not spike heels. Still not the best for walking or running. But Lauren became physically ill at the thought of athletic footwear anywhere other than a health club. I'd opted for black gym shoes.

I stepped into a pool of light from the closest gas lamp. "Denis Jednyak?"

He paused.

I put out my hand to shake. "I'm Quille C. Davis. I'm—"

Denis broke into a run. I bolted after him, grateful for my gym shoes. I hoped Lauren could catch up.

He darted through the Square, narrowly avoiding tourists gathered at the steps of a giant monument, then nearly being run over by a teenager on a scooter. I wove through the people, vehicles, and statues more easily. My training with a retired police academy instructor includes dodging through obstacle courses and following real people.

But Denis Jednyak knew Prague and I didn't. He turned down one street only seconds before me. I followed, but it was as if he'd disappeared. I ran to a cross street. Only a few people walked the sidewalks on either side. I saw no passageways between the designer stores and upscale restaurants. But that didn't mean there wasn't a way to duck into one of them and emerge on another street.

If my sense of direction was right, both this street and the one behind it led to the parklike area along the river. I backtracked and ran on a diagonal toward the Charles Bridge. It, too, is lit by gas lamps that deepen the pockets of darkness in between them. And it's full of tourists, statues, singers, and other performers. In other words, a perfect place for someone who knows it well to get lost. As I ran I dictated a text to Lauren telling her what I was doing.

I spotted Denis the equivalent of a block ahead of me. Luckily for me, he was tall and his pale skin and blond hair caught what little light there was. He glanced back more than once as he hurried along the riverbank, breathing hard. Though sweat coated my skin, I barely felt winded and mentally thanked my instructor for forcing me to practice both distance running and sprints.

I scanned the area for Lauren. She's shorter than me but blond and pale like Denis. I didn't see her. I hurried after Denis, not sure if I ought to confront him alone if I caught up to him. As he reached the bridge, someone touched my arm from behind. I whipped my head around. It was Lauren, her hair tucked under a dark cap she'd grabbed somewhere.

Denis's greater size gave him an advantage over us as he crossed the bridge. People moved out of his way, while Lauren and I had to veer around. My ankle twisted on uneven cobblestones as I tried to avoid two dancers dressed as a bride and groom. I nearly fell. Lauren grabbed my arm to steady me, then almost lost her balance when a face painter waved a brush in her face.

Near the end of the bridge, Denis disappeared from sight. I skidded to a stop several paces from where I last saw him. Lauren almost ran into me. A stone stairway led down to a harbor. The gas lamps below cast barely enough light to show four small boats bobbing there. I could just make out Denis's blond hair as he reached the bottom of the steps. Without thought, I raced after him. The river smell grew stronger as I descended.

The last step was shorter than I expected. My foot hit the ground with a thunk, shooting pain into that same ankle. "Denis, wait, please. I just want to talk."

He leapt onto a boat and crouched to fumble with the ropes.

I had no idea how far he could travel on a small boat like that, but I couldn't let him get away. With Nova who knows where, he was my last chance to get answers. Given the way he fled the second he saw me, he must know something about Randall's murder. Or be the killer.

The boat rocked side to side as I jumped on. Water sprayed my face. I pinwheeled my arms for balance. Light flashed on behind me, casting a bluish glow over me and the edge of the dock.

"I'm recording," Lauren yelled from the dock. "Video. Do not hurt her."

"Hurt her?" Denis stood and pointed at me. "Get off boat."

I raised my hands in a surrender gesture and inched backwards, sliding my feet so we didn't start tipping again. "Is it your boat?"

I didn't care, but if I got him talking about something that felt harmless he might relax.

"It is friend's boat. He is captain. You cannot be on."

"I'm not trying to scare you. I just want to talk. About Randall Petrov."

Denis wrapped his arms around himself, one hand still gripping a thick rope. "He is no one to me."

"But he opened your eyes. That's what you wrote in the tarot deck he bought from you. What did you mean?"

Lauren moved closer, panning her phone to take in the harbor and the bridge above us, then pointing the phone and its flashlight beam at Denis again.

"He bought nothing from me." Denis's free hand closed into a fist, as if he were about to assume a fighting stance.

"From the store, then. But you signed them. How did Randall open your eyes?"

Denis glared, his lips clamped into a straight line.

"Why are you angry? Did Randall hurt you? Betray you?"

Denis expelled a huge breath. "The fault is his, all of it. He made me doubt. Question."

Sweat dripped down my forehead into my eyes. I wiped it away. "Question the Center? Nova?"

"Everything. He made me question everything." Denis crumpled in the bow of the boat, making it sway. I bent one knee and then the other, shifting my weight to stay upright.

Lauren stepped closer to the edge of the dock. "You seriously killed him because he made you think?"

"Lauren!" I bit my lip in frustration. She was sleep-deprived, too, or she never would have spoken. In court or real life, it's easier to get answers step-by-step. Unlike in the old TV law shows like *Perry Mason*, people rarely burst out with a confession because of one dramatic surprise question.

This time, though, it got results.

Denis raised his head from his hands, his face whitening. He squinted at Lauren, blinded by the light from her phone. "Kill him? Randall?" He shook his head as if to clear it, then looked at me as he gripped the side of the boat. "He is dead? Randall is dead?"

If he was acting, he deserved an Academy Award.

"You didn't know?" I said.

"No. Randall was good man. He makes me angry but he is good. He showed me errors. Showed how I fool myself. How I fool others. No, not his fault. Hers."

"Nova's?" Lauren said.

At the same time I asked, "What wasn't his fault?"

"Nova." Denis Jednyak bent forward, curled into a sort of modified child's pose from yoga, resting his forehead on the boat's bottom.

I knelt near him. "What was Nova's fault?"

His body rocked and he made a keening sound.

"Denis?" I rested a hand on his shoulder. "What was Nova's fault?"

"All of it. No, not all. Not all. Because now she is dead. Good Lord in Heaven, she is dead. And that—that is my fault."

CHAPTER 42
CONFESSING

I SAT NEXT TO DENIS. Dampness seeped into the seat of my cargo pants. The fishy river smell filled my nose. I slid one hand into my side pocket where I kept an expandable baton just in case. I didn't think Denis was likely to attack me. But it wasn't as if I knew him. Or knew if he killed Randall. A weapon at my fingertips made me feel safer.

"Nova died?" I said. "Today?"

"This morning."

She must have been dead when I arrived for my reading. I supposed it didn't mean that much that I wasn't told. Any company might need time to sort out how to tell the public about its founder's death.

"How is it your fault?" I said.

Denis hiccupped. "I handle tech for Nova."

"You're the Facebook Group Administrator."

"No, no, no. Or yes. But not only group. For video alchemy sessions. A man joined last session. He talked about father who died. About beloved dog who died. Background check showed all was true."

"And the man turned out to be Randall Petrov," I said.

"What background check?" Lauren said.

"Always we do background check. Nova said to be sure people need help. That they are good people. One person at Center reviews socials before session. I check again during call. Send private message to Nova to confirm and add detail. She says it is to be safe."

"What happened in the session Randall joined?"

"He gave different name. Name he used in group. Name we background checked. But at end of session he say he is Randall Petrov. And somehow he controls session. I could not end it. I could not stop his recording. He send information to all in Chat. He showed everything Nova said came from spirits came from socials. And showed his false profile."

"You must have been angry."

"Angry and shocked." He looked from me to Lauren and again at me. "Who robs people of comfort and faith?"

Lauren sat on the edge of the dock, her phone still aimed toward us. I didn't know if Czech Republic law prohibited recording people. But at least she announced when she did it.

I asked if Nova tried to explain.

Denis, still on the boat floor, stared at his hands. "She say Randall's false story live so strong in his mind that she sensed and believed it. But that is not how Nova always say she works. She hears from spirits. Did unknown spirit pretend to be father of fake man? Did dog spirit pretend to be man's dog? It does not fit."

"And that's why you got in touch with Randall again?" I said.

"No. Nova told me call him because he wrote in Chat he will post video on Internet. I called and begged him wait until Nova and I visit Chicago and talk to him."

"He must have agreed." It explained why the video never surfaced, though not where Randall stored it.

"Yes. He promised to wait if I promise to watch his other videos. He gave me list."

"And you watched them," Lauren said. "You watched and they totally made you question your whole profession."

Denis's chest heaved as he drew a deep, ragged breath. "Yes. I doubted before. For years. But cast doubts aside. Until videos made it all clear. Sometimes I felt gratitude. I sent Randall the signed cards in a fit of gratitude. But more often I felt angry."

"At Randall?" I shifted, easing the pressure on my knees.

"At Randall. At myself. At Nova. And that's why I did it."

I glanced at Lauren. She nodded. She still had the recording going.

"You killed Randall out of anger?" I said.

Denis's head jerked up. He met my eyes. "Killed Randall? No. No, I killed Nova."

I forced myself not to jerk away from Denis. Head on his knees, he looked defeated, not angry. But I had no idea how he'd react if I showed alarm.

"I want to hear about what happened," I said quietly. "But let's get on land. We'll both feel better without the boat swaying under us."

I'd also feel better if Denis couldn't let go of the rope and send the boat drifting down the river with me in it. I'm a good swimmer and the Vltava isn't deep, but I had no desire to jump into it.

He nodded. We maneuvered to a wrought iron bench under a gas lamp. I sat a few feet from him. Lauren stood nearby, light still on, still recording. It was warm out, but Denis shivered. I took off the lightweight cardigan I wore and put it around his shoulders.

"I cannot believe Randall is dead." He rocked forward and back.

"Did you meet him when you came to Chicago?"

Denis shook his head so hard the bench trembled. "No. No. Nova was to see Randall. Ask him in person please not to publish video. But her heart is bad. Doctor wanted her not to go on book tour with me. And I could not meet Randall. I had to meet clients at bookstore in Cleveland Sunday afternoon."

I didn't remember that being on the book tour schedule online. But it could have been a private meeting. If Denis was telling the truth, PRG 830 in Randall's calendar likely referred to a meeting he never had with Nova.

Denis told me his Cleveland meeting went terribly. He broke down crying during it and couldn't finish. He cancelled the rest of the tour, returned to Prague, and meant to take time off to decide what to do with his life.

But the Center's manager informed Denis that Nova had a minor heart attack while Denis was away. She was cutting back to two or three readings a day at most. Denis needed to fill in.

As he worked more, it became clearer each day to Denis that he was doing exactly what Randall said. He used online information about each person, played off their reactions and answers to his open-ended questions, and conveyed comforting words. The clients filled in the blanks and believed.

"When you begin," he said, "Nova tells you everyone psychic. Everyone is emotional alchemist. You only need to get in touch with your psychic side. You start by imagining spirit client asks about. It is like street singer who throws few dollars into hat to start. Now other people think to donate, too."

Denis sounded like the type of person Randall called a Shut Eye. The inscription about opening Denis's eyes made sense now.

He continued, his eyes still cast down. "Nova says you think you imagine but spirit is real. You must listen to it. I try very hard to keep doing it. But once I know is only imagination, only tricks, I cannot. That is when I send cards to Randall."

"And then you did something to Nova?"

As ill as the woman apparently was, she might have had a fatal heart attack and Denis felt guilty, thinking he caused it.

He ran his hand through his hair at the front. "First I try to call Randall for advice but he never returns call. So I make plan. I am ready to carry it out. Then I hear someone from Chicago called to talk to me. I think maybe Randall. Maybe he will help decide what to do with my life now. But no. It is woman."

I shifted further from him, shivering despite the warm air. I'd never forgive myself if I'd prompted him to harm Nova. But no. He said he had a plan before I called.

Lauren crept closer and did something on the screen of her phone. "What was the plan?" she said.

"My mother at end of life had many pills for pain. She died of cancer. Very hard at end. I have all her things."

"How long ago did she die?" I said.

"Six months. Six months and I never hear her spirit."

Denis's head still hung forward, so I didn't think he saw Lauren as she mimed telephoning someone. Then she switched hands and clicked buttons on the phone while keeping the light trained on him.

"What did you do with the pills?" I asked.

"I grind pills. I go to Center early. A death there will make news. All will be exposed. But Nova was in office. She cannot sleep and wants to return to regular work. I tell her I came for quiet contemplation, offer to make herb tea. We drank tea together when she trained me. It is very bitter always. I pour ground pills into my cup. Bring tea to her office. Will be perfect. I will die in front of her. She will feel remorse. But at last moment, I give her my cup. With the pills. She drinks. She slumps on desk. Breathing stops. I run. Return at usual time. They tell me she is dead."

CHAPTER 43
999

Lauren called 999, the emergency number in Europe. She ran to the top of the stairs to watch for the police. I stayed with Denis, holding her phone, and asked him again about Randall.

He insisted he never met Randall in person and claimed he was the only employee of the Center in Chicago at all this summer. Denis knew at the time the identities of the people on the video conference Randall hijacked. But he didn't remember them off the top of his head. The Center had a list. I doubted anyone there would give it to me.

The police reached us and pulled me aside. The officer who spoke the best English asked me what happened. I told him briefly.

At the police station, Lauren and I were separated and questioned. Waiting for my turn was unnerving. The woman who told me when to go into the interview room spoke English to me. But all around me people spoke in Czech, which I didn't understand. I didn't know if they found me suspicious. The officer who questioned me was polite but cool and revealed nothing to me. I couldn't tell if he believed anything I said.

The police confiscated Lauren's phone but eventually returned it after, I assumed, checking for other videos. While I waited, I searched my phone and learned that at least we probably weren't in trouble for making the video of Denis, though I wasn't clear on whether it could be used against him. I saw no news about Nova's death.

Hours later, we were released. Lauren and I compared notes when we got to our hotel room. She felt as uncomfortable as I did and had no idea what the police thought of us. But we were free.

Both exhausted, we fell into the King-sized bed and slept until mid-morning the next day.

I awoke before Lauren. Wanting to feel like I accomplished something, I made the few changes Julia requested to my motion to dismiss Oscar's case. The Wi-Fi at the hotel worked well, so I submitted it electronically to the court. Then I emailed Julia about the trip so far. I kept backspacing and rewording what I wrote, trying to be honest about how little progress we made on Randall's murder while offering some hope.

Then I made a few calls. At the third Cleveland spiritual book-store I tried, an employee confirmed that Denis was there until after seven in the evening the Sunday of Randall's death. It takes over five hours to get to Chicago from Cleveland by car. A flight is much faster. But by the time you add in travel time to and from the airports, Denis couldn't have gotten to Randall's until after midnight. He wasn't the killer.

For breakfast, Lauren and I got a table on the hotel patio with a view overlooking the Vltava River. I ordered off the menu.

While I scoured my phone for news of Nova's death, Lauren meandered through the buffet inside the restaurant. There was no news about Nova yet. From what I could tell based on Czech Republic government sites, with her age and heart problems if Denis hadn't confessed no one would have done an autopsy. The authorities would have assumed death by natural causes.

Lauren set down a plate brimming with bread, sausage, cheese, and salmon. "So who's left?"

"As suspects? Nova if she flew to the States. But Denis is out. Both of them are, if we believe Denis."

"Who was spilling his guts on everything else, so it seriously seems like he told the truth."

"Probably." I thanked the server as she set a bowl of oatmeal, a plate of fruit, and a second bowl, this one filled with thick-sliced bacon, in front of me. "Which leaves me with Randall's brother, Max. Oscar. AngryHusband. And anyone else who was on that video session and doesn't want their name out there."

Lauren spread soft cheese on a chunk of black bread. "Or, like AngryHusband, is mad that Randall shattered all their hopes."

We talked through everywhere Randall might have saved the video. I'd been through all the cloud accounts and computer files I could find and combed through every inch of Randall's office and the new loft. Julia had gone through their home. Randall might have sent the video somewhere on a thumb drive to get the faces and names blurred out. But if he had, the vendor ought to have sent it back by now.

A small, colorful bird hopped onto the table and headed straight for my bowl of bacon.

Lauren shooed it away. "You know what? I think Heather saw that ring Joe bought and her jealousy totally kicked in."

It took me a second to follow the topic switch. Then I nodded. "Probably. She said it confirmed everything she felt in her gut about Joe's feelings for me. Then he never called her after she turned down his proposal."

"And she figured she must be right. Because why else wouldn't he beg her to come back?"

The bird tried again. This time I let it nibble on the bacon. I was done with it.

"It doesn't seem to have crossed her mind that he realized he didn't love her, but it had nothing to do with me."

"That totally gets my vote. And not just because that's the answer I want." Lauren drained the last of her espresso and sighed. "But none of this answers my real question. Does Joe have a commitment problem? Late forties, never married or engaged, proposed only once in his life, under duress."

"Heather says she didn't push him."

"She probably claims she isn't the jealous type, too."

"She does."

We spent the next day and a half sightseeing, with a few breaks for me to answer law firm emails. We visited the castle we saw from the rooftop restaurant. I thought it might well be the model for any number of Disney castles, at least from the outside.

The trip home felt longer, though the La Première lounge in Paris was larger and lovelier than the one in New York. The square footage had to be more than my parents' entire rambling three-story home.

This time I got the facial, which ended with me lying on my back in a darkened room with nature sounds playing. Some sort of cool, moisturizing gel, massaged in by the technician, seeped into my skin. That and the hot towel around my neck left me so relaxed I drifted to sleep. I awoke to the room gradually becoming lighter and the bird songs louder. As Lauren promised, the technician redid my makeup, using a foundation that perfectly matched my olive skin. It, too, was deeply moisturizing.

There didn't seem to be a charge, but I felt sure I ought to tip. Grateful I'd brought cash, I gave her thirty dollars. I slept most of the way home.

At home, after throwing my clothes into the mini-washer in my condo, I called Max to ask if Randall might have stored anything on Petrov's Pizza servers.

"No. He couldn't access the company's network," Max said.

"Did he ever tell you where he stored vital data?"

"Sorry, but no."

Max did say he knew Randall used thumb drives sometimes because for a while he had one on his keyring. That made sense to me. In his sixties, Randall would have grown up using external storage devices. I texted Julia. But she said there wasn't a drive on Randall's keyring now. And I hadn't found any in his office.

Much as I didn't want to deal with Oscar in person until I saw him in court I needed to ask other people at Randall's office if they knew where Randall might have kept a thumb drive.

CHAPTER 44
JUDGMENT

After catching up on other work at my office, I met Detective
Sergeant Beckwell at Café des Livres. We sat outside, Beckwell
with his back to the building. He likes to keep an eye on the
street and on anyone biking or walking by, a habit I'd picked up
as well.

He listened to my story about Denis Jednyak and Nova Moon
and agreed to see if he could verify that Nova hadn't been in
Chicago. So far he had no luck getting any video of the attack
on me on the L platform.

Beckwell agreed with my questions about the strength of Max's
and Oscar's alibis for Randall's murder. Max's ex-wife vouched
for him but might be biased toward him. And Oscar's neighbor, the one who saw him bike riding through the neighborhood and then sitting on his deck the evening of Randall's
death, might be mistaken about the date. Police didn't talk to
him until several days after Randall's death. Plus, earlier in the
year Oscar got the neighbor's son's DUI bargained down to
reckless driving so that he kept his driver's license. The
neighbor might be inclined to think well of him because of
that.

"It still sounds like your best bet is to find that video." Beckwell drank the last of his iced coffee. "Though if someone who attended the session killed Randall, they might already have it. Assuming Randall carried it with him."

That had occurred to me, too. But surely Randall kept more than one copy. With his dedication to exposing fraud, I couldn't see him taking the chance of losing that type of proof. If only I could find it.

Oscar's door was shut, so I asked the other two attorneys in the suite about places Randall might have kept external storage devices. They had no idea. Neither did Flora, who sat in front of her computer, typing.

"What about that padlocked cabinet?" I waved toward a tall, two-door gray metal cabinet in the hall just outside the storage room.

Flora shook her head. "No way. That holds Oscar's supplies. He's paranoid about them being stolen. Back when he had a paralegal, she wasn't allowed to open it. She had to requisition supplies from him."

"Requisition them?"

"Oh, yeah. Like if she wanted a new pen, she had to give him the one that ran out first so he could see it was used up, not that she stole or lost it."

"Were these expensive pens?"

"Cheap Bics. He got a bunch in bulk to save money. But the joke was on him. A year ago he discovered they all ran dry from sitting so long."

"So that cabinet hardly ever gets opened."

"Hardly ever except by Oscar."

The more I thought about it, the more that sounded like the perfect spot for Randall to hide a thumb drive. Julia had told me he felt strongly about the privacy of the people psychics preyed on. That's why he never shared the full videos, only the portions involving him, and blurred all the faces other than the psychic's. If anyone broke into Randall's office or computer they wouldn't find the video recording. What better place to hide something than in a cabinet he officially didn't have access to.

A magician who used sleight of hand, I had no doubt Randall could slip something into the cabinet when Oscar opened it. Or pick the padlock to get into it. I learned to pick locks when I looked into Marco's death. With the right tools and some practice, it's not that hard. And there was the simpler option. Randall might have convinced Oscar to let him store a thumb drive in there.

I sighed. This meant the fun of talking to Oscar again. I could break into the cabinet. I doubted I'd get disbarred if I were caught. But if Oscar reported me to the ARDC I'd be embarrassed, and I might have to answer a lot of questions.

I headed for Oscar's office. He stepped out before I reached his door.

"Your motion," he said. "We can argue it tomorrow."

That surprised me. In Cook County, when a motion is filed, a court date is scheduled as well. But no one argues on that date. Instead, the court clerk gives both parties an order that sets a date for the other side to submit a written response brief, a date for the moving attorney to file a reply to the response, then a hearing date far enough down the road so the judge can read everything before the attorneys argue in person. At least in theory that's how it works. Some judges never read the written briefs.

"But you haven't filed a response," I said.

Oscar shrugged. "Don't need one. There's a question of fact."

"That's not the issue."

Oscar was talking about a different type of motion, one where a party tells the court that everyone agrees on all key facts. If that's true, there's no need for a jury. The judge decides the case. But if there is a question about which key fact is true, the judge has to deny the motion.

I was trying to get rid of the case for a different reason. I argued that even if everything Oscar claimed happened really occurred, it didn't matter. Oscar still couldn't win, so the whole case should be thrown out.

Oscar frowned. "You know what I mean."

"I really don't," I said.

"As soon as I tell the judge that Randall promised me he'd stay for the full seven years you'll lose."

People think all attorneys like to argue. And some lawyers go into law because they enjoy that. But a lot of us like arguing to a judge or jury based on the ins and outs of the law but dislike arguing with anyone else. I'm one of those. I'd rather people get along. And most of the time, maybe all of the time, there's no point arguing with your opponent when a judge will still need to decide the issue.

But Oscar was so off base I couldn't stop myself. "Even if that were true, it doesn't matter what Randall said. Because of the Frauds Act. And the Dead Man's Act. Did you read my motion?"

Oscar gestured toward his office. "I'll read it in the morning."

I'd met attorneys like Oscar before, ones who are sure they're so good in the courtroom it doesn't matter how convincing a written brief is or what the law says. Sometimes they're right.

"If you really want to argue tomorrow," I said, "we need to ask the clerk if the judge has time."

"No we don't." Oscar crossed his arms over his chest. "It's the motion date. That's what we're there for."

That might be true in criminal court, where Oscar usually practiced, but not in civil. One of many reasons getting a lawyer who knows the specific practice area matters.

"No—it's—never mind. I'll call the clerk. But I have a question about Randall."

"Ask me tomorrow. I've got a meeting." Oscar clicked a button on his phone, put it to his ear, and strode out of the suite.

I waited outside the courtroom for Oscar, who rushed in at the last minute. I put a hand on his arm. "Before we go in, did Randall by any chance store anything in your supply cabinet?"

"What?"

"I'm looking for an external hard drive or thumb drive he might have had."

"There's nothing like that there."

"Could we go back to your office after this and check? It's important."

Oscar yanked open the courtroom door. "Let's get this over with. You got a bad draw, you know. Judge Hiller lets everything go forward."

Cases are randomly assigned to judges in the Daley Center. Our judge, though he rarely threw cases out, handled a lot of real estate litigation when he practiced law. That was good for me. I had no doubt he already knew all the law I explained in my motion. He had a reputation, too, for carefully reading the written briefs.

When we stepped up in front of the bench and introduced ourselves, the judge clicked a few keys on his computer.

"I read Defendant's motion." He looked at Oscar. "You're sure you don't wish to file a response, Counsel?"

"Yes, Your Honor," Oscar said. "I'm ready to argue."

The judge nodded. "Go ahead. Why shouldn't I dismiss your case?"

Oscar's chin lifted. "I'm entitled to a trial."

"Has the estate stopped paying rent?"

"Not yet, Your Honor. But they plan to next month," Oscar said.

"Is there some document that's not attached to the Complaint?"

"No, Your Honor. But Randall Petrov knew all about the lease I attached to the Complaint. He promised to abide by it."

The judge glanced at his screen, then at Oscar again. "But you don't allege he promised in a signed writing, as defense counsel points out. All you've alleged is a month-to-month tenancy. The estate can end it on thirty days written notice."

"Your Honor, at trial I would testify under oath that Mr. Petrov promised to remain the full length of that lease."

"I've explained why that doesn't matter, and I won't go into it again. And, for future reference, though there isn't a future for this case, you could never testify to that. The Dead Man's Act bars you."

"I've never heard of such a thing, Your Honor. You can't keep me from testifying."

My jaw dropped. The Illinois Dead Man's Act says a party to a case can't testify to what someone who died said if the testimony benefits the party, as there's no way for the deceased to respond. The law was passed for cases just like this one. It applies in criminal cases, too. I couldn't believe Oscar didn't know about it. Then again, it was unlikely to come up in traffic tickets unless a police officer died, in which case the ticket would probably be dropped.

"I can't," the judge said. "But your trial judge could. If your case got that far. But it won't."

It was almost painful to watch Oscar sputter, stumble, and go red in the face as the judge went on to make all the points I made in writing.

In the end, the judge ruled for me without my saying anything beyond my name. With a more skilled opponent I would have felt proud to win without uttering a word. But this just felt uncomfortable. I'm not a sports person, but I supposed it was how players on a winning team might feel if they won because all of the other side's best players were out due to injury. Still a win, but it doesn't speak to your own skills.

The judge stated that he'd issue a written opinion later that day. Oscar, still red-faced, stalked out before the judge finished talking. That's unheard of for a lawyer to do. He could be held in contempt for that and have to pay a fine or spend time in jail. But Judge Hiller was too kind a person for that.

Not at all to my surprise, Oscar didn't answer the phone when I called. I left a voicemail asking again about his supply cabinet but didn't count on getting an answer.

Julia was thrilled about the case being thrown out and frustrated that there were still no answers about Randall, though she didn't seem to blame me. But I paced my office at the end of the day, wracking my brain for anything else I could do other than break into the cabinet.

But the video was my last hope. I called Lauren, half-hoping she'd talk me out of it. Instead, she offered to help.

CHAPTER 45
THE BREAK IN

IN A QUICK CALL to Flora I learned that the office suite emptied by five-thirty at the latest. Oscar left a bit earlier, though sometimes he forgot things and returned. I'd promised Beckwell to take no unnecessary chances. The police academy instructor I worked with, too, emphasized that point. Most of what he covered with me was spotting danger, avoiding danger, and escaping danger because there was little chance I could win a physical fight with anyone. That was also why I needed more than Lauren to do this right.

I texted Dylan.

Want to put your wrestling skills to use again—maybe? In about an hour?

I take it you're not considering joining a team.

I'm searching an office suite. Could be dangerous. More likely boring.

Dinner after?

Yes. I'm buying for you and Lauren. She's my other back up.

Good choice. She looks deceptively sweet but I wouldn't want to cross her.

Lauren and I entered the Monadnock Building through the south entrance about quarter to six. Lauren headed for the restaurant in the center of the building. From a table there she could see both elevator banks and warn me if Oscar returned no matter what entrance he used.

"Then I'll follow him and try to distract him." She wore loafers rather than heels, showing she'd learned from our time in Prague.

"Distract him how?"

"I'll pretend I'm a real estate agent."

"You are a real estate agent."

"And say I might have a new tenant for him."

"Great."

Oscar might wonder about a real estate agent hanging about after hours hoping to buttonhole tenants. But if it slowed him down, that's all that mattered.

Dylan, in dark khakis, gym shoes, and a fitted T-shirt, appeared a few moments later. Happily, the office suite was deserted. Oscar's office door was shut but not locked. He must not keep any valuable office supplies like Bic pens in there. I flicked on the overhead light and glanced around. It looked different but I couldn't place what was missing or changed.

"Let's start in here." I opened his credenza. "I can explain being in the storage room or the supply cabinet, but not why we're going through his things."

Dylan slid a desk drawer open. "What are we looking for?"

"Zip drives, thumb drives, any kind of external storage device. In case Randall just gave one to Oscar for safekeeping." It seemed unlikely but I didn't want to leave without checking. "And as long as we're at it, anything that suggests Oscar was the one who attacked me on the L platform. Or that just seems like it doesn't belong."

"You realize I've got no idea what belongs in a traffic attorney's office."

I shot him a look and he quirked an eyebrow. "Kidding. I'll look for the one thing that's not like the others."

We found no data storage drives. No red sweatshirt or black face mask either—the clothes the attacker wore. Dylan was thorough but fast, which I appreciated. I didn't want the night janitorial service staff to find us rifling through things. Where I rented space, they started around six.

The storage room's door swung out into the suite hallway. I'd gone through the kitchen area on one end of it and the large file cabinets on the other during the first week of the investigation. But Oscar might have stored something since then. And I hadn't been thinking about external drives.

I asked Dylan to search that room and took out a tension wrench. I placed it at the bottom of the padlock's keyhole and pressed lightly.

"Uh, Quille?"

"Yeah?"

My phone buzzed with a text from Lauren.

Oscar just joined a woman at a corner table. Came from restroom.

I called out to Dylan to let him know and texted back.

Let me know if he heads for our elevator bank.

Lauren sent a thumbs up.

I put my lock picking tools in my back pocket and stepped into the storage room. Dylan pointed at an open metal file drawer. Paper files filled one side. A black gym bag sat in the other, unzipped. Inside was a bright red sweatshirt and a black cloth mask. That's when it hit me. A black gym bag had been sitting on the desk the day I snuck a look at Oscar's calendar.

"I take it that wasn't here the first time you checked out this room?" Dylan said.

"Nope. But a lot of people might have a red sweatshirt and a black mask. The back of the guy's sweatshirt on the L platform had a white stripe across it."

"We probably shouldn't touch it, right? We don't want to add our fingerprints or DNA," Dylan said.

I took a few photos. Dylan found some plastic salad tongs in the kitchen drawer. I recorded it on video as he used them to manipulate the sweatshirt. There was a white stripe on the back.

"He's got to be the one," Dylan said.

"Who attacked me, yes. I don't know if that makes him Randall's killer. He might just have been mad about my defense of the estate."

"He knows Julia could just hire another lawyer, right?"

"With this guy? I'm not sure. Let's see if we find anything else."

I texted the video to Beckwell, then called him and got his voicemail. He returned the call a few minutes after I opened the supply cabinet. I told him why we were looking through the storage room. I skipped over our search of Oscar's office and my use of lock picking tools.

The phone in my back pocket, microphone side sticking out, I used both hands to search the shelves. No storage devices were visible. But Randall might have taped one on the underside of a shelf, where Oscar wouldn't see it.

"You need to leave," Beckwell said. "If he attacked you in public, what will he do if he finds you in his office?"

"I'm just here going through Randall's things. Can you get a search warrant based on what I sent you?" I felt underneath each shelf, but found only stickiness and dust.

"Maybe. But I can't promise."

"Then we'll keep searching. I still need to find that video."

I studied the open cabinet. If I were Randall, where would I hide a storage device? It needed to be easy to find later but hidden so no one grabbed it by mistake.

"Then I'm staying on the line," Beckwell said.

My eyes ran over all the supplies. Stacks of legal pads, boxes of pens, toner cartridges, printer paper. A heavy black two-hole punch. When court documents were filed on paper and in person, it would have been used to punch holes at the top center of thick documents. Metal clips were threaded through and separate fasteners clamped over them. Most people just used the clips and skipped the fasteners when making copies for themselves. Which meant a lot of offices had extra fasteners.

Sure enough, four boxes of fasteners, likely long forgotten, sat next to the punch. The thumb drive was in the second box from the bottom.

As I grabbed it, Dylan appeared. "Quille. She said you didn't answer." He showed me a text from Lauren saying Oscar got in an elevator.

"Putting you on mute," I said to Beckwell. "Oscar's on the way. Listen close—maybe I can get him to say something incriminating." I hit the button, cutting off Beckwell's protests. I returned the phone to my back pocket.

"She can't get in the elevator," Dylan said. "Security."

Unlike my building, the Monadnock must require a key card to operate the elevators after six. Which meant Oscar could use the elevator but Lauren would have to climb eleven flights of stairs.

Footsteps sounded outside the suite.

CHAPTER 46
LIVES AT STAKE

Dylan ducked into Oscar's open office. I put the thumb drive in the front pocket of my jeans and shut the supply cabinet doors. Just as I grabbed the padlock from the printer table to replace it, Oscar entered.

He froze when he saw me. "What are you doing here?"

"Looking for that thumb drive I told you about."

Oscar advanced toward me. "What's that in your hand?"

"Your padlock. I got it open so I could check the cabinet."

His hand shot out. "Give it."

I jerked away involuntarily and banged my elbow on the edge of the cabinet door, sending a tingling jolt of pain down my arm. I stifled a squeal and gave him the padlock.

Over Oscar's shoulder I saw Dylan in the office, silhouetted in the glow of the monitor. He nodded toward the storage room as the same thought occurred to me. Oscar must have put the gym bag inside the file cabinet drawer, and possibly other evidence, too. I might be able to use that to get him to say something rash.

Oscar put the padlock in an outer pocket of his oversized sport jacket, shifting something else aside to make room for it. Given his earlier attack on me, and that he could be Randall's killer, he might be carrying a weapon.

I glanced sideways and back toward the storage room doorway.

Oscar frowned, keeping his hand in his pocket. "What're you looking at?"

"I found evidence. Including your gym bag. Red sweatshirt, white stripe, black mask."

"Anyone could wear an outfit like that," Oscar said.

I sucked in a breath. If those were just Oscar's workout clothes he would have been puzzled by why I cared.

"True," I said, hoping Beckwell was still listening and that I could get Oscar to make a clear admission. "Unless my DNA's on there from when you attacked me."

"I never touched you."

I worked to control my trembling hands. "You did. When I ducked on the L platform your knee banged my forehead."

Oscar shook his head. "So what? Your DNA could've gotten on there when you found the gym bag."

I gritted my teeth. He hadn't said anything a good lawyer couldn't explain away.

"Good point," I said. "And you didn't really hurt me. How about this? I'll leave now. You can take the gym bag out of the cabinet and do what you want with the clothes. And that'll be the end of it. I won't tell anyone you attacked me."

"Not so fast." Oscar nodded toward the supply cabinet. "What were you looking for?"

"A thumb drive. Like I told you. Of Randall's."

It occurred to me now that the drive could be Oscar's. His next words nixed that idea, though.

He advanced toward me. "I don't care if it's Randall's. If it's in my cabinet, I have a right to know what's on it." As he moved nearer, his jacket swayed and I saw the outline of the object in its pocket. Probably not a gun. Possibly a knife.

I had my expandable baton in my back pocket. But if I reached for it now, he'd likely go for his weapon. I still hoped to get out of this without violence. "I'm hoping it has a recording of a video where Randall exposed a psychic."

Oscar snorted. "Sure. Because he did that all the time. What evidence are you really looking for?"

Oscar truly knew nothing about Randall. No wonder he thought Flora, who cared enough to get to know people, was a busybody.

I felt more and more that the video didn't matter. Oscar must have killed Randall and be worried there was something incriminating in the cabinet. The question was whether I could get him to admit it. And whether Dylan and I would survive. Beckwell was on the phone and Lauren on the way. But if Oscar, who was big and had a temper, stabbed one or both of us to death before anyone reached us, it was small comfort that he'd go to prison for it.

"I found the thumb drive already. It's all I wanted. But you can have it. I'm going to reach into my front jeans pocket for it and put it there." I pointed to the printer table near the storage room doorway, then inched my fingers into my pocket.

"What else did you find?" Oscar said.

"Just your supplies," I said. "What else could be there? You're the only one with a key, right? I had to break in."

Oscar eyed me for a moment, then nodded.

"Randall didn't have a key?"

"Right."

My strategy, which I use in cross-examinations, was to try to get him saying Yes to unimportant questions. Sometimes that makes a witness more apt to say Yes to incriminating questions, especially small ones that don't seem to matter much by themselves.

The flaw in my logic chain was that Randall, a magician, no doubt knew how to pick a lock. It must be how he put the thumb drive in there in the first place. But Oscar didn't know much about Randall's skills.

I forced myself to keep my face blank. "And if there was any evidence showing you killed Randall in there, you would have seen it by now, correct? When you went in to get supplies?"

"You could have planted something tonight that incriminates me," Oscar said.

"Check the cabinet yourself." I inched sideways, away from the cabinet and closer to the storage room. My goal was to get Oscar in line with the doorway. "But if I had proof you killed Randall, I'd give it to my client or the police, not plant it, wouldn't I? Because then you'd have a chance to take it out of the cabinet?"

Lines formed between Oscar's eyebrows. "Maybe you're not that smart."

Behind Oscar, in the darkened office, Dylan inched forward.

His pale skin gleamed in the spillover light from the storage room.

"But you think I'm smart enough to prove you killed Randall?"

"You could have videoed something."

Sweat sprang up all along my neck and spine. His words made it sound like he killed Randall. But I wanted it to be too clear to deny later. "Like you jogging on the 606 the night of Randall's death?"

Oscar snarled. "I knew it." He pulled a switchblade from his inner jacket pocket. It snicked and the blade shot out.

I raised both hands in a surrender gesture. "Don't hurt me. I'll give it to you."

"What?"

"The video. It's on another drive. I put it in your gym bag. I was going to take it all to the police. It shows everything—you and Randall arguing, you getting angry, him going over the railing."

If Oscar really thought about it, my claim made zero sense. If I had a video, or simply witnessed the crime, I would have told the police that night and he would have been arrested. And the video would be in the cloud or on my phone, not on an external drive. But, as I'd learned in the course of the lawsuit, logic wasn't Oscar's strong suit. And his emotions were running high, never a great time for careful thought.

Oscar jerked his head toward the storage room, still pointing the knife at me. "If you put it in there, why were you out here?"

I shifted my weight to my right foot so I could pivot easily. "Looking for more proof. I don't try criminal cases. I didn't know if it would be enough."

I'm not above playing dumb if my life's at stake.

Oscar's eyes widened. "It won't. Not without your testimony. And what's that law you like so much? The Dead Man's Act. You'll be dead, so you won't be able to testify."

He lunged. I twisted sideways, away from him and toward the supply cabinet. My left shoulder slammed into it. I howled in pain. But I got behind Oscar, grabbed my baton, and hit the button to make it full length. I smacked Oscar on the back of the head. He bent over and stumbled forward. At the same moment, Dylan barreled out of the office. Together we shoved Oscar all the way through the doorway and into the storage room. We slammed the door. The two of us braced ourselves with our backs against it.

I wiggled the phone out of my jeans pocket and shouted into it. "Did you hear that? Did you hear it?"

"All of it," Beckwell said. "Police will be there any minute."

The door shuddered as Oscar slammed into it over and over. Each time it shook my whole body and sent jolts of pain through my shoulder.

What felt like hours later, the suite door flung open.

CHAPTER 47
TOWARD HAPPINESS

THE PROSECUTOR TOLD Julia that Oscar's words alone, heard by Dylan, Beckwell, and me, might be enough to convict him. While normally out of court statements are hearsay and can't be admitted at trial, these qualified as an admission by a party against his own interests. That meant a jury would likely get to hear them.

Plus there was other evidence. Oscar's switchblade had Randall's DNA on it. Oscar must never have washed it, just wiped the blood away. A video from a store half a mile from where Randall's body was found showed someone with Oscar's build wearing black pants, a black mask, and a red sweatshirt with a white stripe on the back jogging down the street around the time of Randall's death.

Julia filled me in on everything when she and I both took a day off. We ate a late lunch on the patio of Mon Ami Gabi, a French restaurant across from Lincoln Park Zoo. The weather was warm but the tables were shaded. Our iced grapefruit and vodka spritzers kept us cool, too. And tasted wonderful with our shrimp cocktail appetizer.

"What about the neighbor who saw Oscar jogging the night of Randall's death?" I said.

Julia finished her second shrimp and pushed aside her plate. "Oscar was smart in one way. The neighbor was washing his car the Tuesday evening after Randall was found. Oscar stopped and said Hello, acting very shaky. He told the neighbor an old friend was found dead two nights ago. And he added something about how there he was, jogging through the neighborhood Sunday night with no idea anything was wrong, and his friend was dead."

The prosecutor told Julia that by the time the police questioned the neighbor, the idea of seeing Oscar Sunday night was stuck in his head. But on follow up, he agreed it could have been Friday, Saturday, or Monday. Oscar's cellphone records helped build a case against him, too. His phone showed him on or near the 606 where Randall was killed that night.

Then there was Oscar's confession. True to form, Oscar never asked for a lawyer, insisting on representing himself. At the police station, the prosecutor repeated my claim that I recorded the crime. Rather than deny what he did, Oscar stressed that he never meant to kill Randall. He stabbed him in the spur of the moment when Randall refused to change his mind about moving out of the office.

A criminal defense attorney who handled felonies would have told Oscar that the intent to kill isn't required for first degree murder. Only the intent to commit an act the defendant knows creates a strong chance of death or great bodily harm. And Oscar failed to say he was in fear for his life or acted as he did because Randall provoked him. If he proved either, it could lower the charge to second degree murder, leading to a lot less time in prison. The prosecutor told us that was why she offered Oscar seventeen years total rather than thirty. But she added that if he had retained an experienced lawyer, she probably would have gone lower. As it was, she felt fairly sure he'd have been convicted if he went to trial.

Julia's and my lunch stretched to two hours as we both unwound. She told me she still struggled to get out of bed many days. But knowing Randall's killer had been found helped her focus some energy on other things. One of those things was, with Max's and Ivan's help, finding a way to bring magic to sick kids once again.

Colleen Cahill, her family members, and her friends were working out plea deals that included paying reparations and some prison time. Magic Works dissolved. But the volunteers were excited about being part of the new non-profit.

When it became clear Oscar was certain to spend a long time in prison, Joe suggested he, Lauren, and I celebrate by going to Geja's. It's a fondue restaurant in the Lincoln Park neighborhood of Chicago that opened in 1965. It's a wonderful place to go in wintertime, as it's partly underground and lit with sparkling lights everywhere. The flames and the fondue oil keep it warm, and a guitarist plays classical and flamenco music.

But it turned out summer was a good time to be there, too, for those who reserve one of the outdoor tables. There are only six, and they're arranged in a row about six steps below street level on a cobblestone patio.

When Joe messaged to float the idea and a few dates, I took my phone out on my deck and called Dylan. We hadn't seen each other since trapping Oscar, though we exchanged plenty of texts. A few verged on flirty. But he seemed to understand without my saying it that I wasn't ready to date anyone so soon after Ty.

After making sure he liked both cheese and chocolate—my favorite parts of the classic dinners—I told him about the Geja's evening. "Any chance you'd be my sort of non-date date for a dinner there with Lauren and Joe?"

"You want to go on a double date before we ever date? And not call it a date?"

I rested my elbows on the table behind me and looked up at the night sky, feeling the warm air on my face. "That's about it."

"You drive a hard bargain, but I can't resist."

The dates Joe suggested worked for Dylan. He insisted he'd pick me up—Lauren as well if she and I were going together— though I offered to meet him there.

"Not complaining, but why include me?" he said. "Joe and Lauren aren't one of those couples who can only hang out with other couples are they? Is that why Lauren invited me to that charity ball?"

"No, that was purely mercenary on her part. And a bit of meddling. It's just been a little awkward for me with them lately. Lauren's upset at Joe over something. But she keeps saying she's not ready to talk to him about it yet."

"Lauren? She doesn't strike me as holding back when she's got something to say."

"She doesn't. Usually. I keep asking why she's not just speaking her mind. But the main reason I want you to come is you helped stop Oscar, and I want you to share our celebration. It's become a tradition when I end an investigation."

"If I'm especially charming can we call it a date?"

I laughed. "Do your best."

I heard news from Beata in Prague a few days before the Geja's dinner. An autopsy was done on Nova Moon's body because Denis admitted to drugging her. But it turned out she died of a heart attack before the pills did very much. That likely would lighten his sentence significantly, though I was sure he wished he had been a lot less chatty with me.

A newspaper reporter from Atlanta contacted me asking about Nova. She had researched Nellie Havel years ago but never made the connection Randall did between Nellie and Nova. Julia and I talked to her together. Julia hoped the reporter's exposé might convince more people to be wary of psychics and mediums, whatever they called themselves.

When Julia's payment for my final bill came through it included an extra five hundred dollars as a bonus for all the hard work. When I called to thank her, she admitted she hoped it would entice me to handle the appeal she felt sure Oscar meant to file, from prison if necessary, in his civil case against the estate.

Randall's father, Ivan, sent me a note.

Because of you, my son's killer will be behind bars. Thank you.

It wasn't much. But I suspected that was as effusive as Ivan got.

I called my own father after getting Ivan's email. We didn't talk about the distance between us since the Q.C. investigation or rehash anything I learned about him during it. We just slid into a conversation about his plans to expand his music store and my efforts to solve Randall's murder. My dad might not always have been the best husband or the ideal father, but he was still my dad. And everything I heard about Randall's family made me value his quiet emotional support all the more.

It's easy to take for granted the good that's there and focus on what's missing or flawed. I didn't want to do that anymore.

Dylan turned up in an Uber rather than his car the night of our dinner. With neither of us driving, we could both enjoy wine. After reading some reviews, Dylan suggested we get there early to sit at the bar. We shared Pinot Noir, bread sticks, and sharp cheddar spread cheese from the small barrels set out for patrons.

The host found us half an hour later and led us to where Joe and Lauren sat next to each other at one of the outdoor tables. Dylan and I sat opposite them. The Italian three-story restaurant to the west of us cast shade over the whole patio, keeping it from being too hot despite the glassed-in flames flickering in the center of the table.

After the cheese fondue and salad course, Dylan leaned close. "They seem to be getting along."

"Something's off, though," I whispered back.

Lauren was less bubbly than usual, though she didn't seem unhappy. Just thoughtful. I wasn't sure if Joe noticed it or not.

Dylan and I shared the shrimp, scallop, and beef dinner which came with raw carrots, small round potatoes, and onions. All the items had to first be cooked in hot oil, then dipped in one of twelve different sauces. Lauren and Joe's dinner skipped scallops and added lobster. The food platter, with the dips around the outside of it, sat on the long end of the table so we could all reach it, though I had to stretch across Dylan.

We talked about the Chicago music scene, restaurants, and real estate. Joe and Dylan got along much better than I expected. That made me happy. It suggested, contrary to Heather's insistence, that Joe didn't feel jealous or upset over the idea that I might date someone new.

Dessert included marshmallows, graham cracker crumbles, pound cake, strawberries, bananas, and Rice Krispie treats, all to be dipped in dark chocolate fondue. Liqueur floated on top of the fondue. The server lit it and we toasted our marshmallows in the flames. Then we rolled them in the graham crackers and dipped them in the chocolate—after the flames went out and it cooled.

Finished with my marshmallow, I speared a giant strawberry.

Lauren squared her shoulders and stood. "Joe." The firelight glinted off her blond hair and flickered across her face. I couldn't read her expression. Her mouth was set in a straight line, her eyes narrowed. But she didn't look angry. Maybe determined.

Joe froze, fondue fork in his hand. "Lauren?"

She grabbed one of his hands and pulled him to his feet. They stood almost face-to-face, at a slight angle because Joe's right knee pressed against the bench he'd sat on a moment before. The brick half wall and wrought iron railing surrounding the patio was at his back.

"These last two years I've been really happy with you," Lauren said. "I think you've been happy with me."

"I have." Joe glanced around. The diners at the other table had stopped eating to watch.

Dylan raised an eyebrow at me and I gave a slight shrug. Lauren hadn't given me any clue she planned to confront Joe tonight. I felt pretty sure this was spur of the moment. I hoped she didn't drag me into it, though I wasn't sure how she'd avoid it if she meant to confront him about what Heather said.

"Good. Because I have to ask you something. And I want an honest answer."

Joe bit his lip and studied her for a moment. "All right."

"Good." She drew in a deep breath, then let it out. "Will you marry me?"

CHAPTER 48
TROUBLE IN MIND

THE MAN, hidden in shadows, peered down from the rooftop of the Italian restaurant next to Geja's. Broad-shouldered, he was nearly six feet tall with a small scar on his right cheekbone.

The firelight made it easier for him to see the faces of the four people gathered around the farthest outdoor table on the cobblestone patio. Binoculars helped more. Luckily, the Italian restaurant had no outdoor seating on the roof and plenty of shadows for him to blend into. Also luckily, plenty of cash made it easy to persuade the owner to let him stay up here the entire evening. And more cash meant few questions about the film he was supposedly scouting locations for.

He didn't recognize the tall, dark-haired man next to Lauren. The couple on the other side of the table—a slender man and a woman with long dark hair—had their backs to him most of the evening. But they turned their heads many times to talk to one another, so he saw their profiles. The slender man got up once to walk inside Geja's. That's when the man on the roof became certain that the two had been at the townhome open house.

His target might have made friends with them after their walk through. Or they were ongoing clients. But he suspected she called them as protection.

That made him smile. Despite her covering it well, he'd rattled her.

A good start. But he had so much more to do.

Looking for more Q.C. Davis crime stories? Get **No Good Plays** (A Q.C. Davis Mystery novella) and short stories free by visiting LisaLilly.com. You'll also be first to get notice of new releases.

Did you enjoy *The Skeptical Man*? Please write a review at your favorite retailer. It helps other readers like you find the series.

ABOUT THE AUTHOR

In addition to the Q.C. Davis Mystery series, which includes *The Worried Man*, *The Charming Man*, *The Fractured Man*, *The Troubled Man*, *The Hidden Man*, *The Forgotten Man,* and the novella *No Good Plays*, Lisa M. Lilly is the author of the *Awakening* supernatural thriller series.

A resident of Chicago, Lilly is currently working on the next Q.C. Davis mystery. In addition, she hosts the podcast *Buffy and the Art of Story,* and her stories and poems have appeared in numerous publications. Under L. M. Lilly, she writes the Writing As A Second Career series and teaches fiction writing.

Join Lisa M. Lilly's Reader's Group at LisaLilly.com to receive *No Good Plays (A Q.C. Davis Mystery novella)*, short stories, an author e-newsletter, and updates on sales and new releases.

ALSO BY LISA M. LILLY

Q.C. Davis Mysteries

The Worried Man

The Charming Man

The Fractured Man

The Troubled Man

The Hidden Man

The Forgotten Man

The Skeptical Man

Q.C. Davis Mysteries Box Set Books 1-3

No Good Deeds (Short Story for Readers Group members)

No New Beginnings (Short Story for Readers Group members)

No Good Plays (A Q.C. Davis Mystery Novella - also available for download by Readers Group Members)

The Awakening Series

The Awakening (Book 1)

The Unbelievers (Book 2)

The Conflagration (Book 3)

The Illumination (Book 4)

The Awakening Series Complete Supernatural Thriller Series Box Set/Omnibus

Other Fiction

When Darkness Falls (a standalone supernatural suspense novel)

The Tower Formerly Known As Sears And Two Other Tales Of Urban Horror